"RIDERS COMING FAST."

Marie craned her neck, trying to see up ahead, but dust kicked up by the front wheels and the horses obscured her view.

Hardley poked his head out the window on the other side of the coach. "Is it Indians, driver?"

"Not likely," the driver shouted, then whistled at his team. "Indians, especially Apaches, don't let you see them until it's too late to do anything but die."

Hardley jerked his head back in the window and fumbled for the revolver at his waist. "Just in case," he said to Marie.

"Just in case what? You decide to shoot yourself?"

He grinned sheepishly.

"If we have to depend on you, Hardley, to protect us, we're as good as dead. Pull out your pencil and pad. Maybe you can write a story about your own demise."

TONY HILLERMAN'S FRONTIER

People of the Plains
The Tribes
The Soldiers
Battle Cry
Brothers in Blood
Cold Justice

Published by HarperPaperbacks

TONY HILLERMAN'S
~FRONTIER~

COLD
JUSTICE

Will Camp

HarperPaperbacks
A Division of HarperCollinsPublishers

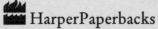
HarperPaperbacks

A Division of HarperCollins*Publishers*
10 East 53rd Street, New York, NY 10022-5299

ISBN: 0-06-101292-0

HarperCollins®, ®, and HarperPaperbacks™ are trademarks of HarperCollins Publishers, Inc.

Cover illustration © 1998 by Hiram Richardson

First printing: July 1998

Printed in the United States of America

Visit HarperPaperbacks on the World Wide Web at
http://www.harpercollins.com

❖ 10 9 8 7 6 5 4 3 2 1

For Ethan Ellenberg,
with many thanks and much appreciation

Santa Fe, New Mexico Territory
October 1858

Standing in the early morning chill outside his quarters just off the central plaza in Santa Fe, Brevet Captain Jean Francis Xavier Benoit III stared to the northeast and watched the sky pale from the unseen sunrise. He glanced at the distant nine-foot walls that surrounded Fort Marcy, his assigned post, though one manned by only a skeleton force while the remainder of the troops in Santa Fe lived and worked in low-slung adobe quarters not far from the governor's palace.

Benoit gazed beyond Fort Marcy toward the Sangre de Cristo Mountains, which glowed red from the sunlight seeping across the peaks' upper reaches. The local Hispanos were a superstitious yet religious lot, Benoit admitted, but as he stared at the stains of red trickling down the mountains he understood why the locals had named them for the blood of Christ.

What he didn't understand was how he had allowed himself to get caught up in a web of intrigue that stretched from Santa Fe to Fort Laramie in Wyoming

Territory, his previous post, and from New Orleans, his home, to Washington, D.C., where he had been assigned after graduation from the United States Military Academy in 1853. From the eastern newspapers that arrived in Santa Fe weeks after their publication, he knew that tensions were running high between the northern and southern states. Abolition, slavery, states' rights, cotton, and tariffs seemed to be the major ingredients in the political stew that was poisoning the Union, but chauvinism, greed, sectionalism, and political ambitions were flavoring that distasteful soup as well. Already there were veiled threats of secession by the southern states if they did not get their way.

Should that day come—and he feared it was inevitable—Benoit would have to choose between state and country. If he sided with Louisiana, the place of his birth, he would break his army oath of allegiance to the United States, a vow he took seriously. But if he chose his country, he would be rejecting his state and his heritage.

He worried about the choice mostly because of one conniving man, Clement "Cle" Couvillion, the junior U.S. senator from Louisiana. A small man with large ambitions, Couvillion had used his political influence to get Benoit promoted to captain and transferred from Fort Laramie to Fort Marcy, where he was to serve as aide-de-camp for Brigadier General Maurice G. Barksdale, commander of the Ninth Military Department and all eleven of its posts in New Mexico Territory.

The honorable senator had had dishonorable intentions, counting on Benoit to spy on the army and to feed him information that could then be used to the advantage of the southern states when they split from the Union. Couvillion's correspondence with Benoit had bordered on the treasonous, so Benoit had burned the senator's letters and any implication he had plotted with the senator. Everything Couvillion touched carried the scent of a skunk with it afterward, and that included his wife, Marie Fontenot Couvillion.

Daughter of one senator from Louisiana and wife of another, Marie Couvillion was an acquaintance he had known as a child in New Orleans, then later in Washington after he had graduated from West Point. Her southern charms—and they were as bountiful as her bust size—had turned randy by the time he had become reacquainted with her in the nation's capital. Further, Benoit knew that her late father, then the senior senator from Louisiana, was the reason he had been transferred from Washington to Fort Laramie four years previously. Aristocratic by nature, Senator Fontenot had felt a junior army officer was not the appropriate match for his beloved daughter.

Benoit thought of Marie, exuberant, demanding, fun, and exhausting. She was a woman better to bed than to wed. She could be sweet as syrup, but in reality she was as tart as a lemon and just as ambitious and ruthless as her husband. Benoit knew he should thank her father for his reassignment to Fort Laramie, but now with her husband as senator, he knew that he was still within reach of the Couvillions, as his transfer to New Mexico Territory had demonstrated.

As the sun peeked above the Sangre de Cristos, it cast a long shadow from Benoit's feet down the dusty street, worn and rutted by years of commerce along the Santa Fe Trail. Benoit shook his head, disgusted that another day had begun, another day during which his only companion would be boredom. General Barksdale was a drunk who had Benoit shuffling papers much of the time and twiddling his thumbs the rest of the day. And when he wasn't busy, which was regularly, he was lonely.

Not only had his promotion been tainted, but it had taken him away from his wife, Inge, who was expecting their first child, and from his best friend, First Lieutenant Jason Caldwell Dobbs, post surgeon at Fort Laramie. He thought mostly of Inge, wondering if she had delivered the son who would carry his name into a new generation. The baby was due at the end of October or in early November, and Benoit fidgeted, wondering if he might be a father and not yet know it. He anxiously awaited every army courier who came from the north, hoping he might carry news of his wife and son-to-be.

Of Germanic stock, Inge was a loving wife and would be a devoted mother. Alongside the pampered Marie Couvillion she might be considered plain, but Benoit found her attractive and sincere. She cooked and cleaned without complaint and would make a man a pleasant home whether he lived under a tree, in a cave, in officers' quarters, or in a mansion. Marie could make a pleasant home only if provided with a mansion staffed with servants. Benoit pulled from his pocket the engraved silver pocket watch Inge had given him for their first anniversary. More important than the time the watch kept was the memory that it offered of her.

As for his friend Dobbs, Benoit could talk with Jace about nearly anything—save maybe slavery and states' rights—and have fun doing it. Dobbs knew a little bit about everything and a lot about many things, whether it was astronomy or geology, politics or religion; he kept a personal library as best he could at a frontier post. Too, it was good to have Dobbs around to patch him up, as over the years Benoit had developed the unfortunate habit of getting into scrapes and fights and needing medical attention as a result. Leaving his pregnant wife behind for reassignment in New Mexico Territory had been more palatable for Benoit, knowing that Dobbs would be there to attend to her and the baby.

He had left others behind in Fort Laramie, including Inge's brother, Erich Schmidt, and her mother. Benoit wondered about Erich, who had been injured in a fall from his horse during a Crow ambush. A big, strapping boy who had learned the ways of the mountain man and had just begun to prove himself an excellent scout, hunter, and Indian fighter, Erich could not walk after the Crow attack. He said his legs were dead. Jace Dobbs had called him paralyzed and had offered little hope that he might ever walk again or, for that matter, father a child, as Benoit had done with Erich's sister. Benoit could not imagine life without the carnal pleasures that a woman could bring a man. He wondered how Erich could live with the knowledge that he might never again have a woman. Dead legs did not kill a man's brain and his yearnings.

Benoit shook his head, then glanced down at the watch in his hand, telling himself he must think of Inge and the child that he knew would be a son. He must hope that he and his son would never face such a tragedy. As his hand slowly slipped the watch back in his pocket he turned and retraced his steps to his quarters, set to join the other officers at the morning mess.

They dined in an adobe dwelling behind their quarters. The single officers and those who had not brought their wives and families to Santa Fe had hired an elderly Hispano woman to cook their meals for them. She worked relentlessly over the corner fireplace to prepare their meals and keep their plates full. Consuela, as she was called, made Mexican pancakes called tortillas that the officers would slather with honey for breakfast or fill with boiled goat meat or mashed *frijoles* for lunch and dinner. The officers had taught her to fry salt pork, which she did well, and to attempt biscuits, which she did poorly, but mostly they ate what she prepared and mostly it was native dishes, often spicy and always filling. She made coffee that the other officers considered superb, but which Benoit thought merely adequate. After all, nobody anywhere on the frontier could make better coffee than Benoit, who used the meticulous methods of his Cajun upbringing and the coffee beans sent to him by his sister Marion from New Orleans. If there was one thing Benoit knew that his good friend Jace Dobbs didn't know, it was how to brew the sweetest coffee.

Entering the officers' mess, Benoit smiled at Consuela as she walked by carrying an earthen bowl of fried bacon and a platter of hot tortillas. Consuela answered with a toothless grin that deepened the leathery wrinkles of her bronzed face.

Benoit snatched a strip of sizzling bacon from the bowl and took a bite, the film of grease that clung to the meat burning his tongue. "*Bueno*," he managed as he slid onto the bench beside Lieutenant Frank Coker, a native of Bellefonte, Pennsylvania, and the only man in Santa Fe who could play a piano. His fingers were supple and delicate, especially for a soldier, and his wit was quick but gentle.

"Hey, Ben-oight," cried Tom Webster across the table, deliberately slaughtering the pronunciation of Benoit's French name, "wait your turn 'fore you eat our bacon."

"And the last shall be first and the first last,"

Lieutenant Coker said softly, cutting his gaze toward Benoit. By the grin on Coker's lips, Benoit knew that the lieutenant was referring not to the purloined bacon but rather to the fact that Benoit outranked the obnoxious Webster, who was twice Benoit's age.

Benoit winked at Coker, letting him know he understood the joke that was too subtle for the thick-headed Webster of South Carolina.

"It's Ben-wah, Weeb-ster," Coker offered, slurring his fellow lieutenant's name as he took the bowl from Consuela, forked several strips of bacon onto his plate, and passed the bowl to Benoit, who straightened in his seat.

Webster slammed his fist against the table. "It's Web-ster."

"Weeb-ster, Web-ster, it's closer to correct than Ben-oight to Ben-wah," Coker replied.

Benoit took some bacon, then passed the bowl to the next officer. Each successive officer took a helping of bacon but was careful not to pass the dish to Webster, who was hated by all.

"It's Web-ster, dammit," he replied.

The now empty bowl returned to Coker. He offered it to Webster, whose eyes widened in anger as Coker informed him, "It's emp-ty, Web-ster."

Webster growled and hit the table again with his fist.

"You rile too easy," Benoit said, offering Webster a couple of strips from his own plate.

Webster waved the offer aside, too proud to admit he had been outwitted by the other officers. Instead he grabbed the platter of tortillas and took a third of them. "I'll make do, Ben-oight."

"Can you pronounce the word *captain?*" Benoit reminded him.

"Captain Ben-oight." Webster spat out the words as though they were rancid butter.

The other officers went about their breakfast, talking among themselves and generally ignoring Webster, who was too loud, too arrogant, and too loutish for everyone. Though a son of the South, he was as devoid of gentility as a jackass was of etiquette.

Benoit much preferred Coker among the other officers at Fort Marcy, admiring him for his patience, enjoying him for his wit, and envying him his intelligence. Coming from a cooler climate than the South Carolinian, his blood did not pulse as hotly as Webster's. He was calm, almost calculating, a soldier much more to be feared in battle, Benoit thought, than the emotional Webster.

"No word from Fort Laramie, Jean?" he asked.

Grabbing a couple of tortillas, Benoit shrugged. "I never knew mail could be so slow. When the courier arrived yesterday afternoon, I hoped he was carrying dispatches from Fort Laramie, but he was up from Fort Fillmore."

"I suspect there is nothing to worry about, not with your friend Dobbs being such a good doctor. Unless, of course, you fear the worst," Coker joked. "A girl instead of a boy."

Benoit grinned. "You've got a point."

Coker shook his head. "That's what I thought until I had my two girls, Annell and Harriet. They can wrap me around their finger, especially the younger one. Why, Harriet's cuter than a bug, and she plays with her dollies like she's a little momma herself. I can't wait for the day when they rejoin me." Coker laughed. "Problem with little girls is that boys want to do with them what we did with their mothers, and that can worry a father as they grow older."

Benoit considered Coker's anxiety, knowing it was grounded in his deep religion. Benoit thought that men and women were made to fit each other and that the difference was to be celebrated instead of worried over. "It's inevitable, Frank, and not to be fought."

"No, it can't be fought," he said, "but decency can be taught."

"Perhaps," Benoit laughed, "but indecency comes naturally."

Coker swatted him playfully on the arm. "You Cajuns have too much French in you. Remind me never to let your son court my daughters."

"He'd only court one at a time," Benoit teased.

They finished their breakfast, then went about their assignments, Benoit visiting the quartermaster at General Barksdale's insistence and checking on the hay and corn that had been purchased from the Hispanos to get the cavalry horses through the upcoming winter. The quartermaster, the son of a Vermont storekeeper, was as thin as the pencils he used to fill his meticulous ledger. If a grain of corn had been purchased, the quartermaster could turn to the ledger and find where it had been stored and when it had been consumed. Thanks to the dedication of soldiers such as the quartermaster, the Ninth Military District was well run despite its drunken commander.

"A dozen more wagonloads of corn," the quartermaster said, "and we'll have enough to get the animals through the winter. As for hay, I've bought some up and down the Rio Grande, but rather than hauling it all here, I'm having the farmers store it for us. They'll do it for free until we need it. It saves the army the cost of having to store it here and some of it can be consumed by cavalry on patrol, saving us those freighting costs."

Benoit nodded at the quartermaster and the clerks standing on either side of him. "Fine work. The army needs good men like you and your clerks."

"Which army, Captain?" the quartermaster asked.

Benoit eyed the quartermaster carefully, fearing he knew what the Vermonter meant but hoping he was wrong about it. "What do you mean? There's only one army."

"Not meaning any disrespect, sir," the quartermaster replied, "but you've heard the talk of dissolving the Union. If that happens, there'll be two armies, one northern and one southern. I was just wondering where you stood."

"I stand with the country I swore allegiance to, these United States," Benoit said, measuring his words and their effect. "To do or say otherwise is treasonous."

"It doesn't stop that damned Tom Webster from spouting off. He talks all the time about Jefferson Davis taking over the army and marching on Washington, taking over the government. Webster's from South Carolina, same as General Barksdale, isn't he?"

"*Sacre bleu,*" Benoit cried, "Tom Webster's an ass. He's not smart enough to empty his boot even if the directions were written on the bottom."

"Everybody knows that, but he ain't good for morale."

Benoit nodded. "That's why he's still a lieutenant. You don't worry about him—just keep up the fine work you're doing. I'll commend you to General Barksdale."

"I'm grateful, Captain, not that it will do any good. The good general remembers to drink his whiskey, but he forgets just about everything else."

Though he felt hypocritical defending the general, Benoit knew it was his obligation to do so anyway. "The general's wife refused to join him in Santa Fe. He's taken to drink to forget the loneliness." Barely were the words out of his mouth than he realized he had chosen them poorly.

"Hell, Captain, he forgets everything, and I suppose he's drunk enough whiskey to forget he ever had a wife."

"Even so," Benoit replied. "I'll put in a good word for you and your men."

"Thank you, sir. We're grateful." The quartermaster and the two clerks saluted Benoit.

He lifted his hand to his forehead in acknowledgment, then turned and walked from the quartermaster's office out into the dusty, rutted street that led to General Barksdale's quarters and office.

Taking a deep breath before he entered, Benoit shook his head, dreading the boredom of yet another day in the small office adjacent to the general's. Soon after Benoit had first arrived in Santa Fe, he had realized that everything the general gave him to do was busywork—shuffling the same papers, signing off on the same meaningless reports. It was almost as if the general realized his own incompetence but tried to disprove it to himself and his superiors by burying them in a blizzard of paper.

Surely his superiors must know of Barksdale's inability, but no one did anything about it. Benoit had learned during his time in the army that it was often easier to ignore a problem than to correct it. Exhaling slowly, Benoit lifted the handle and marched inside, startling Sergeant Hamilton Phipps at his desk.

Phipps dropped the newspaper he was reading to the floor before saluting.

"Morning, Ham," Benoit said, returning the

salute. Smelling the aroma of whiskey, Benoit knew that the commanding officer of the Ninth Military District was in.

The sergeant lifted his finger to his lips, motioning for Benoit to be quiet. "The general's got a hangover, and he's threatened to have me in front of a firing squad if I make any noise."

Benoit extracted an imaginary pistol from his belt and lifted his empty hand in the air. "Ready, aim," he whispered, "fire."

Phipps failed to see the humor and cleared his throat. "After reading the dispatch from Fort Fillmore yesterday, he told me he wanted to see you this morning."

Benoit took a step toward the general's open door.

"I wouldn't go in there yet," Phipps said. "He's been a bear this morning and he'll have forgotten that he wanted to see you. After all, that was yesterday and probably three bottles of Taos Lightning ago."

Benoit halted in the doorway, staring at the general, who was slouched in his chair asleep. Behind him on the wall, a portrait of President James Buchanan stared down at Barksdale, who breathed in spurts through his mouth. Unlike the whiskey he drank, Barksdale was aged beyond his fifty-eight years. When open, his eyes were bloodshot and watery. Even his scraggly beard could not hide all the lines and wrinkles that time and liquor had eroded in his face. Benoit questioned how he could have defended Barksdale to the quartermaster and wondered if being aide-de-camp to such a man would damage his own military career.

Backing away from the door, Benoit retreated even more carefully to the sergeant's desk so as not to arouse the general from his drunken haze. "He's sleeping it off,

Sergeant, and I'm sure he'd have me before that firing squad if I wake him. I'll see him later."

Phipps nodded, then picked up the newspaper from the floor. "Here's a St. Louis newspaper, sir, not four weeks old, if you care to read it."

Benoit took the paper and retreated to his dingy office with a table for a desk and a rough-hewn bench for a seat. No president stared down upon his desk. Benoit shoved open the wooden shutters so a little more morning light could seep inside. He pushed a stack of papers to the edge of the desk, then unfolded the newspaper and laid it flat so that he could read the front page of the *St. Louis Leader*, which was as pro-Union as the Stars and Stripes. Rather than sitting on the unpadded bench, he stood up and leaned over the paper, reading first an article condemning President Buchanan for his efforts to appease the southern states, then a polemic abhorring the institution of slavery, and finally a story attacking a rival St. Louis newspaper for its misplaced allegiance to the iniquitous South. The debate, Benoit feared, was one that would be settled not with words but with war.

The story that he found most interesting, though, ran the length of the left column. Its staggered headline read "Butterfield Mail Route Commences; 2,795 Miles from St. Louis to San Francisco; Trips Completed in Under 25 Days."

Benoit had heard about the new mail route while he was at Fort Laramie but had paid little attention to it, since the Butterfield route ran well south of the territory protected by the Wyoming post. Now, though, he read the article with more interest, for once the route left El Paso, it would cross into New Mexico Territory on the way to California.

The story indicated that the route had been made

possible by an act of Congress the year before, autho-
rizing a government contract for mail to be delivered
twice weekly in both directions. John Butterfield had
been awarded the contract and had commenced delivery in September. From St. Louis the route extended to
Fort Smith, Arkansas, then through north Texas and the
barren wastes of west Texas before reaching El Paso
and turning north into New Mexico Territory, where
the route traversed forbidding terrain to Tucson and
then Fort Yuma. There it crossed the Colorado River
and entered California, heading northwest to Los
Angeles and paralleling the Pacific Coast on into San
Francisco.

Letters were delivered by stage for twenty cents per
ounce, and passengers were carried for two hundred
dollars one way. Benoit paused for a moment, wondering if the mail or passenger rate was the cheaper by
weight, then chuckling to himself as he realized that it
was the kind of question Dobbs would ask. Benoit realized the difference between him and Dobbs: His friend
would take the time to do the calculation, while Benoit
would be amused solely by the question.

The government contract required that mails and
passengers be delivered in four-horse coaches or spring
wagons. The newspaper estimated that the demand for
West Coast mail would result in revenues in excess of a
hundred thousand dollars the first year alone. The story
indicated the company would require 250 coaches,
freight wagons, and tank wagons. More than two thousand men and women would be assigned to two hundred
stations along the route as drivers, conductors, station-
keepers, blacksmiths, mechanics, cooks, hostlers, wran-
glers, and guards. Several times that number of horses
and mules would also be required to operate the line.

The *St. Louis Leader,* being an abolitionist paper, then speculated that the mail route was merely a ploy to develop a route that the southern states could use to convey armies to the gold fields of California when they abandoned the Union. Further, the paper declared that southern leaders such as Jefferson Davis, from Mississippi, hoped to capture those gold fields to finance a war with the United States. Knowing more about military logistics than did the unnamed writer for the *St. Louis Leader,* Benoit could only laugh.

He did realize, however, that the stage might require military escorts from time to time, and he suspected that was what General Barksdale would want to discuss when he was sober enough to speak. The article went on to encourage passengers on the stage to travel well-armed and provisioned. It recommended that passengers take one Sharps rifle and two cartons of cartridges; a Navy revolver with 150 balls; a knife and whetstone; a pair of thick boots; woolen pants; heavy woolen socks; extra undershirts; three woolen shirts; a slouch hat; a sack coat and an overcoat; two blankets in summer, and four in winter; a piece of India-rubber cloth; a pair of gloves; a small bag of needles and pins; a sponge, hairbrush, comb, and razor, and some soap; extra drawers; and some towels.

Benoit had not traveled the route, but he had talked to other officers who had been assigned to Texas or the southern reaches of New Mexico Territory and he knew the commodity often in greatest demand along many stretches of that country was water. He would certainly add a canteen to the newspaper's list of necessities. Benoit opened the paper to page three, where the story jumped, and finished reading the account, which went on to describe John Butterfield as a good businessman who was trying to take his freight and passenger business into parts of the country where there would never be the need for railroads nor any profit in building them.

As Benoit finished the story he glanced at the doorway and realized General Barksdale was standing there, staring absently at him. Benoit straightened and saluted. "Good morning, sir," he said, purposefully loud.

Barksdale winced and half saluted, half waved at him. "Didn't Sergeant Phipps tell you I wanted to see you first thing this morning, Captain?"

"Yes, sir, he did," Benoit replied, "but when I looked in on you, you seemed . . . busy."

"Busy, yes. I've been awfully busy with matters for the War Department, a lot of paperwork, you know? You do know that, don't you, Captain?"

"Certainly, sir," Benoit said loudly again.

Barksdale lifted his palm toward Benoit, silently imploring him to speak more softly. "Please join me in my office." He retreated from the door.

Benoit folded the newspaper, then followed in the general's wake, tossing the paper on Phipps's desk as he marched by and into his commander's office.

Barksdale collapsed in his chair, reached for the bottom left drawer on his desk, and pulled out a half-full bottle of Taos Lightning. It was a wicked local concoction, strong enough to strip the bark from a tree. The general's right hand trembled as he grasped the cork and jerked it from the bottle.

"I haven't been feeling well lately, Captain. Congestion in the chest. Doctor says it's nothing to worry about and the only medicine that'll do much for me is whiskey." He gulped down a couple of swigs.

"Yes, sir."

The general drew the sleeve of his unbuttoned army

blouse across his lips. "How would you like to get away from all the paperwork here, Captain?"

"I'd enjoy that, sir."

"I thought you might, Captain. Have you heard of the new overland mail route?"

"The Butterfield route?" Benoit replied. "I was just reading about it. St. Louis to San Francisco."

"Hell of a stage line, it is, but it needs the army's assistance for an escort."

Benoit smiled. He liked the thought of having a command, no matter how small, and protecting a segment of the route. "I can guard stages."

For a moment the general looked befuddled. He shook his head, then tipped the bottle to his lips. As soon as he yanked the bottle from his mouth he spoke. "Hell, no, that's not the army's job. I need you to ride to Fort Fillmore and escort some damn politician's wife to Santa Fe."

The smile on Benoit's face melted like fat in a fire.

"Do you know a Marie Couvillion? You ought to know her—she's from New Orleans, the wife of Senator Couvillion."

Benoit sighed. He knew her in every possible way a man could know a woman, and if there was one woman he didn't want to see, not when his wife was hundreds of miles away and expecting their first child, it was Marie Couvillion.

"I hear she's quite the looker, this Marie Couvillion, and her husband's a real firebrand for the cause of the southern states, so you—"

"Sir," Benoit interrupted, "I'd prefer you send someone else."

"—have a lot in common with the Couvillions. She's due the last day of the month in Fort Fillmore; that gives you a week to get there."

"Sir, I don't believe you heard me. I'd prefer you send someone else."

Barksdale looked up, his brow furrowed. "Doesn't matter what you want, Captain. The senator's wife specifically requested you, and a politician's wife always gets what she wants in this army."

Benoit grimaced. That was Marie's problem: She had always gotten what she wanted.

"Take a dozen men with you in the morning and bring her back safely to Santa Fe."

"Yes, sir," Benoit said, vowing to himself that she wouldn't get what she wanted from him this time.

— 2 —

Muttering in French, Captain Jean Benoit cursed General Barksdale doubly. First he blasphemed his commander for sending him to escort Marie Couvillion. Then he cursed him as well for assigning Lieutenant Tom Webster to ride with him instead of Frank Coker, his choice for second in command.

Benoit stayed ten yards ahead of Webster, preferring to curse to himself rather than talk with the obnoxious lieutenant. Behind Webster a dozen cavalry troopers rode two abreast.

Overhead a benevolent sun warmed the troopers as they rode toward the Rio Grande southwest of Santa Fe. It was not yet noon and already the trail dust had begun to discolor their uniforms, the dark blue of their blouses paled by the dust loosened by the thousands of other horses, mules, oxen, carts, and wagons that had traveled from Santa Fe to Chihuahua. The Hispanos called the trail El Camino Real de Tierra Adentro, an 850-mile route that was older and longer than the Santa Fe Trail.

The Hispanos also had another name for it: Jornado del Muerto. Translated, it meant "journey of death"— and indeed, many had died along the trail, some from thirst, a number from Apaches. The threat of Apache attacks existed along the entire trail but was particularly intense here, as the Apache hatred of Mexicans had focused their wrath upon them instead of the Americans and their blue-coated soldiers.

Benoit wondered about the Apache and their fighting prowess. He had heard so many tales about the tribe that he could not separate truth from fiction. They were reputed to be so cagey a race that they could catch antelope afoot. An Apache, so he had been told, had learned to rely on an antelope's natural curiosity and lure it into a fatal trap. By tying a strip of colored cloth to a yucca stalk downwind from an antelope and then hiding in the grass beside the yucca, an Apache warrior with patience could entice an antelope to investigate, then jump from hiding and slit its throat with a knife. At least that was how the soldiers told it.

Some even mentioned riding across desert trails where there wasn't enough grass or plants to hide a scorpion, then finding themselves surrounded by a dozen warriors who seemed to spring out of the earth like rabbits out of a hole.

Perhaps it was the instinct for survival that had taught the Apache the art of disguise and stealth upon the desert. In 1835 the Mexican state of Sonora had established bounties upon the heads of all Apaches, men, women, and children: a hundred pesos for the scalp of any Apache warrior fourteen years of age or older, fifty pesos for women, and twenty-five pesos for each child. Further, the scalp was all that was required for a hunter to claim the reward.

The system of bounties had attracted murderous men to Apache country to seek their fortune. A few received substantial rewards for their killing, but in an ironic twist to the law, the scalp hunters, many Anglos among them, found it was less dangerous to kill Mexicans and turn their scalps in for rewards, as their hair was virtually identical to that of Apache scalps. Too, the murderers could always blame a Mexican's death on the Apaches, further fanning the flames of hatred between the two races. Benoit abhorred the practice and knew it was no tall tale, unlike some of the stories he had heard about the Apache.

The thing that worried him most was that he did not know which of the Apache stories to believe. After all, he had never seen an Apache—at least that he knew about. He examined the terrain around him, wondering if his eyes might be missing Apaches hiding in the thin grass or behind the lanky yucca stalks.

Benoit was startled from his thoughts by the sudden sound of galloping hooves behind him. His hand went instinctively to his revolver as he jerked the reins on his gelding around to face whatever threat galloped toward him. The soldiers in his command peeled away from the trail to answer any challenge, but the rider turned out to be one of their own, a solitary horseman in a dark blue blouse and light blue pants. The rider lifted his hat and waved it from side to side over his head and yelled something indecipherable over the pounding of his hooves.

Instantly Benoit recognized Frank Coker.

Benoit turned to Webster. "Have the men fall in line and proceed on, Lieutenant. I will catch up shortly."

Webster saluted lamely. "Yes, sir, Captain," he fairly sneered.

Anxious to see what had brought Coker to join him, Benoit let the insubordination pass. He touched his army-issue spur to the flank of the gelding and rode out to greet Coker, who eased back on his reins, slowing his horse to a trot and then a walk as he came within talking distance.

"What brings you out, Frank? Come to replace Webster, I hope?"

Coker shook his head as he planted his hat back atop it. He undid a button on his blouse and slipped his hand inside. As his hand reappeared Benoit saw a letter. He nudged his horse toward Coker's and snatched the missive from the lieutenant's hand.

"Maybe I'm a papa," he said.

"Courier arrived this morning after you left," Coker told him. "I saw this was for you and convinced the general it should be delivered while I could still catch you."

Benoit was excited as he turned the letter over, then disappointed when he saw the handwriting. The letter had been penned by Jason Dobbs. Then Benoit panicked. Was Dobbs writing him with bad news? Had something gone wrong with Inge or the baby? Instead of the good news he had been expecting, could this be the worst possible news?

Benoit ripped the envelope open and yanked out the letter. He bit his lip as he glanced at Coker, then back at the letter. He caught his breath, then began to read the news.

Dear Jean:

    I have news about your wife and twin daughters. It is neither good nor bad at present.

    Inge had birthing pains early. I was with her almost from the beginning, which is good because it was a troubled birth, lasting some eighteen hours. The babies were turned poorly and resisted coming into this world. Inge was so long in labor that I feared going any longer might kill her, so I decided to free the little ones by cutting into her abdomen, whether or not they were ready to come.

Both mother and babies are weak and I have some worries about all three, but rest assured, Jean, I did the best I could for both mother and girls. I do not know what the future holds for your girls, as I am more worried about them than about Inge. She is strong stock, her German blood thick. Your daughters, though, are tiny and frail, there not being room inside your wife for them to grow fully. Birthing is hard normally and even harder when a baby must be taken this way.

I do not mean to worry you, though I know I can do nothing but by writing this letter, but I wanted you to know the truth. Julius Caesar was born in such a manner, and you know that he lived to be a strong man. Only time will tell your girls' fate. There are moments when a man must turn to prayer; Inge has done so, as have I. Your prayers can only help. Your daughters have your dark hair, your blue eyes, and, I think, your strong will. It will serve them well.

Inge sends her love. She misses you greatly. I must go tend your wife and girls now but I knew you would want to have this news.

Your friend,
Jace Dobbs

Benoit licked his lips, then exhaled slowly as he looked toward Coker.

"Is the news bad?" asked the lieutenant.

He shrugged for an answer, then stared north toward Fort Laramie.

Coker reached for the letter clasped between

Benoit's fingers and gently pulled it away. He read quickly, then refolded the letter and handed it to Benoit, who slipped it back in the envelope.

"I'm sorry, Captain, that there are some complications, but congratulations on being a father. Your daughters will grow on you the way mine have on me. And they will pull through."

Benoit did not know what to say. His emotions bounced between the pride of fathering twins and the fear of losing them before he ever saw them. He wanted so to be with his wife to encourage her and to hold his girls in his arms and help them survive.

Coker reached over and patted Benoit on the shoulder. "The general said I could bring the letter as long as I made it clear you were to continue this assignment—even if the news was the worst."

"Bastard," Benoit mumbled.

"Drunk," Coker affirmed.

Benoit looked at his friend. "I'm grateful to you for bringing me the letter."

"You'd do the same for me, Jean." Coker turned in his saddle and opened the flap on the saddle pack behind him. "I brought a pen, ink, and paper, in case you wanted to write a response."

Benoit pulled the reins on his horse and turned the animal around. He saw his men three quarters of a mile away.

"It must be quick." He dismounted, handed his reins to Coker, and took the paper and pen from him. He propped the paper against the saddle, dipped the tip of the pen in the inkwell that Coker held for him, and began the letter.

To my darling Inge and my daughters,
I have received Jace's letter about your difficul-

*ties. My prayers are with you, and I am with you in
spirit as well. Be strong, and one day soon I will hold
you all in my arms. As I am in the field, I must be
quick, but my every thought will be upon you until
the day we are reunited.*

Your husband and father

He handed the pen to Coker, then lifted the paper
and waved it toward the warm sun so the ink would dry.

"I can address the envelope back at the fort," Coker
volunteered. "You keep the writing materials."

Benoit handed Coker the letter, then slipped the pen,
ink, and paper in his saddlebags. "I wish you were riding
with me instead of Webster," Benoit told his friend as he
mounted his horse.

"I asked the general if I could replace Webster."

"What'd he say?"

"He just laughed and denied my request, saying you
needed to spend more time with Webster and catch his
fervor for the southern cause."

"I took an oath at West Point. My honor is important
to me."

"Neither your honor nor theirs is important to
Barksdale or Webster."

Nor to Senator Cle Couvillion or his wife, Benoit
thought as he gave Coker a final nod. "One day I hope to
return the favor, Frank."

Coker smiled. "We'll worry about that later," he
answered, and rode off.

Benoit spurred his horse into a gallop to catch up
with his men, knowing there would be no waking
moment on the trail to Fort Fillmore that he would not
think of his twins and wife and wonder if they were still
alive.

With the Rio Grande to his back, Lieutenant Colonel Jeremy Sullivan rocked on his heels and stared at the men busily sprucing up the grounds of Fort Fillmore in preparation for the arrival of Marie Couvillion. A slender man with thin lips, narrow eyes, and a pencil-thin mustache, Sullivan saw the visit by the senator's wife as an opportunity to enhance his chances for a promotion. He had planned to give her a tour of the fort and take her to Mesilla, where she could sample the colorful life of the Hispanos. He had also arranged for a special bullfight that Marie might watch and enjoy. Too, he had even sent a vague message to Fort Marcy obscuring the arrival date of the senator's wife so he would have a few extra days to squire her about. He had offered to escort her to Santa Fe himself, but the senator had insisted that Captain Jean Benoit come down from Santa Fe to provide the escort.

Fort Fillmore stood guard between the low hills that marked either side of the Rio Grande. From the front of his headquarters he surveyed the eighteen squat adobe buildings fronting onto the parade ground. Beyond the barracks stood the stables where the fort's horses were fed and groomed.

Beyond the stables and toward the river were the gardens the enlisted men had tilled, planted, irrigated, and harvested since spring. The yellow edges around the leaves of the beans, squash, and melon plants hinted that winter was not far away. The corn stalks were already yellowing. Though his men had paid for the seed and worked the gardens only when they didn't have other duties, Colonel Sullivan saw nothing wrong in taking whatever he wanted from his men and their gardens to put on a good spread for the senator's wife. He would show her that Lieutenant Colonel Jeremy Sullivan knew how to command an army outpost as well as provide her with a touch of luxury that he was sure she would not be offered at any other post.

For her comfort, he had ordered Captain Bernard Roche and his family to temporarily abandon their quarters, which shared half the adobe building that was his own military home. Captain Roche and his family had been outraged at the eviction, but Sullivan was his commanding officer and a young officer's career could be permanently damaged by resistance to any order, no matter how foolish the command or how vain the commander.

The Roches' furniture would stay for the use of the senator's wife, though Sullivan had two soldiers packing straw in a mattress cover so her bed would be soft. The lieutenant colonel had sent six men and a wagon to El Paso to bring back a tin bathtub in which she could wash away the trail dust. From his own pocket, Sullivan had hired a *señora* from Mesilla to serve as Marie Couvillion's maid and servant.

Sullivan studied the two soldiers whitewashing the flagpole in the center of the parade ground. The flagpole would be sparkling by the time Marie Couvillion arrived the next day. Sullivan wondered if he had neglected any detail. If he had, he would simply blame Captain Roche. After all, what were subordinates for?

In the morning he would send out hunting parties to bag antelope for the evening meal. When she arrived in the midafternoon, he would have the soldiers ready for inspection. He'd already threatened thirty days in the stockade for any man who was out of place in formation or out of step in march. He wanted everything to be perfect because he wanted the promotion he deserved. A commander at a post as isolated as Fort Fillmore had few chances to distinguish himself in front of his superiors. Having a senator's wife at the fort was one of those rare chances. He must make the best of it.

Captain Roche approached him and saluted.

Sullivan nodded without lifting his hand. "What is it, Captain?"

"The stables have been cleaned, sir."

"They'll be dirty by tomorrow, Captain. I want them cleaned again by noon tomorrow."

"The men have other chores, sir, and those assigned to clean the stables again won't have time for their main meal."

"Then they'll just have to miss their dinner, won't they? I want the stable clean by two o'clock tomorrow."

"It's not fair that some men'll miss a meal."

"The order stands, Captain, but to make it fair, no men will be allowed to eat a noon meal. It's your job to see that they all stay busy. I also want you to take three men from each company to the gardens at noon. Pick for me the fullest ears of corn, two bushels of beans, a bushel of squash, and the ripest melons so that I can provide a fine meal for the senator's wife."

"But sir, the gardens belong to the men. They paid for the seeds, then planted and cultivated and irrigated them on their own time. We shouldn't take their vegetables. That will be bad for the men's morale."

"The men's morale be damned. Do it! This is not the men's army. It's my army. Another thing—send out a squad of hunters tomorrow to bring back a half dozen antelope so the cooks can prepare it for tomorrow night's dinner."

"Yes, sir." Roche saluted, then strode angrily away.

"And Captain," Sullivan called after him, "you and your wife are invited to dinner tomorrow with the senator's wife. I hear the men have volunteered to provide vegetables for the affair." Sullivan laughed as Roche continued walking. He knew Roche had heard but had chosen to ignore him. That was not a wise thing for the captain to do. After all, Sullivan would be ripe for a promotion after tending to the senator's wife. Then Sullivan would be in a position to help an officer such as Roche, a fact the captain seemed to ignore.

Sullivan turned and walked away from the parade ground toward the bakery. He entered and found the baker and his two helpers pulling fresh loaves of bread from two stone ovens. The aroma was enticing. He stepped to the table where the loaves were lined up like soldiers for inspection. He grabbed a loaf and tore a chunk off the end, the heat stinging his fingers. He bit into the hunk of bread and chewed it quickly, then waved the baker toward him.

"Yes, sir?" the baker said, wiping his hands on his apron.

"Tomorrow there will be no noon meal, as the men will be busy finishing their chores for the arrival of the senator's wife. Have all the men's bread done by one o'clock. Then I want you to bake the best cake as well as some fresh loaves of bread for dinner tomorrow night. I shall be entertaining the senator's wife and I want everything to be perfect."

The baker scratched his head. "Yes, sir, but did I hear you right about the men? No noon meal for them?"

Sullivan stamped his foot on the wooden floor. "You did. Are you questioning my authority?"

"No, sir, just making sure I understood your command."

"Very well then. Carry on, but remember I want everything to be perfect tomorrow night."

"We'll do our best, sir."

Sullivan nodded slowly as he stuffed the remainder of the bread in his mouth. He chewed it quickly. "Just be sure your best is good enough." He turned and walked away.

The lieutenant colonel spent the rest of the afternoon inspecting the fort, assigning housekeeping chores to his men so that the fort would be perfect and his name would be spoken of favorably in Washington.

Before he retired to his quarters, he inspected the rooms where Marie Couvillion would be staying. He was pleased with the tin bathtub, which would certainly impress the senator's wife. Then he stepped back outside, examined the parade ground a final time, and slipped into his own quarters. He walked through the parlor and into a smaller room, where an orderly stood at a table that could seat eight.

"Are you ready to eat, sir?" the orderly asked.

"I am indeed. Tomorrow's a big day for Fort Fillmore." He unbuttoned his blouse and took his seat at the end of the table.

"Yes, sir." The orderly stepped into the kitchen and returned moments later with a tin plate of baked quail, two boiled eggs, candied yams, and fresh bread. He placed the plate before Sullivan and disappeared again into the kitchen.

Sullivan lifted his knife and fork, then attacked the quail. The orderly came back with a tin cup of coffee. Sullivan tapped his tin plate with his fork, then pointed at the tin cup as the orderly placed it before him. "Tomorrow night we will use china to impress our guest. She must know that even an isolated post like ours is capable of providing the amenities of life found back east—that is, if the right commander is in charge."

"Certainly, sir," the orderly answered as he retreated into the kitchen.

Sullivan smiled as he dined. He had seen to everything. Nothing could possibly go wrong with Marie Couvillion's visit the next day.

The coach rattled and creaked as it followed the road along the Rio Grande north from Franklin toward Fort Fillmore. As the wife of a U.S. senator, Marie Couvillion had demanded and gotten a seat by the back window. She was packed into the coach with six other people, three each sitting on the front and back seats and the odd man out sitting on the bench seat between them.

Marie Couvillion had voiced her displeasure innumerable times at the cramped compartment, the rough road, and the indignities that she had to endure. Even her traveling companion, J. Ernest Hardley, a reporter for the *New Orleans Picayune*, had grown tired of her whining. The senator himself had insisted that Hardley travel with Marie and report back to the newspaper with accounts of her doings.

Marie figured the reporter had merely been sent along to spy on her and make sure she didn't get in another man's bed, especially Jean Benoit's. Since leaving St. Louis on the stage, there had been no opportunity nor any man available to satisfy her. Hardley, with his black hair, full beard, and black eyes, might have been acceptable were it not for his spectacles and the twenty extra pounds he carried everywhere with him. And she still might consider bedding him, because then he wouldn't be tempted to report back to Cle Couvillion any infidelities she might commit.

As the desert landscape passed by her, she thought about the many times she had had Jean before he was reassigned by the army to Fort Laramie, far away from her in Washington. At first she had been mad at her father for arranging the transfer, and she even informed him that she and Benoit had made love in his favorite room of their Washington home, the library. She still remembered the look of shock and disappointment upon his face at her bold announcement.

But for all the heartache her father had created in breaking off Benoit's courtship, he had been right about her. She never would have been satisfied as the wife of an army officer. A senator's influence and prestige were much more suited to her tastes. Just as she had grown up the daughter of a Louisiana senator, she had continued that life by marrying the man who since had become another senator from Louisiana. Still, she wondered if she might have been happier with Benoit. He was, after all, more passionate than Couvillion. Though the senator was without doubt a jealous man, having killed a man in a duel at Fort Laramie after discovering he had bedded Marie, her husband's passion was reserved for his true mistress, politics.

Marie always wondered what Couvillion would do if she slept with Benoit again. She knew her husband risked their being together again so Benoit could pass information to her that might be useful to the South should war come. She was only too glad to help, since it would allow her to rekindle the flame her father had extinguished four years before.

She was jarred from her thoughts by the shout of the coach driver. "Riders coming fast."

Marie craned her neck, trying to see up ahead, but dust kicked up by the front wheels and the horses obscured her view.

Hardley poked his head out the window on the other side of the coach. "Is it Indians, driver?"

"Not likely," the driver shouted, then whistled at his team. "Indians, especially Apaches, don't let you see them until it's too late to do anything but die."

Hardley jerked his head back in the window and fumbled for the revolver at his waist. "Just in case," he said to Marie.

"Just in case what? You decide to shoot yourself?"

He grinned sheepishly.

"If we have to depend on you, Hardley, to protect us, we're as good as dead. Pull out your pencil and pad. Maybe you can write a story about your own demise."

From up above came the shout of the driver. "It's cavalry." The stage began to slow.

Marie peeked outside once again and saw two dozen soldiers approaching. She hoped one of them was Jean Benoit. The stage came to a stop as a captain rode up to the driver. "I'm Captain Roche of Fort Fillmore. Is this stage carrying Marie Couvillion, wife of Senator Couvillion?"

Marie opened the coach door and leaned out. "I'm Marie Couvillion."

The captain removed his hat. "Allow me to introduce myself, ma'am. I'm Captain Bernard Roche, here to escort you back to Fort Fillmore."

Marie cleared her throat of the trail dust. "I had assumed Captain Jean Benoit from Fort Marcy would be here to accompany me. Is he with you?"

"No, ma'am. He is not scheduled to arrive for a few days, as I understand, though that is a matter attended to by my commander, Lieutenant Colonel Jeremy Sullivan."

"The senator's instructions were for Captain Benoit to meet me here. Was his message not delivered to your commander?"

"Yes, ma'am, I believe it was."

"I must have a talk with your commander, then."

Oddly, the captain seemed to grin slightly as Marie pulled herself back inside and shut the door. Then the driver shouted at the horses and the stage lurched forward again.

An hour later the stagecoach dipped down an incline toward the wide valley that had been carved out of the earth over thousands of years by the Rio Grande. The stage skirted the bank of the river, then lunged past a few rolling hills, and as it made a curve in the road Marie Couvillion saw the modest buildings of Fort Fillmore. They were the color of earth and as plain as a box. Over them all flew an American flag from a flagpole that sparkled white in the bright sunlight. As the stage passed the first of the outer buildings Marie brushed her blond hair.

The coach rumbled past several of the buildings, then stopped beside the parade ground, where soldiers stood ready for inspection. The coach halted, and instantly a soldier opened the door.

The senior officer stepped to the coach, removed his hat, and looked inside. "Welcome to Fort Fillmore," he said.

Marie leaned out the door and gathered her skirts before stepping onto New Mexico soil. As she looked around, she wondered how any information Jean Benoit might have acquired in this godforsaken territory could possibly help the South.

"I am Lieutenant Colonel Jeremy Sullivan," announced the commander.

"Where is Captain Jean Benoit?" Marie demanded.

"Who?"

"Captain Jean Benoit. He was to meet me here from Santa Fe, and I do not see him."

"He may be a few days late, ma'am."

"And why is that?"

Sullivan seemed to gulp. "The distances, ma'am. It takes a while for us to pass orders along."

"The senator will be greatly disappointed, as am I, Colonel. Now, show me to my room and have your men bring my trunks—there are two of them."

"Would you care to join me and a few officers for dinner?"

Marie shook her head. "I am tired and desire rest." She turned and looked at the stage as Hardley emerged. "Were Jean Benoit here, I might have joined you, but perhaps Mr. Hardley, of the *New Orleans Picayune*, would care to have dinner with you. Now, take me to my quarters."

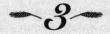

3

Lieutenant Colonel Jeremy Sullivan paced back and forth in front of his desk. It was almost noon, and he had not seen nor heard from Marie Couvillion. Still stung by her rebuke the afternoon before, he worried about his chances for promotion. Even worse than her rebuke were the smirks of his soldiers. They were laughing at him, enjoying her curt refusal to join him for supper, a supper largely taken from their gardens. Though not one soldier or officer had said a thing, Sullivan could read the glee in their steps as they carried out their chores. He cursed them to himself, resolving to deal with them after the senator's wife left for Santa Fe.

For now, he had to win back Marie Couvillion's favor. She was a striking woman with blond hair and cornflower blue eyes that seemed inviting even when refusing an invitation to dinner. Even in her dust-powdered overcoat, she cut a striking figure with her inviting hips, narrow waist, and ample bosom. Sullivan was expecting Captain Benoit to arrive from Santa Fe the next day, and the lieutenant colonel knew he must take her that afternoon to Mesilla and to the bullfight he had carefully arranged.

As he paraded back and forth in front of his desk, he heard Captain Bernard Roche clear his throat. Sullivan turned and answered Roche's salute with a nod. "Yes, Captain?"

"The woman you hired to attend the senator's wife says Mrs. Couvillion would like to see you in her quarters."

Sullivan nodded. "I shall go immediately."

Roche turned smartly and disappeared from the doorway.

Sullivan grabbed his hat, raced briskly out of his office and past the lieutenant who worked the desk, then strode outside and across the parade ground, scowling at a pair of soldiers who grinned while they scooped up horse apples and dumped them in tin pails. He could read in their eyes how much they relished his failure the previous afternoon, and it only fueled his ire.

Reaching her quarters, he knocked on the door. "Mrs. Couvillion, it is Colonel Sullivan." At first he heard no response. "Mrs. Couvillion," he called again. Then he heard the muffled sound of her voice from the back of the house.

"Please come in."

Sullivan lifted the handle and entered, looking for her in the parlor and listening for the sound of her footfall upon the floor. Wondering where she was, he removed his hat and stood for a moment, waiting for a noise. He heard the sound of water being poured, and thought for a moment that it was she who had to do her own dishes instead of the *señora* he had hired to attend to those matters. He made a mental note to reprimand the *señora* and reduce her pay. He stepped down the hall, checking the dining room on the left, then glancing at the bedroom on the right, where the bed had been made. He heard the sound of water again but was confused by the location. It sounded as if it was coming from opposite the kitchen. He stopped at the kitchen doorway and looked around, taking in two kettles of water heating on the stove.

Then he heard the water sound again in the back bedroom opposite the kitchen. That bedroom was the room where he had had the tin bathtub placed. Was she bathing? What should he do? Walking in on her might anger her further, ending his hopes for a promotion.

"Mrs. Couvillion," he called, "may I do something for you?"

"Certainly," she cooed, her voice almost seductive. "Come in."

"Are you presentable?"

"Indeed."

He pushed the door open, then caught his breath. She sat naked in the tub facing the door, her arms resting on either side of the tub, her breasts drooping into the water, which was milky from soap. The water hid her nipples and her legs, but when she straightened, her breasts jiggled clear of the water.

"Wouldn't you say I'm presentable, Colonel?"

He licked his lips, his lust desiring her but his ambition for a promotion holding him back. "Indeed, Mrs. Couvillion."

"We didn't have the chance to get acquainted yesterday. The ride tired me out." She sat forward in the tub and dropped her right hand between her legs. When she lifted her hand, her fingers held a cloth. "Colonel, could you wash my back?" she teased, throwing back her shoulders so her breasts lifted. "I can't reach it."

Sullivan hesitated. Would this lead him to a promotion or a demotion? His mind urged caution, but the rest of him opposed restraint. He took a step toward her, then two, and suddenly found himself beside her. With his right hand he took the cloth while his left hand still held his hat. Marie Couvillion leaned forward. He bent slightly and gently swabbed her back. She moaned her approval.

"How's that?"

"It will do," she replied. When he lifted his hand she leaned back in the tub, her bosom rising and falling with the gentle swell of each breath.

Sullivan stared and offered her the cloth.

"Don't you plan to do the front?"

Sullivan hesitated.

"Aren't you under orders to attend to my every need, Colonel?"

He nodded.

"Then do it." Her voice turned momentarily cold.

"Yes, Mrs. Couvillion." He lowered his hand toward her, then hesitated a moment to close the final inch between his hand and her bosom. She saved him the trouble by arching her back and lifting herself against his hand. He warmed quickly to the soft touch of her breast, like a potter handling clay.

She twisted in the tub, then grabbed his wrist and guided it to her other breast. She moaned. "You should have had Captain Benoit here so you wouldn't have to endure this, Colonel."

"It is no problem, Mrs. Couvillion."

She laughed wickedly. "Please, Colonel, don't remind me I'm married, not that it would make any difference."

He washed her bosom carefully, enjoying the softness of her breasts. He continued until she pushed his hand away into the water, wetting his sleeve. Sullivan feared her fickle nature was to tease a man without giving him release. He backed away.

She lifted her hand toward him. "Help me up, then fetch the towel." Her wet blond hair was plastered against her head.

He dropped the cloth and took her hand, pulling her up from the water. She shivered as the air hit the water dripping from her body. Sullivan was close enough to see the goose bumps prickling her skin.

"The towel," she reminded him.

Hat still in hand, he retreated to the chair, grabbed the towel, then offered it to her.

Marie Couvillion jerked it from him and quickly dried down to her knees, then stepped out of the tub. Sullivan's eyes were riveted to the tiny V of silky blond hair where her legs met. She tossed the towel to the floor, then grabbed his belt and pulled him to her.

Sullivan was tempted to kiss her full upon the lips, but this woman worried him. Her deft fingers, though, left no doubt of her intentions as she quickly unbuttoned his pants. He flinched at the touch of her cold fingers, but even that could not douse his ardor.

Sullivan stiffened his back and tightened the grip on the brim of his hat. He closed his eyes until she released him.

"Take me," she commanded.

When he opened his eyes, he saw her bending over the tub, bracing herself against it and widening her feet upon the floor. Sullivan approached her and took her, never loosening his grip on the brim of his hat. Their bodies locked in passion's embrace, she began to moan, then cry and finally scream with excitement.

Though he wanted her to hush, he didn't want her to stop her carnal assault, so he said nothing until his lust was drained away. She screamed a final time, then jerked free of him and lunged for the towel. Grabbing it, she wrapped herself so quickly that Sullivan was stunned by her false modesty.

He awkwardly fixed himself and buttoned his pants, covering himself with his hat.

Marie shook her head. "I've never seen a man so partial to his hat."

Suddenly the hat felt odd in his hand, but he didn't know whether to put it on or not.

"You married?" she asked.

"To the army."

"A bachelor, then?"

"Yes, ma'am."

"That's too bad, Colonel."

Her reply confused him. "Why is it so bad?"

"Those are your quarters next door, are they not?"

He nodded.

"I thought my screams just might break up your marriage if your wife overheard them." She laughed.

Sullivan grimaced. He had never known a woman as conniving as she. Marie Couvillion was dangerous indeed, and he regretted not sending the request for Captain Benoit to Santa Fe sooner.

"My husband," she bragged, "once found out that I was diddling an Indian agent at Fort Laramie—George Teasley was his name—and my husband challenged him to a duel."

Sullivan didn't care to listen. He stepped away.

"Teasley fired first, creasing my husband's left cheek, leaving him a scar he still wears today," Marie continued. "Then my husband—he was only a congressman then, not a senator—fired. He didn't aim for the heart, nor for the head. No, he aimed for the gut, going for his privates. Teasley died an agonizing death two days later." Marie smiled. "My husband is a jealous man, and I do everything I can to keep him that way."

Sullivan had faced enemy cannon in the Mexican War. He had fought Indians on the northern plains, where he had been outnumbered two to one, but he had never been as scared as he was by this woman. Had he ruined his chances for a promotion—or at the very least, for one based on his ability to run a fort? Had he diddled away his own career, his very life? His knees felt weak.

"Run along, Colonel, so I can get dressed. But before you go, tell me—what do you have planned to entertain me until Captain Benoit arrives?"

"The village of Mesilla, north of here, is a quaint little place, with musicians who sing on the town plaza in the evening, and I have even arranged for the Hispanos to perform a bullfight tonight for your entertainment."

"What is so entertaining about watching bulls fight?"

"It is a man against a bull. It is a favored sport and spectacle among the Hispanos. There is no more dangerous sport than bullfighting."

"Now, Colonel, I am intrigued. I shall be glad for you to take me," she answered.

Sullivan turned and left, uncertain just what she meant.

Jean Benoit had pushed his men, arising two hours before dawn and riding for an hour after sundown each day. He was anxious to finish his assignment and return to Santa Fe, where he might learn more of his wife and girls. He craved news of them more than he desired rest. Often along the trail he had pulled

Dobbs's letter from his pocket and reread it, looking for some sign of hope that he might have missed before. Dobbs had written with heartfelt emotion, but gave no real clues, just a recitation of facts about his family's chances. If his daughters did not live, Benoit knew he would never have a chance to lay his eyes or his hands upon them. Should the girls die, he hoped Inge would at least save him locks of their hair for remembrance.

Benoit had not shared his news with his men, so he had not told them why he was driving them so hard. By moving at such a pace, he had picked up most of a day and would arrive the next morning at the fort instead of the next evening. He was close enough to make it to Fort Fillmore that night, being but four miles from Mesilla and a little over ten from the fort itself. However, the sun had set and darkness was enveloping the land. He figured he would camp on the outskirts of Mesilla and let the men visit the cantinas in town. They could have a good time, provided they were ready to leave by mid-morning.

The soldiers riding behind him had not been pleased with the long days. Their dissatisfaction had been stoked even further by Lieutenant Webster, who complained incessantly about Benoit's leadership to his subordinates. Most of the men, though, seemed to despise Webster as much as Benoit himself did.

Despite Webster's carping, the ride had been uneventful save for one moment earlier in the afternoon. Riding beyond a bend in the Rio Grande, where yucca and ocotillo sprang from the earth like the devil's hangnails, Benoit had glanced toward the river and had seen an Indian standing behind a yucca plant. Or at least he thought he had seen an Indian. In the blink of an eye the man was gone. Had it been a man or an apparition? Benoit did not know. He wondered if he had heard so many stories about Apaches that his mind was playing tricks on him. He had seen—or thought he had seen—a warrior with straight black hair hanging to his shoulders. Beneath his dark eyes was a white stripe going from cheek to cheek, over his nose. The warrior was shirtless, his bronzed chest traversed by a cartridge belt. He wore a breechcloth and leather leggings and held in his hand a carbine.

Benoit had blinked, and the man had disappeared. Benoit felt a chill run up his spine. Had he imagined things, or could the man have disappeared into thin air? He had encountered Indians in Wyoming Territory, including the vicious Crow, but never had he felt such uncertain fear.

The encounter—if it had been an encounter at all— occupied his thoughts until sundown, when Lieutenant Webster rode up beside him. The lieutenant saluted. "You going to keep the men riding until it's too dark to see, like you've done every night out of Santa Fe?"

"Is that a problem, Lieutenant?"

"It sours the men's morale."

"Your badmouthing my decisions doesn't help morale either, does it, Lieutenant?"

His question first surprised and then angered Webster. "Who said that, Captain?"

"I'm not blind, Lieutenant. I know what you're doing. That's one reason I'm a captain and you're still a lieutenant."

Webster's jaw snapped shut with a click of teeth.

"That's why I requested Lieutenant Coker instead of you, but General Barksdale ordered otherwise."

Webster spat between their horses. "I can't figure

you out, Benoit. You're from the South. When war comes, this'll be a northern army we're in. Doesn't that bother you?"

Benoit pointed his finger at Webster. "I took an oath, Webster. That's what bothers me, that and your insubordination."

Webster grumbled indecipherably.

"What was that, Lieutenant?"

"What shall I tell the men about tonight?"

"I'll tell them."

"Request permission to join the others, Captain," he sneered.

"Permission granted."

Benoit led his men forward. When he got within a mile of Mesilla, he stopped his procession and turned his horse to face his troopers.

"Men," he called, "I know we've ridden long and hard the last few days and you're tired."

A couple of men answered, "Yes, sir."

"I had my reasons. One of them was that I wanted to give you a night of entertainment in Mesilla, unless you're too tired, of course."

"No, sir," they answered in unison.

"Be ready to ride out at midmorning. We'll make the rest of the way to Fort Fillmore quickly, and likely start the return trip tomorrow afternoon."

"Thank you, sir," said one soldier. "We knew the things the lieutenant was saying about you weren't true."

"Webster," Benoit called.

"Sir?"

"What is it you've been telling the men?"

"Just that we need to be careful not to push our horses too hard, sir, or we'll wear them out."

Benoit heard the snickers of several soldiers.

"Very good, Lieutenant. Once we reach Mesilla, I want you to look after the horses while the men go to town."

"Yes, sir," Webster replied, anger in his answer.

"Let's ride to the outskirts of town, where we'll camp." Benoit turned his horse about and led the procession toward Mesilla. About a half mile from town, toward the river, Benoit made out the campfires of a party he took to be freighters, the men who carried goods from Santa Fe into Mexico and returned with bags of money. Benoit led the soldiers around the freighters' camp and picked out ground closer to Mesilla for the night.

He halted the column and dismounted. "Stake your horses and walk the rest of the way to town. Just be sure you can walk back tomorrow."

The men jumped from their mounts, hurrying to unsaddle and stake them. A few unrolled their bedding, but most opted to head for Mesilla immediately. Benoit rode among the men on his horse, waiting until the last man was gone so Webster wouldn't command any of them to handle his assignment. When the last soldier had left the camp, Benoit nudged his horse toward Mesilla, deciding to check out a cantina first, then go see what the ring of torches on the far side of town was about.

He found a cantina on the town square, dismounted, and went inside. A couple of his soldiers were already drinking, but their merriment dimmed when he walked in. Benoit nodded at them, deciding to take one drink and leave, so as not to diminish his men's celebration. He ordered a whiskey at the bar, which was nothing more than two planks across empty whiskey barrels.

As he drank the liquor he watched two men sitting

in the dim light of the far corner. One was a short man with unruly brown hair framing a bronzed face beneath a slouch hat. He had a hard look about him. The other was taller and thinner, except for a round face with little pig eyes and a snout of a nose. Both looked like men seeking easy money, but neither was dressed suitably for a gambler. Benoit might have studied them longer, but out of the corner of his eye he saw his men casting furtive glances at him, so he finished his drink, nodded to his soldiers, and exited the cantina.

He mounted and turned his horse toward the ring of torches on the far side of town. As he neared the lights he made out three dozen torches around a circular corral. In the fringe of the torchlight, he saw several men, all in uniform. He dismounted and introduced himself to the nearest soldier. "Captain Jean Benoit from Fort Marcy," he announced to a sergeant.

The sergeant saluted. "Welcome, sir. Colonel Sullivan wasn't expecting you until tomorrow afternoon or later."

Benoit glanced into the corral. "Is he here?"

"Yes, sir, with the senator's wife."

Benoit pointed to the corral and a man standing with a sword and cape. "What is this, Sergeant?"

"It's bullfighting, a local sport, sir. They'll let a bull in the ring and it will be up to the matador, as they call him, to slaughter the bull."

"A gun would do the job quicker."

"But that's not sporting, sir."

Benoit grinned. "Take me to Colonel Sullivan."

The sergeant nodded and started around the corral. "The senator's wife's a looker, sir, and stories are going around that she's not chaste."

"Marie Couvillion is a longtime friend of mine," Benoit said, then laughed.

"Sorry, sir, I spoke out of line," the soldier apologized.

"But Sergeant, the stories may be true."

Both men were sill laughing when they approached a stand where the colonel, Marie Couvillion, and a nattily dressed civilian sat on a bench overlooking the corral.

"Isn't this exciting," Marie said, clapping her hands together.

"They have been jabbing the bull with arrow points," Sullivan announced. "When they let him into the ring, he will be furious."

Benoit poked the sergeant. "Do they always fight at night? I wouldn't want to be in a half-dark ring with an enraged bull."

"I think the colonel paid them extra to do it under the torches." The sergeant stepped to the stand and saluted. "Colonel."

"What is it, Sergeant?" The colonel turned from Marie.

Holding his salute, the sergeant announced, "Captain Jean Benoit from Fort Marcy reporting to you."

"Jean," Marie exclaimed, bolting up from her seat, running down the steps, and throwing her arms around Benoit. "I'm so glad to see you. We have so much to catch up on, things Cle wants to know."

"I'm sure he does," Benoit answered, then saluted Sullivan.

"How are you?" Marie demanded.

"Married."

She laughed. "But what does that matter?"

Benoit turned to face Sullivan, who arose and returned the salute. "Evening, sir."

"Welcome, Captain. I've just been entertaining Mrs.

Couvillion and her friend, Mr. Hardley of the *New Orleans Picayune*. You are welcome to join as we watch an encounter between man and beast. It's a favorite sport of the Hispanos."

Benoit untwined Marie's arms from him, removed his hat, and followed Marie up the five steps to the bench. He shook Hardley's soft hand. By the smirk on the newspaperman's face, Benoit could tell he wasn't going to like Hardley.

"They're about to release the bull," Sullivan announced. "Take your seats and watch the spectacle."

"Oh, yes," Marie exclaimed. "I can't wait." She grabbed Benoit's hand and pulled him onto the bench between her and Hardley.

Two men in the corral opened a gate, and the mottled brown bull with wickedly curved horns charged into the ring. The young man in the middle twirled his red cape. Bewildered and angered from the torture, the bull pawed at the ground, tossed its head, then snorted.

The matador whistled at him, and the bull shuddered with anger, churning dirt with its front hooves. The bullfighter, who looked no more than nineteen in the dim light, moved to the center of the ring, where there was even less light. He came within ten yards of the bull, then kicked dirt at the animal. The bull lowered its head and charged for the man, who dropped the red cape to his side, then twirled it and danced away as the bull rumbled by.

"How thrilling," cried Marie, squeezing Benoit's hand.

The bull spun around. Instantly the matador lifted and flourished the cape to entice the bull to make another charge. The animal bolted forward, lowering its head and gouging at the cape as it charged by. With a compact move, the matador merely twisted away in a quarter turn as the bull lumbered by, its horns slicing at air.

"The colonel tells me," Marie exclaimed, her breath heavy with excitement, "that after he kills the bull with his sword, the bullfighter will cut off its tail and present it to me."

Benoit snickered. "I can think of a more appropriate part he should cut off for you."

Marie slapped his arm. "Jean, you haven't changed." She saw the bull make another pass at the bullfighter. "The sport," she said, "is to let the bull come as close as possible without getting gored."

On the next pass, the matador whirled the cape out of the way and slapped the bull with the side of the sword as it flew past.

The bull headed straight for Marie, and she cried with excitement as the soldiers cheered. The bull stopped suddenly, tossing its head in the air and snorting, then spun around so quickly that it kicked clods over the reviewing stand. The animal bellowed.

The bullfighter retreated to the center of the ring. The bull galloped forward, passing to the bullfighter's right, just as it had every time.

Marie twittered with excitement. "He stands so close to the bull. I have never seen a braver man."

The bull veered around without pausing and charged again. Head down, the bull shot toward the lone man, churning up the dirt. As the bull neared, the fighter waved his cape at the two thousand pounds of charging muscle.

The bull charged within three feet of the bullfighter, who raised his sword in the air. The bullfighter stepped to his left, expecting the bull to pass on his right, as before.

Instead the bull darted left.

The bullfighter reacted too late.

The crazed animal bore into the bullfighter's knees, then jerked its head upward, one of its horns catching the matador in the side and spinning him like a doll.

The man screamed as he flew through the air, then landed hard on the ground, staining it with a puddle of blood.

The bull circled about, lowered its head, and thundered across the ring, digging into the matador with its horns again and tossing him into the fence in front of Marie.

Benoit jumped to his feet. Before anyone could react and distract the enraged animal, the bull gored the young man in the gut, slicing open his belly.

Marie cried with excitement as the bull hooked the matador on its horns and smashed him into the fence with such force that the stand shook.

She and Sullivan shot up from their bench. Sullivan leaped from the stand to the ground, then turned, holding up his arms to catch Marie. "Jump, Mrs. Couvillion. Hurry before it breaks through the fence."

Though Hardley abandoned his seat with a scream, Marie ignored the colonel's call and smiled perversely at the bull, still digging its bloodied horns into the limp mass of meat that had moments before been a handsome young man.

Benoit popped open the snap on his pistol scabbard and jerked open the flap. His fingers grasped the butt of his revolver and jerked it free. He stepped to the edge of the corral, then leaned over the high rail until the barrel of his gun pointed at the ear of the bull. He pulled the trigger and the gun exploded, hitting the bull on the thickest part of the skull.

Staggered but not killed, the bull half lunged, half tripped into the corral, shaking the stand backward. Marie screamed and bounced into Benoit, knocking him toward the ring.

Benoit lost his balance and fell forward, clinging to the top rail as the wounded and angry bull tossed its head toward its new tormentor. One of its horns hooked on a rail, lifting both it and Benoit for an instant.

Benoit cocked his pistol again and fired, but the percussion cap was defective. The pistol merely clicked.

The bull pulled its horn from beneath the rail and lowered its head to slash at Benoit again.

So close to the bull that he could smell the aroma of sticky blood on its horns, Benoit pulled back the hammer on his pistol again.

The bull's horns started toward him.

Benoit fired at the bull's black eye, then instantly cocked his revolver and shot again, this time at its neck. Both bullets hit their mark and the bull dropped to its knees, then lunged forward, dying atop the dead bullfighter.

"*Merdé!*" Benoit exclaimed as he peeled himself from the fence. For a moment everyone looked in silence, awed by sudden death. The quietude was suddenly broken by Marie Couvillion laughing, then applauding.

Several Hispanos, including one screaming young woman, scrambled into the ring to attend to the young man. A few soldiers helped pull the bull from atop its victim.

"Colonel, that was exciting," Marie cried with the glee of a girl who had just ridden her first pony.

Benoit saw the distaste in the colonel's eyes, then turned from Marie and reholstered his pistol. Examining his uniform, he noticed a smear of blood where the bull's horn had brushed against it. Other than that, he was all right, save for the churning disgust in his stomach. Marie was a cold woman.

"Colonel, colonel," she cried, "bring me the tail of that bull. I shall have many exciting things to tell the gentle ladies back in Washington when I return."

The torchlight was adequate for Benoit to see Sullivan's loathing. Benoit let out a deep breath, then jumped from the stand to the ground. He had seen enough of the bloody spectacle and more than enough of Marie. Walking around the review stand, he dreaded the long ride with her to Santa Fe. Benoit approached the colonel as he turned to one of his men.

"Son," Sullivan commanded, "snip the tail of that bull and give it to the lady." By the inflection on the last word, the commander made evident his feelings about Marie.

"Jean," cried Marie, ignoring Hardley's proffered hand, "come help me down."

Benoit paid no attention to her. "Colonel," he said, "I've had enough for the night. My men will be at the fort by midmorning. I hope to start the return trip by one o'clock."

"The sooner the better," the colonel replied.

Benoit walked to his horse.

Marie's voice trailed after him. "Jean, where are you going? We've much to visit about. News from Washington."

Benoit found his gelding, mounted the animal, and returned to camp where a sullen Lieutenant Webster waited near the campfire he had started.

Before dismounting, Benoit called to Webster, "Lieutenant, you can go into town with the others, but be back in time to ride. We'll have another long day tomorrow."

Without a word Webster slipped away in the darkness, and Benoit slid off his horse, silently unsaddled the animal, and rubbed it down. He made his bed and waited, the horror of Marie's bloodthirstiness pushing aside temporarily his worries about his wife and young daughters in Wyoming Territory.

After midnight the men began to straggle back into camp in pairs and trios, a couple singing off key until another one informed them that it was Captain Benoit, not Lieutenant Webster, on his bedroll just beyond the glow of the dying campfire. Benoit finally fell asleep, only to wake an hour before sunrise. He decided to let his men sleep off the night's reverie, at least until the sun was ready to peek over the horizon.

When the men were up and ready, he led them to Fort Fillmore, arriving an hour before noon. The colonel already had an army ambulance with a canvas top loaded with Marie Couvillion's two trunks when they arrived. The colonel dashed out of his headquarters the moment Benoit dismounted.

"I'm glad you're finally here. I feared you'd deserted and I'd be stuck with that woman," he said, waving away Benoit's salute.

"She wasn't always like this," Benoit answered. "She didn't benefit by the man she married."

"Senator Couvillion?"

Benoit nodded.

"She brags he killed a man who had cuckolded him."

"Happened at Fort Laramie. She probably wishes Cle had been killed instead, but she's too vain to give up the privileges of being a senator's wife."

"I thought she might help my career."

Benoit shook his head. "She only helps herself to whatever she wants, like the bull's tail. What kind of woman would want that?"

Sullivan shrugged. "You can ask her on the way to Santa Fe. You'll have a lot of time to talk."

"I know, Colonel, but let's change the subject. Can my men mess with your men, get a decent meal before they start back? They're dragging this morning. I let them spend the night in Mesilla."

"I don't know that you can call the mess food decent, but it's better than trail food."

Benoit told his men to join the soldiers of Fort Fillmore for lunch while he and the colonel dined together. The colonel escorted him to the officers' mess hall, where they took chairs at a table with a white linen cloth. Shortly the cooks brought them beefsteaks and sweet potatoes as well as cups of steaming coffee.

"I have arranged, Captain Benoit, for you to accompany a Mexican caravan from Chihuahua up the trail to Santa Fe."

"That won't be necessary, Colonel." Benoit took a bite of steak and savored its flavor.

"I must insist, Captain, my thought being that there's more safety in numbers."

Benoit pointed his fork at the colonel. "But why? We all know Apaches hate the Mexicans, but there haven't been reports of Apache attacks on soldiers."

"Absolutely not," Sullivan answered, hitting the table with his fist. "To the best of my knowledge, there's never been an attack on U.S. soldiers by Apaches."

"Then why the worry, Colonel? We can make better time without the freighters."

"You have but a dozen men, and I would hate for

the first attack to be on a party that included a senator's wife, even Marie Couvillion. There's safety in numbers, even with Mexicans."

Benoit was against the idea because he knew the freighters would slow him down. Yet he had pushed his men hard, and perhaps a slower pace, at least for a couple of days, would replenish his men's energy. He could at least accompany the caravan for the remainder of that day and the next. That would be adequate. Then he could leave the freighters to their own devices.

"I'll accept your offer, Colonel."

"I will rest much easier, Captain. The freighters will be ready to move once you reach them. They are camped by the river, north of Mesilla."

"I think I saw their camp last night."

The two officers talked about mutual army acquaintances and army gossip for the remainder of the meal. After seconds and a slice of mincemeat pie for each, the two officers arose and headed for the parade ground, where the men had reassembled to await Marie Couvillion's emergence from her quarters. She appeared wearing a full blue silk dress with lace around the collar, sleeves, and hem. She opened a parasol as Hardley joined her, then both strolled across the parade ground. She twirled the parasol on her shoulder and carried in her other hand a coil that looked like a quirt.

Not a pair of male eyes at the fort failed to watch. She was striking, Benoit had to admit, even with a reporter at her side.

She stopped in front of the officers. "Good afternoon, gentlemen," she said, then pointed at Benoit with the hand that carried the coil. "You should not have left so soon, Jean. I thought surely you would want to see this." She flicked her wrist and the bull's tail unfurled in her hand. She held it by the tassel. "Only the one who killed the bull can give it away, and that is you. Who shall have it?" She shook the tail.

Benoit bent at the waist and bowed toward her. "I can think of no one more appropriate than you."

She smiled. "You always were a charmer. I look forward to visiting with you on the trail."

Benoit smiled. "Lieutenant Webster will be assigned to you, Marie. Hardley will ride in your wagon with you. As commander, I must ride ahead of the men."

"A shame," she said. "We have so much to . . . explore together."

Benoit turned and ordered Webster to escort Marie and Hardley to the wagon. Then he instructed the men to mount up.

Within minutes the dozen soldiers and the army ambulance with Webster, Marie Couvillion, and J. Ernest Hardley was turning toward Santa Fe.

Benoit kept his men on the trail through Mesilla while he rode ahead to the freighter camp. He found the freighters where he had seen their camp before. He greeted the *jefe*, a small, muscular man who carried a whip in his hand. Though Benoit had expected a caravan of wagons, what he found instead was a single Conestoga wagon, two *carretas*—wooden wheeled carts— drawn by oxen, and forty mules laden with packs. Benoit soon realized the traders had sold their goods in Mexico and were now returning with the proceeds of their commerce. He could tell by the way the mules were packed that some carried gold and silver.

The *jefe* spoke broken English. "Welcome, *señor*, glad we are that you have joined us." He pointed to two men sitting on horseback a hundred yards away. "*Dos hombres muy males*, very bad."

Benoit recognized the two as the men he had seen in the cantina the night before.

"Who are they?"

"*Se llama* Jim Morehouse. A scalp hunter he is. And Harold McRae. Hated by the Apache. Feared by the Mexicans. Your soldiers protect us they will."

"You'll be protected." Benoit pointed to the northeast. "Follow my finger and we shall join the soldiers."

The *jefe* issued commands in Spanish, and the wagon and the *carretas* began to roll, followed by the forty mules, a dozen muleteers working among them, whistling, cursing, and shouting. The wheels of the *carretas* turned on ungreased wooden axles, squealing as if protesting every movement toward Santa Fe.

For miles Benoit kept looking over his shoulder, unsettled by the two riders who seemed to be tailing them. After the caravan joined Benoit's soldiers and Marie's ambulance, the two riders turned around and headed back for Mesilla.

Riding until sunset, Benoit finally ordered his men and the Mexicans to make camp. Soon the Mexicans had started campfires and began cooking meals that seemed more flavorful than the jerked beef and hardtack that his own men and Marie were eating. A couple of times Marie started toward him from across camp, but he always jumped up to find something to do in the opposite direction.

He instructed Webster to keep her away from him for the night, and for once the lieutenant followed his orders without hesitation. After checking on the posting of guards, Benoit settled into his bedroll, wondering about the health of his family and fearing Marie's machinations.

His band was small, only nine men, three wives who had accompanied their husbands, and Crooked Tooth, a woman whose fierceness in battle had earned her a reputation equal to that of any male warrior. One Who Hears Like a Coyote knew when he left camp that Mangas Coloradas did not favor his raid. But Mangas Coloradas was growing old and the Chiricahua must one day choose a new leader. One Who Hears Like a Coyote wanted to be that leader instead of Cochise, the wily buck who had married the daughter of Mangas Coloradas.

Rather than go into Mexico, One Who Hears Like a Coyote had ridden east from the camp of Mangas Coloradas and roamed along the Rio Grande. He had hoped to find a party of traders along the river, but instead he had seen but one small band of soldiers.

The caravans heading south were always to be preferred. While the traders on the return trip north usually carried gold, silver, and other items of little use to the Chiricahua, the southbound traders carried great riches, including calico, flannel, broadcloth, and linen as well as buttons and beads that the Apache women favored to adorn their clothes. Often the freighters carried rings, bracelets, necklaces, and earrings as well as mirrors, copper pots and pans, candlewicks, and other goods the Apache women could use. But most important of all, the trade wagons carried gunpowder, rifles, percussion caps, flints, lead, knives, axes, and arrow points, good both for killing game and for killing enemies.

And the Chiricahua had many foes of long standing, most certainly the Mexicans, whose chiefs had placed bounties upon the heads of all Apaches. Rogue Mexicans hunted Apaches like animals. Even some Americans had joined them in their perfidious war against the Apaches.

Among the dozen scalp hunters the Chiricahuas knew by name was one in the land claimed by the United States. He was called Jim Morehouse, and he roamed within a two-hundred-mile radius of Mesilla and was especially vicious to Apaches. But bad though the scalp bounties had been on the Apaches, they were probably worse on the Mexican people themselves. With Indian blood in their veins, the Mexicans were darkskinned and dark-haired like their Indian cousins. Evil men such as Morehouse often killed Mexican families and turned their scalps in for the reward money.

In fact, the Mexicans often had more to fear from the scalp hunters than did the Apache, because the Apache roamed the region while the Mexicans were bound to a piece of ground that they tilled or ran livestock on, making themselves easy targets for the scalp hunters. They were foolish, the Mexicans, not to roam the land, as did the Apache.

One Who Hears Like a Coyote looked around the small camp in the hills overlooking the river. Over a small fire roasted strips of venison from a buck deer that Crooked Tooth had killed that afternoon. The other three women cooked, but Crooked Tooth sharpened her knife, always glancing toward the river. Though a good-looking Apache woman, she had never taken a husband after the death of Spotted Dog, who had been her lover six winters previously. Spotted Dog had been killed by scalp hunters, and Crooked Tooth had avenged his death, but she vowed not to stop her warlike ways until all scalp hunters had disappeared from the land.

Crooked Tooth had trapped Spotted Dog's killers by walking naked and unarmed into the camp of the three scalp hunters who had killed him. Observing Spotted Dog's scalp upon the belt of one man, she had gone over to him.

The murderers suspected Crooked Tooth of treachery until she patted the crotch of her betrothed's killer. Then the Mexicans started whooping with anticipation. She led the scalp hunter to his bedroll. So anxious was the man to have her that he unbuttoned his fly without removing his pants. When he laid upon her, she kept her legs tightly together, making him struggle as she worked open his collar. When the base of his neck was exposed, she bit into it, severing his jugular vein and spitting out a hunk of flesh, and simultaneously reached for his knife.

As he screamed and rolled over, she pulled the knife from his scabbard and buried the blade between his ribs. Either wound would have killed the scalp hunter, but he lay thrashing for an instant as she leaped to her feet. She lunged for the second of the scalp hunters and sliced open his belly so adroitly that he did not understand what had happened until he looked at his shirt and saw his guts oozing out. He fell to the ground and died.

The surviving scalp hunter had grabbed his gunbelt and managed to extract his pistol, but it was not properly primed and merely clicked when he pulled the trigger.

Crooked Tooth had plunged the knife into his heart, and he was dead before he fell.

Though Apache women sometimes took up arms against enemies when they were threatened, only Crooked Tooth rode as a warrior without question among the men. One Who Hears Like a Coyote knew that he must develop a reputation as fierce as Crooked Tooth's if he was one day to replace Mangas Coloradas as leader of the Chiricahua. The warriors with him were good fighters as well, especially He Is Building Something, Flat Nose, and He Is Wide, though none of them was as ambitious as himself. They and the others relaxed around the fire, eating pinyon nuts as they waited for the venison to cook.

Flat Nose looked at One Who Hears Like a Coyote. "Winter storms will come early this year," he said. "The signs show it." He pointed to the venison. "The coat of the buck was thick, and the birds fly overhead toward the south earlier than I can remember. And the pack rats scurry to gather as many pinyon nuts as they can. It is wise to return to the camp and help prepare for the winter."

One Who Hears Like a Coyote shook his head. "We must return with our hands full of presents for our people. It will help them get through the cold months ahead."

He Is Building Something grabbed a strip of venison from one of the sticks over the fire, tossing the sizzling meat from hand to hand until he could stuff it in his mouth. He chewed, then smiled. "The meat is sweet."

The others stepped to the small fire and helped themselves to the venison. They ate and talked, debating when winter might arrive and arguing where Mangas Coloradas's band should spend the cold moons. They were camped farther east this year than they had ever camped before. Some argued that they should stay where they were, but others suggested they move south into Mexico, where it was warmer.

Gradually dusk settled over their temporary camp, which they had chosen because they could see for miles in each direction along the river. Crooked Tooth arose from the ground and moved to her horse. One Who Hears Like a Coyote watched her and thought it a shame she had never taken a husband.

Even though his belly was full, One Who Hears Like a Coyote took a final strip of venison. A man of the desert could never eat too much, for he never knew when sustenance might again be available. He ate the sizzling meat, slowly savoring its sweetness, then stood and stretched. He moved away from camp to survey the length of the river. First he looked north, in hopes that he might see a camp of freighters. Disappointed that all was darkness, he glanced south. In the distance, perhaps three miles away, he saw a fire. It was a big fire to be so easily seen from the distance, but that was like the freighters. The Apache built small fires because they were much less wasteful of scarce wood. Their enemies made large fires that betrayed their presence and made them easy targets.

Knowing the restlessness of his band, he decided that they must raid the camp the next day. This caravan would be heading north, so it wouldn't have much, save the gold and silver that the whites and Mexicans found so valuable. He watched the campfire for many minutes, then returned to his own, where the burning embers gave off a soft glow. He squatted among the others. "Traders are coming from the south. Tomorrow we shall raid them and return to our people."

Flat Nose stood up to look at the whites' camp. "Attack at sunrise?"

"I will scout the camp first, then decide." One Who Hears Like a Coyote moved to his horse, where he encountered Crooked Tooth.

"Traders are camped down by the river," he said.

"I know," she replied. "I've been watching them since before we made the fire."

"Why didn't you tell me?"

"You are the leader who looks out for us all. You certainly saw them before I did."

One Who Hears Like a Coyote grabbed his bow and arrows as well as a hand ax he tucked in his belt beside his knife. "I will spy on the camp and return with plans for tomorrow," he told Crooked Tooth. He picked up his carbine and a belt of ammunition.

Crooked Tooth said nothing, but One Who Hears Like a Coyote could almost feel her hard gaze. He retreated to the others still lounging by the fire, telling them he would return. "Be ready to ride before sunup," he said, then trotted away from camp.

He moved carefully down the slope toward the river bottom. Reaching the level plain, he trotted toward the distant fire, weaving between the shrubs and cacti he could just make out in the darkness. Once his eyes adjusted further, he picked up his pace and ran with measured breath and long, even strides. Apache boys learned early in life to run and pace themselves, so the effort came easily to him.

Running as fast as he could in the darkness for two miles, he then eased back so he would approach the camp with even breath. When he was within a hundred yards of camp, he heard the restless stamp of the mules and the braying of a pair. They had picked up his scent.

He backtracked, then moved around the camp to make sure he was downwind from the animals. Coming within fifty yards of the camp, he bent to his hands and knees, advancing slowly from bush to bush, ever vigilant of any guards who might be posted. He hid behind a yucca bush and watched. He was disappointed to find that the camp was composed not only of traders, but also of United States soldiers. He saw one who seemed to be the chief and recognized him as the officer who had seen him three days before on the trail heading south.

Perhaps he should call off the attack, thought One Who Hears Like A Coyote, since the Chiricahua had never attacked U.S. soldiers. Then he saw something that changed his mind. There among the soldiers was a woman unlike any he had ever seen. Instead of hair as black as the darkest night, like Apache women's, this woman had hair as fair as corn silk. He knew he must capture the woman and have her. With time, perhaps he could even make her his wife or slave.

She seemed to be the focus of the soldiers' attention, though she was generally ignored by the Mexicans. One Who Hears Like a Coyote watched her, thinking he could return with no greater trophy than the woman with corn-silk hair. Satisfied that he knew the number of soldiers and Mexicans, he retreated from the enemy camp and returned to his own.

The others were still talking around the remnants of the campfire when he arrived. "We will attack tomorrow at dusk."

"But why not morning?" He Is Wide wanted to know.

"Because soldiers travel with the traders. We shall wait until the afternoon, when the soldiers' horses are tired and the sun is in their eyes."

"These soldiers," Flat Nose asked, "are from the United States, not Mexico, no?"

"Yes," One Who Hears Like a Coyote replied.

The members of his band chatted among themselves, then He Is Building Something shook his head and pointed his finger at One Who Hears Like a Coyote. "Our band has never attacked the blue-coated soldiers. It is not wise. Mangas Coloradas will be unhappy."

"Mangas Coloradas is a great warrior, but he is old and his vision is bad. He cannot see that all soldiers are bad."

The men questioned the wisdom of an attack. Only Crooked Tooth did not complain. One Who Hears Like a Coyote gestured toward her. "Among warriors, it is a woman who does not speak against the attack."

The men murmured at the insult. Even the three wives who had accompanied their husbands whispered excitedly to each other.

Crooked Tooth spoke. "I will follow my leader, whether I agree or not." Her words shamed the men. One by one the men nodded.

"We will rise early," One Who Hears Like a Coyote said. "We shall go a day's journey and wait in ambush. We will take women for captives. I did see one. And we shall take the mules and horses, as many as we can capture. Then we shall ride hard back to the camp of Mangas Coloradas, our leader. We will be received as heroes."

Jean Benoit decided they had traveled enough for the day. As he had foreseen, the freighters had slowed his return to Santa Fe, and, like him, the soldiers were restless. Come morning, he would leave the traders behind so that they could move more quickly toward Santa Fe. All the men were tired of Marie Couvillion's aristocratic manners and of Hardley's meddling. For once, Benoit actually felt sorry for Lieutenant Webster, who was riding in the wagon with them.

Though tired, Benoit dreaded the end of the day's march because Marie would start pestering him. Finally, however, Marie's whining and the screech of the *carreta* wheels got the best of him. Though a couple of hours of sunshine still remained, Benoit lifted his hand and halted the procession. Immediately the Mexican freighters started unloading packs from mules. The soldiers dismounted, and Webster abandoned the ambulance, leaving Marie to get down for herself. Marie looked around, but no soldier moved to help her, forcing Hardley to assist. Benoit sat amused in his saddle. She was, after all, only a senator's wife, not the queen of Sheba.

Amused at her regal manner in the desert, Benoit rode toward her. She brushed the dust from her dress and glanced at Benoit.

"When do we dine?" she asked nonchalantly.

Benoit took off his hat, looking beyond her to the granite mountains that were pink beneath the descending sun. "On the trail, Marie, we just eat."

Marie cocked her head. "You've changed, Jean," she said.

"Times change."

"Once you were fun and carefree. You remember all the time we spent in my father's library, wondering if Father would catch us?"

"I'm married now."

Marie laughed wickedly. "So am I, but that doesn't stop me."

"We're different, Marie."

"We're both flesh and blood."

"I have twin daughters."

Marie seemed perplexed. "Well, well. . . congratulations. That German girl—Ingrid, wasn't it?"

"Inge is her name."

"And your daughters' names?"

"I don't know."

"Inge won't tell you," she shot back sarcastically.

Benoit slapped his hat back on his head. "Good day, Marie. I will see that Lieutenant Webster attends to your needs."

"He can't attend to them all. I was hoping you could."

Ignoring her, Benoit rode away, issuing orders to his men to set up camp, gather firewood from the stand of trees near the riverbank, and stake their horses.

Benoit turned toward the Rio Grande, then rode along the river, its waters glistening in the late afternoon sunlight. The waters were quiet, and Benoit advanced until he came to a clear pool that stood at the foot of a backwash where runoff had gouged out a gully that seemed to stretch all the way to the mountains.

Sliding off his horse, he held the reins and squatted over the clear water. He dipped his cupped hand into the pool and lifted it to his lips. The water was cool, the taste bitter, like Marie. He remembered a young, fun-loving girl who was pampered but not mean, unlike the present Marie. Had Cle Couvillion changed her so? Was that the price of marrying an ambitious politician? Cle was ruthless in politics. Was he the same with his wife? Benoit had never respected Cle. But after Cle caught Benoit's own brother, Theophile, in his sinister web of political intrigue, Benoit had even less respect for him. His brother, enrolled in the U.S. Naval Academy, had answered Couvillion's call for Louisiana and the South, agreeing to turn his back on his oath of allegiance to the United States should a separate nation be formed. Benoit cursed the senator for his deviousness and his brother for his foolishness.

Standing up, Benoit let his horse drink, then jerked the reins and turned the animal toward camp, preferring to walk. By the time he got back to camp, the mules were herded together and the men were collecting around fires to cook their supper. The soldiers were boiling salt pork and potatoes. Marie wandered from fire to fire to see what was cooking, but not bothering to help. Spotting Benoit, she strode toward him. Drawing up in front of him and his gelding, she planted her feet on the ground and placed her balled fists on her hips. "That slop, is that what we're having to eat?"

"This isn't a drawing room in Washington, Marie. These men are soldiers, not your cooks and servants."

"I am the wife of a U.S. senator." She stamped her foot.

"And the daughter of one," Benoit reminded her. "I'd say you did better by the father than by the husband."

She lifted her arms. "I suppose I could've been an army officer's wife, eating slop for food and only dreaming of ever being in a Washington drawing room. I've met the president, been to balls, even met the ambassadors from England and France. I deserve better than this from the United States Army."

Benoit realized the soldiers were beginning to notice their conversation, and he knew he must make a statement. "Unlike your prissy husband, who wears his silk cravats and diamond stickpins in the halls of Congress, these men wear ill-fitting uniforms and rely on firearms that don't always work because Congress didn't lay out enough money to give them dependable weapons. The army owes you nothing. It's your husband that owes the army. And he's not producing."

Marie crossed her arms over her bosom, her bottom lip protruding in a pout. He'd seen that hurt look on her face in the past when she didn't get her way. Now, he knew, she was embarrassed because of his insult in front of the men. He no longer cared. Maybe if he angered her, she would report back to her husband that he no longer had the same passion for Couvillion's conspiracies.

"I'm not hungry," she said. "I don't want any of this slop."

"Very well. I'm not sure there was enough to go around, anyway."

"Should I remind you that you would never have gotten promoted to captain, certainly not at your age, without my husband? Don't you forget that. My husband and I made you a captain."

Benoit nodded. "I didn't ask for any help."

"No," she said, "I did."

Benoit turned to walk away, but she grabbed his arm. He took another step, pulling her with him.

"I won't ever ask Cle to do you another favor." Then she smirked. "And I won't have him help out your brother, either. I've seen the letters Theophile has written, they're—"

"Hush, Marie," Benoit commanded, looking around and seeing several soldiers within hearing range, including Lieutenant Webster. "Let's go for a walk."

Marie nodded.

Benoit turned the horse around and started back toward the river. They walked along its bank until they reached the pool where Benoit had tasted the water. He tied his horse to the limb of a giant fallen tree carried by floodwaters past to that location.

"You've changed, Marie, and Cle's the one who did it."

She shrugged. "Politics make for strange bedfellows and marriages."

"Hotheads like him will ruin Louisiana and the South." Benoit eyed her closely. No matter what she said, he did not trust her.

Marie unbuttoned her left sleeve cuff, then her right.

Benoit studied her face, ignoring the movement of her fingers.

Then Marie's fingers began to dance up the front of her blouse, dislodging button after button until her blouse fell open. She pulled it off and tossed it toward the horse's rump.

Benoit backed away.

She began to unbutton her undergarment, then slid it down until it hung limply over her belt. Her breasts jutted out like mountains waiting to be scaled.

Benoit shook his head, then glimpsed Lieutenant Webster hiding down the bank. "Cover yourself, Marie. Don't act like a whore."

"Just once for old times' sake, like things used to be."

Suddenly Marie lunged for him. She flung her arms around his chest, then screamed and slid down in his arms. As she did so, Benoit felt a burning sensation in his breastbone.

Behind him he heard a scream, more shrill and frightening than Marie's, followed by the sound of pounding hooves.

Benoit caught Marie, his hand brushing against a shaft in her side. She whimpered as his hand jarred the wood. Benoit glimpsed an arrow buried in her side.

Glancing at her bosom, he saw that the point had exited her and hit his chest. He realized a uniform button—and Marie's flesh—had softened the blow to him.

Webster shouted from downstream and drew his pistol, firing an instant later. For a split second Benoit feared Webster was shooting at him.

A horseman galloped by, then a second and a third, racing down the river toward Webster and the camp. By the uprooted tree, Benoit's horse fought against the reins, then jerked free and bolted for camp.

Benoit hurried to get Marie behind the downed tree for cover. He broke the end of the shaft off at her rib, then jerked the arrow by the point, pulling it from her body. Marie passed out, her weight falling full in Benoit's arms. He staggered and dropped to the ground just as a warrior galloped past. He could have sworn he was seeing things—the rider appeared to be a woman, her breasts bouncing as she passed.

Benoit leaped up from behind the tree and quickly pulled his revolver as two more Indians galloped by.

Then a single Apache charged out of the backwash astride a gray pony. The warrior was low in his saddle, leaning beside his mount's neck and drawing the bowstring, preparing to loose another arrow.

Benoit recognized the dark face with the white paint traversing his face from cheek to cheek. It was the warrior he thought he had seen on the trip to Fort Fillmore.

"Damn you," Benoit cried, cocking the hammer on his pistol and pulling the trigger. The gun exploded with a puff of smoke that temporarily blinded him. Benoit ducked behind the log and heard the swish of an arrow overhead.

Benoit raised his head.

The Apache was riding toward Lieutenant Webster.

Benoit fired again, then checked Marie. She was still breathing, but a pink froth came out of her nostrils. Her chest was bleeding. He grabbed her discarded blouse and pressed it against her wound. He looked downstream. Webster had disappeared. He heard the gunfire and men shouting at the camp. Benoit cursed his luck.

If the Apaches returned, he knew he could not hold them off.

It was a bitter irony that he might die with Marie Couvillion.

One Who Hears Like a Coyote had licked his lips, pulled back his bowstring, and sent the arrow flying toward the army officer just as the woman with the corn-silk hair had lunged toward the white man. By her scream, he knew he had hit her instead.

He had shouted for the others to attack, and they raced from hiding and down the riverbank toward the camp. One Who Hears Like a Coyote had run back for his horse, leaped astride it, and charged for the soldier he had meant to kill. The soldier had dropped the woman behind the tree trunk and scrambled over himself. One Who Hears Like a Coyote had lowered himself on his horse, notched another arrow, and pulled the bowstring taut.

The soldier had fired at the same instant that One Who Hears Like a Coyote let fly his arrow. The soldier's aim was off, and the warrior was unhurt. But the soldier had ducked, too, and the arrow flew harmlessly overhead.

One Who Hears Like a Coyote had raced by, striking his horse's neck with his bow, imploring his animal to fly. He'd heard a shot from behind him and passed a second soldier who seemed to have him in his sights. One Who Hears Like a Coyote had flinched, riding so close to the soldier that he could have reached out and touched him. This soldier's aim seemed true.

One Who Hears Like a Coyote had gritted his teeth for the expected blow of the soldier's bullet. The soldier had snapped the trigger, but his gun had not fired.

Now One Who Hears Like a Coyote charged into the camp. Before him soldiers scrambled for cover and their guns. The Mexican freighters ran terrified toward the wagon.

Releasing the reins of his horse and guiding the animal with his knees, One Who Hears Like a Coyote drew an arrow and fluidly slipped the notch over the bowstring. His strong arms pulled on the arrow until the bow warped. Seeing a soldier take rifle aim at one of his men, he pointed the arrow at his enemy and released the bowstring. The bow vibrated as it propelled the sharp metal point to its target. The arrow struck the soldier in the ribs just beneath the shoulder of his uplifted arm. The soldier dropped the rifle, the weapon discharging at his feet as he fell upon it.

Out of the corner of his eye, One Who Hears Like a Coyote saw an Apache warrior leaning over the neck of a wildly galloping pony and charging for two soldiers. One Who Hears Like a Coyote galloped through the camp, jerked the reins of his horse, and wheeled the animal about, ready to assist the foolhardy warrior. He jerked another arrow from his quiver, then realized the warrior was not a man but Crooked Tooth.

She charged between the two soldiers, her reins in one hand, a war ax in the other. Yanking the reins, she stopped the horse between the two men and leaped off her mount. She struck one soldier with a blow across the neck before he could even fire. Then, while the soldier on the other side of her horse tried to shoot her over the top of her fretful mount, she darted under the animal's neck and chopped at the man's shoulder. As he screamed and collapsed beneath her horse Crooked Tooth grabbed the man's carbine and jumped atop her mount again.

"Aaaahhhwoooo," she screamed, slapping her horse into a gallop.

Crooked Tooth was no man, thought One Who Hears Like a Coyote, but she was a warrior.

One Who Hears Like a Coyote saw a Mexican running for the wagon. He twisted and shot the arrow, which struck the man in the thigh. The trader tumbled forward, then crawled on hands and knees for cover behind a dead mule.

The sound of growing gunfire told One Who Hears Like a Coyote that the soldiers had recovered from the attack enough to answer with lead. He shouted at his band to escape. Just as quickly as they had run upon the camp, they departed, herding as many horses and mules as they could.

Shouting and screaming, his band hit the water, trying to keep the horses and mules together, but many of the animals balked and turned away, retreating toward camp.

With the soldiers firing bullets at them, One Who Hears Like a Coyote did not care to risk injury in pursuit of the fleeing animals. His band would escape with enough horses and mules for the raid to be a success. The horses splashed across the river, never in water more than chest deep.

Emerging from the river, One Who Hears Like a Coyote glanced about to make sure he was the last warrior to cross. He raised his bow over his head, then turned in triumph to follow the warriors racing for the hills, where they would meet the three wives and head back for the Chiricahua camp.

One Who Hears Like a Coyote counted his braves and was heartened to discover that not a one was lost. After they had ridden a couple of miles and were certain the soldiers were not following them, they slowed and herded their stolen animals together so they could count their take. One Who Hears Like a Coyote tallied twenty-one mules and six horses. He was disappointed that they hadn't gotten more horses, because it meant that the soldiers might give chase, though that was unlikely with wounded men.

One Who Hears Like a Coyote rode among the warriors, commending each for his bravery. He stopped opposite Crooked Tooth. "I have seen no warrior kill an enemy as bravely as you. I have heard stories of your courage but until today I had never witnessed it."

She lifted her war ax and ran her finger through the blood, then sucked the stain from her finger. "The blood of enemies is always sweet." Her eyes were as cold as her words. He knew of no Apache warrior who burned so hot for the enemy, any enemy. She seemed so harsh that One Who Hears Like a Coyote felt a current of fear pulse through him.

One Who Hears Like a Coyote turned away from Crooked Tooth and addressed all his warriors. "We will return to camp with many animals and many successes. Mangas Coloradas will remember our deeds, and soon others will follow us on raids because we bring back many mounts and we return without wounds."

Flat Nose looked oddly at One Who Hears Like a Coyote. "Mangas Coloradas does not want you to lead his people. You may return victorious with animals, but he tells all of Cochise's bravery."

"Crooked Tooth is a greater warrior than Cochise."

"I will not argue that," Flat Nose replied, "but Mangas Coloradas is against you, more so than even Cochise—no matter your bravery, no matter your success."

"Triumph speaks louder than an old man," One Who Hears Like a Coyote said.

"But Mangas Coloradas has many more triumphs than all of us. The people will listen to him."

One Who Hears Like a Coyote clenched his fist in anger. "They do not have the sense of a tortoise."

He Is Wide rode his horse between the two men. He pointed to the west. "The sun is disappearing and does not want to hear your bickering. We must find the women before dark and ride to the others. Only then will we know what Mangas Coloradas believes and what the people want."

One Who Hears Like a Coyote turned angrily away. "I shall lead you today, and I shall lead the people the day that Mangas Coloradas dies."

Jean Benoit staggered under the weight of Marie Couvillion as he carried her back to camp. He saw the Apache racing toward the river herding many animals, but half or more of the terrified mules and horses veered away from the water.

The heavy fire laid down by his men discouraged the Apache from trying to retrieve them. Benoit half ran, half stumbled toward the ambulance. He saw Lieutenant Webster shooting at the Apache.

"Lieutenant," he cried, "get the men to round up as many animals as they can."

"Yes, sir," cried Webster, issuing a torrent of commands.

Benoit squatted to place Marie gently on the ground. Her blouse, which he had used to cover the wound, was soaked with blood. He thought of his friend Jason Dobbs, the surgeon at Fort Laramie, and wished that he were here to attend to her, though he would have settled for any doctor at that moment.

Marie groaned as he pulled his hands from beneath her. Her head rolled to the side. He placed his finger in front of her nostril, concerned that her nose no longer bubbled with that pink froth; he wondered if she might be dead. Then he felt the slight wisp of a breath.

"Hold on, Marie, we'll get you to a doctor," he said, wondering if she would last long enough for him to get her in the wagon, much less survive the ride to Fort Fillmore.

Lieutenant Webster approached Benoit. "Is she alive?"

Benoit nodded. "For now, but we must get her back to Fort Fillmore."

"We lost six horses, and the Mexicans lost half the mules. We don't have enough for everybody."

"What about the men?"

Webster darted away, calling out the names of the soldiers, then going to each downed man.

Benoit pulled Marie's two trunks out of the ambulance and dumped them on the ground. He bent down, picked her up, and placed her in the back just as Webster returned.

"Two men dead, four wounded, one seriously, his shoulder cut like a side of beef," the lieutenant reported.

Benoit did some quick calculations. "We had eighteen horses, counting the four for the wagon—that leaves us twelve. There were fourteen men, including you and me, so we're down to twelve men, with one who can't ride. What about the other three wounded? Can they ride?"

"Should be able to, Captain. They have flesh wounds, painful but not usually fatal unless gangrene sets in."

"Put the one who's badly wounded in the wagon with Marie. That leaves us eleven men with twelve horses, four of which we'll need for the wagon. Someone'll need to drive the wagon, but we'll still be short. Have Hardley ride in the wagon with you, and the others double up on horses. Tell the men to saddle up and hitch up the team. We're returning to Fort Fillmore."

Webster hesitated. "Night's approaching."

"So's death for Marie and the soldier if we don't get moving."

"Yes, sir," cried Lieutenant Webster as he ran off, issuing orders.

Webster returned shortly with the leader of the Mexican freighters, who was talking faster than a snake-oil salesman and gesticulating wildly with his hands.

"What's he saying?" Benoit asked.

"He wants to know when you are going to retrieve his mules."

"Tell him we must get the woman to the fort to see a doctor."

"What about his wounded, he wants to know," Webster translated.

"They can follow us on mules, but we're not waiting."

Webster explained to the Mexican, who turned and jabbered disgustedly to one of his men.

"Only two of the freighters were wounded," Webster said.

Benoit helped two soldiers lift their seriously

wounded comrade to the floor of the ambulance. He heard
Marie groan. He looked at her and realized he hadn't even
covered her bosom. He crawled into the wagon, pulled her
undergarment up and slipped her arms through the arm-
holes, and buttoned it down the front, keeping her blouse
inside for a bandage.

Two soldiers moved quickly to hitch the team to the
wagon. One of the two horses, however, had not been
broken to the harness, having been a mount instead. The
horse shifted and stamped, only reluctantly allowing the
soldiers to hitch it to the wagon.

"Be sure there's a couple of canteens of water in the
back for the wounded," Benoit commanded.

A soldier brought him a horse. "Here, captain."

Benoit realized his mount had been one that was
lost. *"Merdé!"*

When the soldiers finished hitching the team to the
ambulance, Webster hopped into the seat and grabbed
the reins, quickly releasing the foot brake.

"Okay, men," cried Benoit, "mount up. Let's ride as
fast as we can while we still have a little light."

Benoit guided his horse into the lead and waited for
Webster to fall in behind him with the wagon, then
started south toward the fort.

"What about the two dead?" cried one soldier.

"Damn," Benoit said, halting his horse. "Any volunteers to bury them?"

All the men offered to help.

Benoit nodded. "Webster and I will start back. The
rest of you bury the dead, then catch up with us as best
you can."

Then the wagon turned about and headed south.
Benoit and Webster rode a half hour before darkness
slowed them. A half moon arose later in the night, giving

them enough light to find their way, but the going was slow, the men still on edge after the attack.

Benoit guided his horse beside the wagon to check on Marie.

Webster smirked. "Won't look good on your record, Captain, that the senator's wife was wounded on your watch."

"Can't be helped."

"Won't look good, either, when I tell Colonel Sullivan you were about to rape her."

"That's a lie."

"A woman don't take off her top to discuss religion," Webster said contemptuously.

"Lieutenant Webster, I'm ordering you to shut up. Once you get to Fort Fillmore, you can tell whatever lies you want to Lieutenant Colonel Sullivan. Until then, shut up."

"Yes, sir," Webster replied.

They rode in silence until midnight, when the troops rejoined them. The men sat tired in the saddle through the night, at times the wounded soldier growing delirious and crying for reinforcements to fight the demons.

Marie moaned occasionally. Three times they stopped the wagon long enough to attempt to give the two seriously wounded sips of water and to moisten their faces and lips.

The night seemed as though it would never end, and when dawn finally came they were still ten miles from Mesilla. With daylight the soldiers moved faster, skirting Mesilla and arriving in the early morning at Fort Fillmore, angling across the parade ground for the hospital.

Their appearance caused a commotion as soldiers ran from their posts to watch.

By the time they reached the hospital, Sullivan had joined them. "What happened, Captain?"

"Apache attack."

Sullivan looked in the wagon and saw Marie Couvillion. "Oh, my God," he said, "my career is ruined."

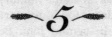

The post surgeon pushed Lieutenant Colonel Jeremy Sullivan aside and climbed into the wagon. Jean Benoit studied the doctor, waiting for an assessment of Marie's chances, but he struggled to hold his eyes open. Exhaustion had set in. Lieutenant Webster and J. Ernest Hardley climbed down from the wagon seat while the doctor checked Marie Couvillion and the injured soldier.

"Take them inside," cried the doctor.

Sullivan ordered others to help carry the wounded inside. In seconds Marie and the soldier were hauled into the hospital.

Turning to Benoit and Webster, Sullivan spoke abruptly. "You two come with me. I want a full report. Damn, why did this have to happen to me? Why now?" As Sullivan started toward headquarters, he grabbed the arm of a passing soldier. "Find Tim McManus and deliver him to my office, soldier." The soldier darted away, and Sullivan looked over his shoulder to confirm that Benoit and Webster were following him. They were, but slowly.

Sullivan wondered if he would have an army career

any longer. Marie Couvillion had brought nothing but bad luck to Fort Fillmore. Now her injury—or death, perish the thought—might ruin his career. He had to get results to salvage his life in the military.

Sullivan strode into headquarters. Benoit and Webster slouched in behind him. Both men fell into chairs as Hardley entered on their heels.

"What do you want?" Sullivan demanded.

"To find out what you're going to do about this attack," Hardley replied, "so I can inform my readers."

"Get out," Sullivan shouted. "You'll be told in good time."

Hardley retreated. Benoit shook his head, partly at the reporter, partly at the muddle in his brain.

"What happened, Captain?" Sullivan asked.

Benoit explained how they had stopped for the night and how Marie had resented the lack of special treatment. "We walked down to the river to talk about it outside the hearing and viewing of the men."

Webster perked up. "Hell, you went down there to rape her. She was half naked when the Indians attacked. I saw her."

"Webster was spying on us when the Apaches attacked. They shot her with an arrow, I dragged her to cover."

"Dammit," Webster said, "he was about to poke her."

"She's a loose woman," Sullivan said icily.

"To Webster's credit," Benoit went on, "he fired and alerted the camp. If he hadn't, more would have died. We lost two men as it is." Benoit shook his head. "Traveling with the Mexican freighters slowed us down."

Sullivan glared at Benoit as a rough-hewn man barged in.

"Call fo' me, did ya, Colonel?" came a booming voice.

Sullivan turned to the interloper, a man no more than five and a half feet tall with a full beard framing a bronzed face beneath a slouch hat that he made no effort to remove. His pants disappeared into knee-high boots and his shirt looked neatly starched and pressed beneath a clean vest.

"Tim McManus, have you met Captain Benoit and Lieutenant Webster? They ran into trouble on the way to Santa Fe."

"So I heard. Also heard they was travelin' with Mexicans."

Benoit nodded. "Upon Sullivan's orders, we did."

"'Paches, they hate Mexicans. Scalp hunting made 'em enemies."

"McManus should know," Sullivan said. "He was raised by Apaches."

McManus's dark eyes narrowed. "Me ma was Mexican, me pa Irish. 'Paches killed 'em, stole me. Kept me eight years 'fore I escaped, but I learned how the 'pache thinks. It wasn't smart, Colonel, sendin' 'em out with Mexicans."

Sullivan shrugged. "More safety in numbers."

"Not when the numbers are Mexicans." McManus scratched his chin. "I don't recall any 'pache raids on U.S. soldiers."

"And a senator's wife," Sullivan added.

"How many was there, Cap'n?" McManus asked.

"Maybe a dozen," Benoit answered.

"Likely a raidin' party, maybe young boys practicing so they can join the fall raids into Mexico."

"These were men," Webster said.

Sullivan slapped his desk. "Think you can find and

kill them, McManus? Several army careers may be ruined if you don't."

"Yours be one of them, Colonel?" McManus laughed.

"Everyone in this room would suffer, Tim."

"'Cepting me, of course," McManus replied.

"I want to report to Washington the savages were killed, if you can find them."

McManus nodded. "Done. Who'll be leading the expedition?"

Sullivan pointed at Benoit. "He's the one that let it happen."

For a moment Benoit was in that fog somewhere between being asleep and awake. When he realized what the colonel had said, he snapped alertly. "Colonel, I must report back to Santa Fe first."

"What were your orders when you came here? To deliver Marie Couvillion safely to Santa Fe. You failed, Benoit. Now's your chance to redeem yourself."

Benoit gritted his teeth. He wanted to return to Santa Fe to learn more news of his family. "Sir, I request that you appoint another officer to lead your men. They are, after all, your men, not men I've trained with."

"They're soldiers. They'll fight under any man who's not afraid to lead them."

"I've been riding for more than twenty-four hours. I'm exhausted."

"Then you'd better catch a few winks. I'm ordering my men to depart by one o'clock. You'll be in command, Benoit, with Webster as your second in command. Any questions, Captain?"

Benoit sighed. "Where's the nearest bed?"

The Apaches circled Jean Benoit. He tried to run but he could not lift his feet. He tried to scream but his voice hung in his throat. Just beyond the Apaches was the army camp where a hundred soldiers were fixing supper. How could his men not hear the Apache yells? All his men stood with their backs to him, ignoring him.

Benoit lifted his pistol but it would not fire.

The ring of Apaches tightened like a noose.

Benoit reached for his saber, but it would not budge from the scabbard. He felt the sweat beading on his face. He tried to curse but, like the saber, his words were stuck.

The Apaches came within reach, and he stood helpless, paralyzed with fear. But why? It was all so confusing.

Then one of the Apaches reached for him, grabbing his shoulders and shaking him. Benoit knew the warrior was about to strangle him.

"Cap'n, Cap'n," came the voice.

The Apache spoke English and knew his rank. Odd?

"Cap'n, it's time to get up."

Slowly the fog faded in his mind. Benoit shook his eyes open and looked up at Tim McManus.

"You're a mite jumpy, Cap'n."

Benoit rubbed his eyes. He had caught maybe four hours' sleep, but it had passed like four seconds, and his spent muscles seemed to be melting away in the bed. Breathing deeply, he tried to push himself up. He failed. He finally struggled to a sitting position, his hands dropping to his knees. He was uncertain whether he could stand, and if he could, he was doubtful he could walk, much less ride a horse across New Mexico Territory in search of Apaches.

"Men are a-waitin', Cap'n, ready to ride out for 'paches."

"What about Lieutenant Webster? Is he up?"

"Ya betcha, Cap'n. I wokened him first, I did. I know about rank, cap'ns outrankin' lieutenants and everybody outrankin' scouts like me."

Benoit struggled to his feet. He spent no time getting dressed because he had never undressed, merely removed his hat. Reaching for his hat, Benoit licked his lips and realized how dry his throat was.

"Where's water, McManus?"

"I brought a water pail, Cap'n. Left it outside. I figured ya might be thirsty. I grabbed a couple boiled taters from mess for ya, figurin' ya'd be a mite hungry."

Benoit straightened. "Good man, McManus."

"I been in your boots, Cap'n, so tired I couldn't arm-wrestle a horsefly without getting whipped. I once went thirty-six hours in the saddle without sleep and collapsed for two days. I didn't have the strength to break wind."

Benoit was too tired to laugh. He eased out the door, briefly blinded by the afternoon sunlight. He squinted at the ground. Spotting the pail and a drinking dipper, he hobbled over, bent, grabbed the dipper, and lifted it to his lips, gulping down the water quickly. It felt smooth upon his rough, dry throat. He drank until his thirst was sated.

Removing his hat, he bent over, filled the dipper, and poured the water on his head. The liquid jarred him from his drowsiness. He doused himself two more times before dropping the dipper and shaking his head like a dog coming out of a river. He yanked his hat down on his forehead, then straightened, realizing that the soldiers he would be leading had been watching.

"I didn't impress the men, McManus, did I?"

"Hard to say, Cap'n. Some figure you're sleepin' off a drunk, and that's something the men can't help but admire. I do, bein' of Irish descent. I figure I got as much whiskey as blood in me."

Benoit wiped the water from his eyes. "I'm gonna like you."

"That's a good thing, Cap'n, 'cause we're gonna get to know each other pretty well chasing 'paches, which is like playing hide-and-seek with the devil. They're everywhere and they're nowhere."

"With you, McManus, I've a feeling we're on even footing with the devil."

McManus shook his head. "I'd rather be on even footin' with the 'paches. I figure I can take the devil a mite easier."

"I've fought Crow and other northern tribes. What's the difference from fighting Apaches?"

"Ya fought them in the high country, didn't ya?"

Benoit nodded.

"This is desert we're fightin' in. 'Pache can go days without water. He knows where every drop of water is on the desert, and when that's gone he'll drink blood from a horse or mule. He's on a first-name basis, he is, with every snake, lizard, rock, and cactus. And he's got a mean disposition."

"Sounds like Crow to me."

"'Paches got a mean streak in 'em that'll make the Crow look as tame as missionary women at prayer time."

"McManus, I don't know whether to believe you or not, but I won't find out until I start riding, now will I?"

"No, sir," McManus answered, pointing across the parade ground, "but ya might linger."

Benoit turned to see Lieutenant Colonel Sullivan striding toward him. Benoit saluted.

Sullivan nodded. "The doctor says it'll be touch and go with the senator's wife. She's lost a lot of blood, and it's possible the arrow had some type of poison on it."

"We'll get the 'paches, Colonel," said McManus.

"Do that, but don't let any of my men die in the process."

"There's always that chance, Colonel."

"Just kill more of them than they kill of you."

Benoit nodded at the colonel. "With your permission, sir, we'll move out."

"There's a hundred rounds of ammunition and seven days of rations per man. There's plenty of grit in my men," Sullivan said.

"But they ain't fought 'paches yet, Colonel. That's when we see how much grit they got."

Benoit and McManus marched to their horses and quickly mounted up. Benoit was relieved to see the *Picayune* reporter watching from the hospital. He didn't trust Hardley any more than he did Marie, and he was glad the reporter hadn't insisted on accompanying the expedition. When he gave the command, the procession of forty soldiers fell in behind Benoit. McManus headed the men toward the Rio Grande.

About a mile short of Mesilla, McManus looked toward the town, then stood in his stirrups and cursed. "I afeared that," he said.

"What are you talking about?"

McManus pointed toward Mesilla. "Riders, eight of 'em."

"It's not Apaches."

"Worse. They're scalp hunters, the cause of trouble on both sides of the border."

"What do you think they want?"

"To travel with us."

"They can't."

"Sure they can, Cap'n. They'll circle around us like buzzards over spoiled meat."

Benoit realized the scalp hunters were intending to intersect his path on the other side of the Rio Grande.

At the river's edge Benoit studied the water.

"We may get across without wetting our tally-whackers," McManus said, "river being down, but it's a good idea to protect our powder."

Benoit ordered the soldiers to carry their powder and guns overhead, then motioned for the column to proceed. He led the cavalrymen into the water, which reached his knees as his horse plowed across the Rio Grande. The cold water invigorated him despite his exhaustion as he emerged on the opposite bank.

"With the river down that much, water's gonna be scarce wherever we go, Cap'n."

Across the river, both Benoit and McManus looked upstream at the scalp hunters, drawing closer. Benoit had seen the two in the lead in the cantina in Mesilla as well as trailing the Mexican freighters until Benoit had joined with them to take Marie Couvillion to Santa Fe.

"Jim Morehouse, he's the one on the bay, Cap'n. He's as cruel as the 'paches but without any of their finer qualities. He's so mean, he won't waste a bullet on a baby. He'll just brain 'em with a club or slit their throats. I'd as sooner sleep with a rattlesnake as ride with 'im. His partner, the one on the gray, is Harold McRae. He's got a decent streak in 'im, killing kids and babies with bullets. He's loyal as a puppy to Morehouse, though I can't figure why, 'less it's pure ignorance."

Benoit eyed McManus. "What's different between him and you wanting to kill Apaches?"

McManus bit his lip, then spoke. "I'm not killin' for money, but for my murdered parents and the eight years the 'pache took from me. The 'pache ain't done nothin' to Morehouse." McManus laughed. "But they sure will if they ever catch 'im."

The path of the soldiers finally intersected that of the scalp hunters a mile from the river, where the ground was as barren as a scalp hunter's soul.

Jim Morehouse halted his small band in front of the cavalry, lifted his right foot from its stirrup, and hooked his leg over the saddle horn. He cocked his head and waited, taking time to pull out a plug of chewing tobacco.

Benoit halted his column and motioned for McManus to advance with him. As Benoit approached, Morehouse eyed McManus, then Benoit. The captain studied Morehouse. Benoit did not care for his looks. His eyes were the color of the tobacco stains on his teeth, and there was a meanness in them. Morehouse was lean as a buggy whip, with stringy brown hair sprouting from beneath his hat. The drips from his nose fertilized a lush mustache that ran into a thick, wild beard. Benoit wondered if Morehouse was just as ugly underneath all that hair.

McRae was better-looking, the way the back end of a horse looks better than the back end of a mule. He carried more weight and less hair than Morehouse and had a broad nose and piggish eyes. A missing left ear gave his head a lopsided look.

Morehouse spoke first. "I hear you're hunting Apaches."

When he spoke, McRae cupped his left hand to the side of his head to hear better.

"Damn shame about that senator's woman," Morehouse continued. "Restores my faith in the United States Army to know you're going for the savages."

"Touching," Benoit replied.

"I figure you can use a little help from me and my volunteers." Morehouse eyed McManus. "You'll need it with him as your scout."

McManus cursed. "You damned son of a bitch."

"We're not interested in your assistance, Morehouse," Benoit said.

"That could be a mistake, a big mistake, Captain. You don't know Apaches."

Benoit nodded. "McManus does."

"Don't believe what he tells you." Morehouse looked beyond Benoit at the string of troops behind him. "Your men are green."

"They'll do."

Morehouse laughed. "You'll be singing another tune when you run into Apaches. You ran into them once and pretty near got yourself and the woman killed. All we're asking is to ride with you, Captain, and teach them Apache a lesson."

"And pick up any scalps you think you can sell for bounties."

Morehouse grinned. "A man's got to make a living."

"Not that way he doesn't."

Morehouse shrugged. "Once you get into the Apaches you'll regret not having us on your side."

"Don't think so, Morehouse. Now, I'm ordering you and your men to get out of our way so we can proceed on army business."

Morehouse smirked. "You can't keep us from following you. And you can't keep us from collecting scalps."

Benoit pointed at Morehouse. "What I can see, I can stop. Now get out of the way."

Morehouse removed his hat and grinned. "You can't stop us from following you," he repeated.

"You come within a half mile of my camp, and I'll fire on you."

"You'll be sorry if you do."

"You'll be sorry if you don't move—right now, Morehouse."

Morehouse slid his leg back over his saddle and his foot into his stirrup. "Let the toy soldiers pass by."

"Yeah," McRae said, as if wanting Benoit to know that he too had a tongue, if Morehouse would ever let him use it.

Morehouse, McRae, and the six other men moved off the trail.

Benoit turned in his saddle, nodded at Webster, and waved his arm forward. The soldiers advanced, McManus spitting at the ground beneath Morehouse's bay as they passed.

"No love lost between you two?"

"I'd love to kill 'im, 'cept I don't want to deprive the 'paches of the pleasure. They can kill a man so slow it takes a lifetime for him to die, and every second is pure horror."

The cavalry passed the scalp hunters and continued northwest until dark. They made a cold camp, not lighting any fires, upon McManus's recommendation. But a half mile behind them they saw the fires of the scalp hunters.

"The bastards," McManus said. "Any 'pache that couldn't see us in the daylight'll know we're here now."

Benoit half nodded. The exhaustion he had fought all afternoon gradually enveloped him in a foggy haze as sleep darted back and forth across his mind, even as he sat opposite McManus.

"Any man that rides with Morehouse is a fool, Cap'n."

"How's that?" Benoit heard himself ask.

"McRae's the only partner who ever seems to return with 'im from his scalp hunts. Seems the others get killed. And from what I heard, it ain't the 'paches that kill them, but Morehouse. I heard tell one man always gets his throat slit in the night and next mornin' Morehouse blames it on the 'pache for slippin' into camp and doin' the dirty work. But it ain't 'paches, no sir."

Benoit grunted. "I'm retiring, McManus. Make sure that Webster has posted the guards. I'm too tired to care."

"Cap'n," McManus said, "I'm surprised ya made it this long."

As soon as he had lain down on his bedroll, Benoit fell into the deep, restful sleep that only pure exhaustion can bestow. If he dreamed, he did not remember. If he moved, he could not recall.

Come morning he awoke with the stirrings of camp. The men ate hardtack, which challenged their teeth, and jerked beef, which challenged their innards. They saddled their horses and were riding by good light.

Benoit felt better than he had the day before, realizing that he had ridden on sheer willpower. McManus, who had been talkative the day before, seemed strangely quiet.

"Something bothering you, McManus?"

He shook his head. "I'm gettin' serious about findin' the raiders' trail." That was all he said until an hour before high sun, when he stopped his horse and dismounted. Holding the reins of his gelding, he started walking up an easily discernible trail. "Follow me, but not too closely," he instructed Benoit.

As McManus advanced he moved from side to side on the trail, well marked by the hooves of forty or more animals. He left the trail and examined the ground splotched in three places. "There's at least three women with them," he announced.

"How do you know?"

"Here's where they peed. A woman pees in a puddle. A man leaves a puddle and a trail."

Benoit nodded. It made sense, reading sign, but a man had to know the sign, just the way a man opening a book had to know the alphabet to read. Benoit had ridden with good scouts before, but never one who seemed to read sign so thoroughly.

"I thought I saw a woman among the attackers."

McManus stopped in his tracks and stared at Benoit. "How'd ya tell?"

"Rider had tits, but I thought I was imagining things in the surprise battle."

"Maybe you saw Crooked Tooth."

"Who's Crooked Tooth?"

"I always thought she was a legend, but supposedly she's a woman warrior who's ridden with the men."

"Never heard of such."

"Women ride with their husbands on raidin' parties and have been known to fight beside their men when attacked in camp, but Crooked Tooth rides with the men and fights with them."

"So there's she-devils among the Apache?"

"I reckon so."

"Answer me this, McManus. If you ever came up against her in battle, could you kill her, her being a woman and all?"

McManus considered the question for a moment, then started walking along the trail, looking for more sign. "A man's got to protect hisself." He pointed at the trail, then bent and picked up a dumpling of horse manure. Breaking it apart in his fingers, he studied it, then spoke. "They're a day and a half to two days ahead of us. The manure is still moist in the middle."

Benoit turned his gelding and stood in the stirrups, stretching his legs and looking a half mile behind his troops to where the scalp hunters, buzzards that they were, watched. Settling back into his army-issue saddle, Benoit shook his head. "Will we ever lose the scalp hunters, McManus?"

"Not 'less we kill 'em ourselves, Cap'n. Some men need killin', and I'd say those fellows need it bad." McManus paused long enough to pull himself into his saddle. He looked west toward the distant mountains, then to the north, studying so intently that Benoit felt edgy.

"What is it? Apaches?"

McManus shook his head. "Weather. Signs not good. I ain't seen any dung beetles around the horse apples. I ain't seen any lizards neither, now that I think of it. We could be in for bad weather."

"It's almost November. The chill's in the air at night."

"Yeah, but I'm not talkin' about a normal cold spell, Cap'n, I'm talkin' about an early winter storm." He pointed to the western sky. "See the geese?"

Benoit shook his head.

"I've counted a dozen flocks of 'em over the last few minutes. Too many for there not to be a storm brewin'."

"All the more reason to keep moving so we can get our business done and return to Fort Fillmore."

McManus nodded. "But the 'paches'll have something to say about our business, Cap'n."

The camp was touched with fever. More than half of the Chiricahua were stricken, clinging lifelessly to their blankets, barely breathing as the fever warred against their bodies. The men and the women would recover, but the weak—the young children and the old folks— might die.

Mangas Coloradas shivered with the fever, sometimes almost delirious and at other times as clear as his reputation for being one of the great chiefs of the Apache. He had lived many more summers than he could count and he wondered if the summer just ending might be his last. Already five women, three children, and a man Mangas Coloradas had in his own youth admired as a great warrior had died. Two babies had died as well.

Even if he died, though, Mangas Coloradas knew his people would survive, for his daughter had married well. As was the custom of his people, a man married into his wife's family and abandoned his own to live with her. His daughter, Dos-teh-seh, had married Cochise, a strong man, a crafty warrior, and a source of wisdom for all.

Others among his people, principally One Who Hears Like a Coyote, aspired to be his successor, but only Cochise was a leader who could command the respect of all. One Who Hears Like a Coyote was hot-headed and not given to careful thought.

As long as Cochise was strong and well, the Chiricahua would be a strong people. But at that moment Cochise too was stricken by the fever; he would recover, for he was too strong not to, but the camp was vulnerable with Cochise and so many other warriors sick.

Though Apaches were raised to trust no man but their fellow Apache, the Chiricahua trusted the Mexican least of all, for it was they who had put bounties upon the Apaches' scalps. The Americans, who had taken what they called New Mexico Territory from the Mexicans ten summers before, initially had seemed more interested in possessing the land on paper rather than in body. They had ignored the land until some prospector uncovered precious metals, metals the Americans called copper, silver, and gold.

At first the Apache had hoped to trust the Americans more than the Mexicans. And their conquest had benefited the Apache, for neither side was supposed to cross the border between their countries. Thus the Chiricahua could rest in relative peace in the United States without fear of the Mexican soldiers following them after their raids.

By his power of mind and by his commanding body he had persuaded the warriors to follow his guidance, for an Apache could not order another Apache to do anything. He could not understand how the soldiers in the Mexican and American armies could follow their leaders when the leaders ordered them to do chores, told them when to sleep, and commanded them to go into battle.

In his younger days, his body had been as strong and powerful as a grizzly bear's and his mind had been as cagey as a mountain lion's, but he was aging, his strength diminishing. And because of the periodic delirium brought on by the fever, he wondered at times if his mind was vanishing, too.

And then he fell into delirium again, his thoughts going back to the time a white man had given him an officer's blouse and a pair of blue army pants with a wide red stripe running down the side of each leg. He remembered the cotton cloth, the colorful beads, the tobacco—ahhh, the tobacco—the tinwork, the pistols, the carbines, the arrow points, the ammunition. Had the pants and the other goods brought by the white man into Apacheria merely been goods for trade, or had they been tools to make the Apache greedy and vulnerable to the ways of the white man? Mangas Coloradas did not know which of his thoughts were the ramblings of a fevered mind and which were the truth.

For all his trade goods and the limitless supply of weapons and ammunition, the white man was not a good warrior. At the sound of a gun, a white man would run to the spot and risk his own death, but the Apache would slip away, then stealthily approach the place to determine the cause of the trouble and to preserve his own life. The white man viewed the Apache as cowards, but the Apache thought themselves wise, for they had learned to survive in the harshest of all lands—the desert.

Mangas Coloradas startled on his blanket. His eyes focused on the twigs and branches that formed the rounded top of his wickiup overhead. He seemed to be burning up now, and his face was moist with the sweat that the fever boiled from his body. His throat was parched and he wanted water.

He tried to prop himself up, but he was so weak he could merely turn his head and look at the clay olla that contained the water. He crawled like a snake away from his blanket, then grabbed the neck of the olla with both hands, as if he were choking an enemy. He tipped the water to his face and felt its coolness trickle down his throat and down his chin. But the water did not quench his thirst nor cool his fever. He dropped the olla and crawled back to his blanket and into delirium, thinking he heard the sound of a raiding party returning from preying upon Mexicans. He listened to the shouts of One Who Hears Like a Coyote coming triumphantly into camp. Was it a dream or not? He could no longer tell. Had he died? Mangas Coloradas did not think so, but now everything was so confusing.

Then Mangas Coloradas heard the voice of Cochise, weakened by fever also. It no longer mattered whether Mangas Coloradas was imagining or hearing things. As long as Cochise was there, the Chiricahua would be fine.

At the sound, Cochise arose from his blanket. He reached for his carbine, picking it up a moment, then leaning it back against the curved wall of the brush wickiup. It was too heavy. He picked up instead his bow and arrows, lighter, but he feared he could not pull the bowstring and fire an arrow that would harm an enemy. He stepped out of the wickiup and squinted against the burning sun.

A rider, his head held high, led a string of mules and horses through the camp. It was One Who Hears Like a Coyote, a man Cochise trusted less than the meanest rattlesnake in the desert.

One Who Hears Like a Coyote reined up in front of Cochise. "I have horses and many mules. There is cause for celebration."

Cochise felt his head droop. He used all the strength he could muster to lift his head. "There will be no celebration."

"Cochise is fearful that I will follow Mangas Coloradas as leader of the Chiricahua," One Who Hears Like a Coyote replied.

"The camp is sick. A bad fever has left us powerless. A few braves are well, but most are ill. The women who are not sick are tired from keeping us fed and watered."

One Who Hears Like a Coyote looked around the camp. What people he saw, no more than ten, were listless, with half-closed eyes and limp arms. He glared contemptuously at Cochise. "The mighty Cochise is sick."

"We will celebrate another time, when more warriors and women will be able to see your vanity."

"Your words are as sick as you are, Cochise."

"Take the horses and mules to the herd and help with the sick."

"I do not answer to you, Cochise."

"No Apache does," Cochise replied, "but you should answer to your people. They are sick and need help."

"Someday I will be leader of the Chiricahua."

"Someday I will be well," Cochise replied. "Now move your horses."

One Who Hears Like a Coyote signaled for his men to drive the animals through camp. He stared at Cochise, who watched a pair of mules pass by, then a horse.

Cochise saw a saddle.

He twisted his head to study the saddled horse and saw the brand on the gelding's rump. It was the same as the markings on all horses ridden by the bluecoats. Then another saddled horse trotted past, and Cochise feared he saw blood upon the saddle.

"One Who Hears Like a Coyote," he called as strongly as his weakened voice could manage, "where did these saddled horses come from?"

"We stole them."

"Did you attack the bluecoats?"

"We stole their horses."

Crooked Tooth rode up and stopped beside One Who Hears Like a Coyote. "We fought the soldiers," she said.

"Ride on, woman," One Who Hears Like a Coyote cried. "She does not know the ways of men and the ways of war."

"Crooked Tooth knows to speak the truth, so she is wiser than you." Cochise turned to Crooked Tooth. "Did the soldiers attack first?"

Crooked Tooth shook her head. "One Who Hears Like a Coyote wanted to steal from the bluecoats a woman with pale hair, so we attacked them."

Cochise stepped toward One Who Hears Like a Coyote, wishing he were well enough to challenge the wayward warrior. "Upon the wisdom of Mangas Coloradas, we were never to attack the soldiers in blue coats. We have enemies to the south in Mexico; we cannot have enemies to the north, because we cannot survive between two enemies."

"Under your leadership, no, Cochise, but under mine we can. And Mangas Coloradas is an old man. The Chiricahua should follow young men like me."

"Then you shall have your chance for the Chiricahua to follow you, because the soldiers will surely come, and this camp cannot defend itself. You must take the men in your party and lead away from this camp any bluecoats who come or we shall all die. But the women of your party will stay here to help with the sick."

"Crooked Tooth goes with me," answered One Who Hears Like a Coyote.

The woman warrior shook her head. "I would rather

live like a woman than ride behind a man who tells lies."
She jerked the reins of her horse and rode away.

"It is not your place to send me out to fight the soldiers," One Who Hears Like a Coyote said to Cochise.

"It was not your place to fire upon the bluecoats. You have endangered all of us when we must be gathering food to get us through the winter. The mesquite beans are ripe and the pinyon nuts are plentiful, and even if we were well, now we could not gather them without fear that the bluecoats would attack us."

"Is the brave Cochise scared of the soldiers?"

"I fear for my people, not for myself. You think not of your people, but only yourself."

"Cochise has the heart of an old woman."

"You have no heart."

One Who Hears Like a Coyote made a motion to dismount, but He Is Wide rode up and grabbed his arm.

"Cochise is right," He Is Wide said. "Many are sick. If we do not lead the bluecoats away, they will find our camp and kill us."

"They will not find us," One Who Hears Like a Coyote replied.

Cochise coughed, then spat yellow phlegm from his mouth. "You bring a string of forty animals to our camp. A dead man could follow that trail. And you forget that one we raised as our own, the one we called Rolling Thunder but the soldiers call Mac-man-us, scouts for the bluecoats. He is shrewd and knows our ways and our places to hide."

"I will kill him first," One Who Hears Like a Coyote bragged.

"You talk more than you think, One Who Hears Like a Coyote. If you do not leave soon, he may kill you before you finish speaking."

One Who Hears Like a Coyote yanked the reins around and galloped through the camp, yelling as though he were attacking an unseen enemy.

Cochise turned to He Is Wide. "The camp is too weak to defend against so many bluecoats. Do not let him return until he has led the bluecoats away from our camp."

He Is Wide nodded. "I will not let you down."

"I am of no matter," Cochise said. "It is your people that matter."

6

The Apaches had neither disguised their trail nor scattered, as if they feared no retribution from the army. Captain Jean Benoit pushed his men down the trail, and by midmorning of the fourth day, when the mountains loomed like giant tombstones in front of them, they came to a fork in the trail. McManus dismounted and studied the sign.

He pointed to the southwest. "This is the older trail where they took the stolen mules and horses, likely to their village." He squatted and examined the tracks more closely. "Then they returned and angled off in this direction." He pointed to the northwest. "They're decoyin' us away from their village." McManus yanked himself atop his horse. "Which way, Cap'n? There's 'paches at the end of both trails."

"Which ones do you think are the raiders?"

"The smaller trail. They've been sent back to lead us astray."

"Sullivan ordered us to attack the raiders."

McManus nodded. "Then it's into the mountains."

"Could it be a trap?"

"No indication they know we're followin' 'em,"

McManus said as he rode beside Benoit. "Don't know that they've been tracked before by United States cavalry. Chances are we might never see them—until it's too late, of course."

McManus looked around, then pulled his pistol. He studied the terrain, jagged foothills spiked with yucca and agave and splotched with pinyon and juniper bushes. There were a thousand places to hide, and every hill, ravine, bush, and cactus was a refuge for the Apache. McManus looked northwest.

Benoit alternately studied the scout and the adjacent terrain. The land told him nothing, but he saw worry in the scout's eyes.

"Tell the men to pull their weapons," McManus whispered.

He lifted his pistol and twisted in the saddle, motioning for his men to do likewise. Suddenly the quiet was shattered by the noise of galloping horses and screaming Apaches.

The attackers swooped in from behind them, coming up a ravine, then skirting the edge of a hill opposite them. They fired wildly, then disappeared behind the hill so suddenly that even with their weapons drawn, the soldiers had fired barely a dozen shots, none with effect.

Benoit shouted the command, and his troops charged down the slope, across the shallow ravine, then atop the hill where the Apaches had disappeared. The troops rode like demons across the foothills, catching periodic glimpses of the Apaches and occasionally firing.

"Can we catch them?" Benoit yelled over the pounding of hooves.

"Our horses are grain-fed and stronger. We'll catch them eventually, if they don't split up."

They chased the Apaches for two hours, the Apaches always close enough to be seen but too far away to be shot. As the soldiers pursued the attackers higher into the mountains, the cacti, pinyon, and juniper gave way to oak woodlands on the south-facing slopes and ponderosa pine on the north-facing slopes. Eventually the pines surrounded them and the Apache vanished among the timber and the boulders that offered a million hiding places.

Without warning, a volley of carbine fire spat from behind trees and rocks. The men scurried for cover, dismounting and jumping behind trees, holding the reins to their horses.

Benoit ordered his men to fire. They did, but at what? No gunfire answered. The men shot until he ordered them to halt. "Anybody wounded?"

"Nobody hurt," Lieutenant Webster replied.

"Mount and ride," Benoit commanded. Shortly they were mounted again, moving deeper into the mountains, as if they were chasing ghosts. By dusk they had ridden far into the timber. The day had been hard and without result, save for winded men and animals. To Benoit's knowledge, the Apache had not lost a drop of blood, but neither had his men. He would follow the Apaches another full day, then swing around and threaten their village to draw the raiders out.

"McManus," Benoit shouted, after ordering his men to halt for the night, "should we make a cold camp?"

The scout pointed skyward. "Clouds movin' in. It'll be cold. I'd let the men make a few fires."

"Will the Apaches take potshots at us in the firelight?"

"They're toyin' with us so we won't give up the chase."

"We might force them to fight if we backtracked and searched for their village."

"It might work," McManus replied.

Benoit stared back down the mountain but could not see far for all the trees. For the first time in days he did not see the fires of the scalp hunters behind him. "I don't see sign of Morehouse and his men."

"They probably found other carrion," McManus replied.

Jim Morehouse sneered as he watched the cavalrymen disappear down the ravine. "McManus ain't got horse apples for brains," he announced to Harold McRae.

McRae nodded without understanding why. It was always easier to agree with Morehouse than to risk his wrath disagreeing.

"McManus took the wrong trail. There's a warrior band leading the soldiers into the mountains on a wild-goose chase."

"Yeah," McRae said.

"You know what that means, McRae?"

McRae shrugged.

Morehouse grinned. "That means their women and children will be unguarded. We can kill and scalp 'em, then get out of here before their men get back. The Apache men'll think they're leading all the danger away from camp. We can waltz right in, kill 'em all. If the camp is big, we could make a thousand dollars in bounties."

McRae grinned. "I'd buy a new knife, a sharp one that'll scalp 'em quicker. Make me even more money."

Morehouse found his tobacco pouch and bit off a chew, grinning widely at his men. "The army's done us a favor," he announced. "All we have to do is sharpen our knives, ride into camp, and take scalps."

The men nodded to one another. A couple pulled knives and fished whetstones from their pockets to sharpen the blades.

They were a motley crew, all with ragged beards and sinister eyes. Some wore buckskin britches and shirts; others wore various garments so covered with filth that the material could no longer be determined. They were well-armed but lazy, their weapons showing the rust of inattention. Their ears perked up at the sound of gunshots up the trail the cavalrymen had followed. The men put away their knives and drew their carbines.

Morehouse pointed to a circle of rocks crowning an adjacent hill and motioned his men in that direction. "We'll wait there. Apaches'll lead the soldiers deeper into the mountains and dumb old McManus'll follow them like a dog after a gut wagon."

The men laughed as they rode toward their rock fortress. They took up positions behind the rocks, hobbling their horses and preparing for a fight in case soldiers or Apaches retreated. They waited two hours and saw no sign of either.

While they waited, one man pulled a bottle of whiskey and passed it around. When McRae tipped his head to draw a swig, he saw a line of gray clouds to the north. They hung low and menacing over the mountains. "Think winter's coming?" he asked no one in particular.

"Too soon," Morehouse replied. "But it'll be three weeks or more before real cold weather hits us. By then we'll have our bounties and be in town drinking whiskey and bedding *señoritas*."

McRae studied the clouds. They looked like snow to him, but he didn't argue with Morehouse.

By the time Morehouse felt certain neither the Apaches nor the cavalry would be returning, it was time for them to eat lunch. The men grumbled about not having anything better than tortillas, and Morehouse, certain the threat of both Apaches and cavalry was past, decided to let his men hunt for meat. He assigned the better shots to bring in game while he instructed the others to gather firewood from the draw. They whiled away another two hours waiting for the hunters to return with a small deer and then an hour cooking and eating the venison along with their tortillas.

When they finished their meal in the midafternoon, they mounted and followed the wide trail southwest toward what they expected to be the Apache village. For three hours they followed the trail through the foothills, traversing draws that provided cover and in some cases water. Just before dusk Morehouse topped a hill and then quickly retreated. He had spotted the camp a mile and a half away in a wide draw. He signaled for his men to fall back, hoping the Apache had not seen them. "Apaches, a little over a mile away," he whispered.

"Should we attack?" McRae asked.

"Too late. Too many can hide in the dark. We'll wait until sunrise, then attack. That'll give us all day to scalp 'em and get away before their warriors return. We'll keep a cold camp."

"Good thing we ate before," McRae observed.

"We'll camp here and post a guard, hour-and-a-half shifts. I'll take the first shift, then McRae," Morehouse announced, then went around the circle assigning watch order. "Remember who follows you and wake him up when your shift is done. Any questions?"

"Yeah, Morehouse," said one of his men. "Why do you get the first watch?"

"Because I'm in charge and I'll slit the guts of any man who questions me. That a good enough reason for you?"

The other scalp hunter nodded. "That'll do."

"Now," Morehouse said, "who's got the bottle? I need a little nip to warm me up before I stand my watch."

McRae looked to the north and the low rolling clouds. "There's gonna be a chill in the air tonight."

Morehouse laughed. "And there's gonna be blood on the ground tomorrow." He grabbed the whiskey bottle from one of his men and took a sip much too generous for his share. He came up for air. "Yes, sir, there's gonna be blood on the ground tomorrow."

Crooked Tooth fretted. Just before dusk she thought she had seen a man on horseback atop the hill that stared down at the Apache camp.

All around her was fever and sickness, but she feared that death waited beyond the hill. She carried water to the sick and cooled their fevered foreheads with wet cloths. She and the other women offered the sick pinyon nuts and a soup of boiled meat. As she went about her chores, she debated whether she had seen anything or if she was imagining enemies the way fevered warriors did. Was the vision just a warning the fever was to strike her? Or was it white men who might attack the camp?

As she entered each wickiup she counted the sick among men, women, and children. Of more than a hundred people, only nine women, two warriors, and four children were well, but the two men had to guard the horses and the nine women were exhausted from tending the sick.

Crooked Tooth knew she could not leave her apparition to chance. She must see for herself and for her people. When darkness came, she found the wickiup where Gray Eyes tended the great Mangas Coloradas. Gray Eyes was an aging woman, but she had been known to fight when she was younger. Though Gray Eyes had never achieved Crooked Tooth's renown among the men, she was a woman of great courage.

Crooked Tooth lowered her head in respect for both Mangas Coloradas and Gray Eyes when she entered his wickiup.

Gray Eyes nodded. "Our chief is out of his head, Crooked Tooth. And Cochise is no better. If the bluecoats come, we will die."

"I know, Gray Eyes. That is why I have come to you, for you are wise in the ways of war."

"You honor me by your words."

"Tonight before darkness came, I fear I saw an attacker briefly on the hill toward the east. Perhaps I am succumbing to the fever."

Gray Eyes touched her hand to Crooked Tooth's forehead. The older woman shook her head. "You are strong and well and you must remain so, Crooked Tooth."

"Then I must scout beyond the hill. When it is late, I will leave the camp afoot. If I have not returned by sunrise, you will know of the danger beyond the hills."

"Should we kill our fires? The skies are shivering and the cold is approaching."

"If it is our enemies, they know we are here and are waiting for morning to attack. If it is our friends, the fires will help them find our camp."

"You are wise, Crooked Tooth." Gray Eyes clasped the younger woman's arm firmly. "Go with the caution of the puma, the wisdom of the owl, and the speed of the antelope."

"I will find you first when I return," Crooked Tooth said, then lowered her head in respect and backed from the wickiup.

Crooked Tooth tended the sick until midnight, then retreated to her wickiup for her knife, bow, and arrows. She left her guns, as they were heavier and more apt to brush against a bush or rock and make a noise that might awaken the potential enemies beyond the hill.

When the overcast sky was at its darkest, Crooked Tooth slipped from camp, moving slowly downwind from the hill so as not to alert any horses of her approach. When she came within a hundred yards of the hill, she slipped her bow over her head and across one shoulder, then tucked the quiver of arrows in the back of her belt. She pulled her knife from its sheath and advanced on hands and knees so that if she was seen, she might be mistaken for an animal.

She moved slowly, stealthily, measuring each movement as though she were the hunted rather than the predator. As she neared the peak of the hill she heard the snorts of men sleeping. She tensed. Surely they did not sleep without posting a guard.

Crooked Tooth crawled forward, looking for that guard and finally spotting him sitting on a rock just around the hill. He was a dark splotch against a darker sky and he seemed to be dozing off.

She inched toward him.

He stirred.

She froze.

He shook his head and seemed to settle back into a doze.

She moved closer and closer until she could smell

him. She eased behind him, then when he shook his head, she sprang for him, jerking her left hand over his mouth and pulling his head back. She sliced his throat, cutting his windpipe so that he whistled rather than spoke.

Crooked Tooth felt his blood spurt oven her hands, and she let him slide to the ground.

Beyond the sleeping men, the horses had heard her victim's whistling last breath and stamped and blew. She slipped down the hill to get close enough to the camp to count the number of men who threatened the village. She counted seven lumps beneath blankets. She might be able to kill them all, as she had the sentry, but if she failed and awoke just one, he might kill her. Her death would threaten her own people. Rather than risk discovery or death by killing another, she went back to the dead sentry, took his pistol, carbine, and gunbelt, and retreated to her village.

Once back in camp, she found Gray Eyes in her wickiup. "I did not imagine things. Seven men are camped beyond the hill."

"What will we do, Crooked Tooth? The men are weak."

"We will hide in ambush, all who can fight, and when they come we will attack."

"Because of you, Crooked Tooth, we will be ready."

One Who Hears Like a Coyote could see the glow of the soldiers' campfires through the trees. Three times during the day his warriors had fired on the soldiers, drawing them farther and higher into the mountains. He had been surprised at how readily the soldiers had trailed them, especially with Mac-man-us leading them. Didn't he realize they were moving farther from the village?

The soldiers no longer worried One Who Hears Like a Coyote, because he had been watching the clouds move in. The clouds were pregnant with snow and would surely blanket the mountain heights before morning. One Who Hears Like a Coyote could lead the soldiers farther into the mountains for another day, or he could evaporate with his band into the night and hope the snow came before sunup. Snow would delay the soldiers for certain.

He called his warriors together. "We have led the soldiers away from our camp and our families. We have done our duty."

He Is Wide pointed to the clouds. "The breath of winter is near. I can feel it within my soul."

"The signs," said Flat Nose, "point to a winter early and hard. The geese have been flying overhead for days, but not today. Winter may hit us during the night."

"We should have Crooked Tooth here," said He Is Building Something, "to warm our beds and our loins in the cold."

The men laughed as Flat Nose said what each knew. "She would cut our loins and slash our blankets."

One Who Hears Like a Coyote, still stung by her rebuke before Cochise, changed the subject, asking each man his opinion on what the weather would bring. When the last warrior had spoken, he nodded.

"It is settled," One Who Hears Like a Coyote announced. "We will leave when the bluecoats' fires burn down. To hinder them, should the snows not come, we will steal their horses."

The others nodded their approval, eating pinyon nuts and jerked venison until the darkness was full and the fires of their enemy began to die down. Then One Who Hears Like a Coyote, Flat Nose, and He Is Building Something slipped away from camp afoot and armed with only their knives, hatchets, and bows and arrows.

The breeze was the slight breath of the clouds moving in from the north. With caution instilled since childhood, the Apaches cut across the mountainside toward the south so they would remain downwind from the camp and the horses would not pick up the scent and alarm the soldiers.

The three warriors inched carefully through the woods, their slight noises hidden by the rustle of the wisp of a breeze through the trees. Creeping from tree to tree, they studied the camp, looking for the posted guards. One Who Hears Like a Coyote noted three. He had hoped that the soldiers had tied their horses to a picket line, the way the cavalry often did, but instead he saw that each man had staked and hobbled his horse adjacent to his bed. That would make it more difficult to steal some, but an Apache could do it.

With his hand, One Who Hears Like a Coyote signaled each of his companions to cut four horses free. Then, on his signal, they would each mount one of the animals and stampede the others through the camp. The likelihood was good that several of the still-hobbled horses would break their legs in the stampede.

The three warriors spread out, taking positions on their bellies midway between the guards, watching and waiting for the soldiers to fall asleep. Having ridden all day, the cavalrymen were tired. They did not visit or joke around but checked their horses, then fell onto their bedrolls and crawled under the covers to ease their aches and to hide from the encroaching chill. When the campfires were but a mere glow, the three warriors slipped among the soldiers. One horse nickered as One Who Hears Like a Coyote reached him.

The animal seemed skittish until One Who Hears Like a Coyote lifted his foreleg and removed the hobble. He removed the hobble from the second leg, then slipped in front of the animal and cut the rope that held him to the picket stake.

One Who Hears Like a Coyote saw Flat Nose and He Is Building Something moving among the horses, quietly doing their work. Periodically One Who Hears Like a Coyote and the others checked the guards, but they always checked outward as well, away from the camp. They knew danger could come from any direction.

One Who Hears Like a Coyote unhobbled and cut the tie ropes of three more horses, holding the line to the last one. He watched Flat Nose and He Is Building Something until they quit moving among the horses. The time was now. He waved his arm and his two allies arose with him.

One Who Hears Like a Coyote bounced onto the army mount, whistled, then yelled shrilly. He slapped his horse on the rump and sent the others stampeding. First the unhobbled horses charged through the camp, stepping on bedrolls and men. Then startled soldiers arose from their bedrolls, momentarily confused. Next One Who Hears Like a Coyote chased after the animals, whooping as he pulled an arrow and strung it across his bow.

Behind him charged Flat Nose and He Is Building Something, screaming and whistling. The hobbled horses panicked and kicked at the ground and at the soldiers getting up around them.

One Who Hears Like a Coyote saw a silhouette against the glowing embers of the fire and released his arrow, which struck his target full in the chest. The soldier fell backward into the hot coals.

Then the Indians raced beyond the camp, trying to herd the stolen horses toward their own men. Ahead of them, the other Apaches were mounted to herd the stolen horses away.

Shots whizzed through the night from the cavalry camp, but One Who Hears Like a Coyote did not care. The soldiers would not hit them because they were shooting blindly in the dark.

Quickly the horse thieves rejoined the other Apaches and exchanged stolen mounts for their ponies. Then One Who Hears Like a Coyote led his band north of the cavalry camp so the animals would pick up his scent and fret. That would worry the soldiers even more.

They passed the enemy camp, making enough noise to keep the soldiers on edge. One Who Hears Like a Coyote knew the soldiers now would be imagining an Apache behind every tree and in every whisper of the wind among the branches. He was proud that he had outsmarted Mac-man-us, who was a coward for ever leaving the Apaches.

The band herded the stolen horses down the mountain, then around the base of the next peak. Sometime after midnight the wind picked up from the north and the hint of bitter cold became reality. At first the wind howled through the trees; then it merely moaned, as if the mountains had souls complaining to the sky.

Later the snow came, first in large flakes, then in frozen pellets, and finally in great flurries. Come morning, the mountain would be covered with snow and their tracks would have vanished beneath a white blanket. One Who Hears Like a Coyote smiled. He had made the right choice, the type of decision that other warriors

would look favorably upon. One day he—not Cochise—
would be the leader of all the Chiricahua, he vowed.

Jean Benoit had barely unlimbered his revolver before
the Apaches had disappeared into the trees, stampeding with them several horses. The soldiers fired into
the darkness, shooting at demons they had barely
glimpsed and could no longer see.

Over the retorts of the carbines and revolvers, Benoit
heard the scream and then the whimpering of a man.

"It's Webster," cried a soldier. "He's been hurt bad."

Benoit turned toward the noise and saw two men
grab Webster by the legs and pull him from a pile of
glowing embers. Seeing an arrow protruding from
Webster's chest, Benoit ran to help. Holstering his
revolver, he squatted beside the lieutenant and turned
him on his side. He swatted at the hot coals embedded in
the back of his uniform. Another soldier brought a canteen to pour water over his army blouse, but the water
was frozen. He quickly held the canteen over the fire
until the water melted, then doused the hot spots.

Soldiers gathered around the lieutenant as Benoit
eased him onto his back. They must get the arrow out,
but it was embedded deep in his chest. They could not
push it through for fear of doing more damage. Benoit
touched the base of the shaft and tugged.

Webster screamed with pain, then whined, "Water."

Three men bolted from the circle and returned with
their canteens, holding them low over the remains of the
fire to melt the water.

"Captain," Webster managed.

Benoit bent closer to him.

"Don't let them watch me die."

Benoit waved the soldiers away. "Take up positions around the camp perimeter and make sure the Apaches don't return."

A few men hesitated.

"All of you," called Benoit.

Three men offered him canteens, which a fourth man grabbed from them. Benoit looked up to see Tim McManus with the canteens.

McManus squatted beside Webster. "You're the only man that got off a decent shot, Lieutenant."

In the dim light from the campfire, Webster seemed to smile for an instant. Then his face distorted cruelly.

Benoit took a canteen and uncorked the neck. He offered it to Webster, lifting his head slightly. The lieutenant made no sound. Benoit tipped the canteen against Webster's motionless lips. The water spilled over his cheeks and chin. Webster was dead.

Benoit let the soldier's head down gently, then grimaced. Benoit had never cared for Webster, but he didn't wish to see any man die in the service of his country and especially not like this, away from home on a cold mountainside where he could not even have a decent burial.

"I'm sorry, Cap'n. I let us down, not thinkin' the 'paches would attack."

Benoit waved his apology away. "You were right, though."

"About what?"

"The Apaches. They're meaner than the Crow and as elusive as the wind."

McManus nodded, retreating to Webster's bedroll and pulling his blanket free. "I'll wrap 'im in this and bury 'im in the morning."

"Please." He turned and walked away, not needing

to announce Webster's death. The soldiers knew, and each man was left to his thoughts.

Benoit doubled the guards and gave orders when they were to be relieved. He told two soldiers to get a count on horses, then cursed when both men came back reporting they were at least a dozen short. They had lost too many horses to continue the pursuit, but Benoit did not want to return unsuccessful to the fort.

Deciding to reconsider his options after a night's sleep, Benoit thought he felt specks of snow hitting his face as he crawled beneath his blanket. He covered his face with his hat and was still awake when the wind picked up, then began to howl through the trees. The temperature dropped so quickly that Benoit felt he had plunged into an icy stream. Suddenly the skies spit snow and sleet, propelled by the great winds.

Benoit could not remember spending a more miserable night in his life. The wind died down but the snow and sleet continued unabated. The snow was so heavy that Benoit had to keep brushing it off his blanket and the hat covering his face. Even so, the snow piled on top of him. When the snow finally stopped, it was replaced by freezing rain, which turned to ice almost the instant it touched trees, rock, or snow. Then daylight pried its way beneath the low clouds, revealing a landscape that looked as white as a death shroud. When Benoit finally pushed his way up through the snow and emerged into the world, the snow was two feet deep around him and glazed over with a quarter inch of ice.

The beds of the soldiers were marked by a few mounds where snow had piled up on top of them, but most of Benoit's troops seemed lost beneath the white carpet. Even the guards were wrapped in snow, like snowmen come to life. The horses looked pitiful, their coats powdered with snow and ice hanging from their tails and manes. Some hung their heads, as if they had given in to the evil storm, while others tossed their heads, as if refusing to surrender to the cold. All had tiny icicles hanging from their nostrils where the moisture in their breath condensed as soon as it hit the frigid air.

Benoit heard a sharp pop and flinched, grabbing instinctively for his gun. The sound, though, was followed not by another Apache attack but by the crash of an ice-clad limb no longer able to stand the weight. The Apaches had left him skittish, Benoit thought. He punched a hole through the ice and snow so he could stand up. As he did, he heard the crunch of someone approaching. He saw McManus, a grimace on his face.

"Poor time for an early storm," he said. "I should've read the sign better, Cap'n."

"We followed the raiders like the colonel ordered. It's time for us to turn back."

McManus shook his head.

"We can't do that, Cap'n, until it warms up a mite."

"Why not?"

McManus bent and broke off a shard of the ice that had frozen atop the snow. "The horses can't take it, Cap'n. Every step they take, they'll have to break through the ice. Every sliver of ice'll be as sharp as a knife. We won't be two miles 'fore their legs'll be cut and bloodied. We'll lose horses, and even more of us will be afoot. We need to wait until it warms enough to melt that ice."

"How long will that be?"

"Hard to say, but a couple of days if we're lucky. A week if we're not."

Benoit sighed. "All of this because of a senator's wife."

Jim Morehouse cursed when he awoke. First, the ground was powdered with snow, and second, whoever had had the last guard had not awakened the men in time to be ready to ride at good light. It was already well past sunup, and the men still clung to their blankets for what warmth they could muster.

Morehouse arose, walked over to Harold McRae's bedding, and kicked his partner in the side.

McRae sat up with a start. "Whatsa matter?"

"The bastard that had last watch didn't wake us."

"I was supposed to have last watch," answered the one McRae knew only as Sam, "but no one woke me."

"Well, you go find that lazy son of a bitch, McRae, and bring him back to me," Morehouse demanded.

McRae got up slowly and stretched. "Snowed last night," he announced, as if Morehouse weren't smart enough to figure it out on his own.

"Bring me the guard."

"Give me a minute."

"Now," Morehouse shouted.

McRae grumbled, then started up the hill, carefully approaching the crest, as he knew his dark clothes would stand out against the snow.

Down in the draw the Apache camp was still asleep, save for the smoke rising from their campfires. At first McRae did not see the guard, thinking the lump of snow was just that. But then his eyes fell on the pink hue in the snow. Blood! He bent and brushed the snow aside, gasping when he uncovered the man's head and neck. His throat had been cut. McRae was puzzled that Morehouse had already killed one of his men, as he didn't usually start that until after they had taken scalps. He grimaced, then retreated to the camp.

Morehouse, standing with arms akimbo, scowled. "Well, where is he?"

"He ain't coming," McRae replied, "and you know why."

"What are you talking about?"

"He's dead."

"I said—" Morehouse stopped, the full impact of what McRae had said hitting him like a hammer between the eyes. "Dead?"

By his expression, McRae realized Morehouse hadn't murdered the man. He felt suddenly fearful. "I seen his body beneath the snow, throat cut."

"Why didn't you bring him back?"

"I didn't want the Apaches to know we're here."

"You fool," Morehouse replied. "If he's dead, the Apaches must already know we're here."

"Then you go get him."

Morehouse stormed up to the top of the hill, disregarding the Apache camp in the distance. He studied the body for a moment, then fished for the man's legs in the snow. Grabbing the frozen limbs, Morehouse dragged the body and pulled it to camp, leaving a dark trail through the snow. As he dragged the body the head bobbed, barely attached.

Once Morehouse yanked the body out of sight of the Apache camp, the other scalp hunters gathered round. The body was stiff and splotched with snow and dirt. The scalp hunters gasped at the man's butchered neck.

"Damn," said one, turning away from the gruesome sight. "Maybe we better leave these Apaches alone."

"You turning coward on us? Nobody's leaving this

camp unless I say so, and I ain't saying so. Anybody tries'll have to kill me."

The men grumbled.

"Gather your bedrolls and let's get mounted. We'll attack them now and get our revenge."

"I don't like it," McRae said. "I saw the camp. It looks lifeless, like they're waiting on us."

"It's cold, dammit. You think those half-naked savages'd be out in the cold like this? Hell, no. What warriors there are must be sleeping with their squaws to keep warm. After we kill what men are around, we can use the squaws to warm ourselves. Get moving."

The men shook their heads, then ambled off, grumbling under their breath at Morehouse, the cold, and their own fear of attacking the Indian camp. Their fingers, stiff with the cold, seemed to tremble as they tied their bedrolls and checked the loads in their guns. The men weighed whether it was safer to challenge Morehouse and risk death at his hands or to follow him blindly into the Apache camp and face death at their hands.

"Hurry up," Morehouse commanded as he placed himself astride his mount. "The camp seems slow to awake. We'll ride in at a walk unless we see they're preparing to fight, then we'll charge. Their horses must be up the draw. We can take them later. We'll have plenty of scalps and horses. If we're not careful," he added with a grin, "we'll all wind up rich after this."

"If we don't wind up dead," answered Sam.

McRae shared the man's foreboding. This did not seem as certain as other raids on Apache camps. This camp was larger and more sinister than any he had ever seen.

And if the Apaches didn't kill them in the attack,

they might capture and torture them. The Apache were supposed to be the cruelest of all creatures, McRae thought, and he didn't care to learn for himself just how cruel they really were. One by one the men mounted, McRae being the last one in the saddle.

"Don't fire till I give the signal," Morehouse said, "and don't anybody dismount till we're sure we've killed most of 'em. We'll have our way with any women who survive the attack."

He motioned for the men to follow. They fell in single file behind him as he topped the hill and aimed down the draw toward the Apaches. Except for plumes of smoke from morning fires, nothing moved. Seemingly undetected, the scalp hunters advanced. As the men neared the camp they heard eerie groans. A chill raced up McRae's back. It was as though they were advancing on a ghost camp.

McRae did not like the feel of it. He looked around and saw that his companions seemed as nervous as he did. Maybe the camp was sick. He thought about smallpox and hoped Morehouse didn't lead them into the contagion.

They made half the distance between the hill and the village without seeing movement. Then McRae saw what looked like a woman carrying wood from wickiup to wickiup. Maybe Morehouse had been right; maybe the warriors—at least those who hadn't led the cavalry into the mountains—were asleep with their squaws.

"They haven't even seen us," Morehouse said softly. "If we charged in rather than walked, they'd be shooting us now. This'll be as easy as stomping baby chickens."

McRae didn't feel so confident. He felt antsy.

The men around him cocked their weapons, their

nervous grimaces gradually transforming into more confident smiles.

Three quarters of the way to the Apache camp they still had not seen a single sign of life, save for the wood-hauling woman who had caught McRae's gaze.

Morehouse chuckled. "Boys, I think we can just ride right into camp without them knowing a thing."

McRae doubted that. His lip quivered, and he knew it wasn't from the cold.

Morehouse laughed—too loudly for McRae's comfort, as if he was daring the camp to awake. Still, stare though he did, McRae spotted no threats.

The men approached to within fifty yards of the camp. Everyone was ready to shoot, but they had no targets. Even the woman carrying wood had not reappeared. At the moment the men arrived at the edge of the camp, out of the corner of his eye McRae saw a bush suddenly turn into a warrior. A fraction of a second before the first shot was fired, McRae realized Morehouse had led them into an ambush.

7

Dawn came cold and gray. The Apaches—at least those well enough to fight—awaited. Crooked Tooth had positioned them around the camp: two youths, Long Arrow and Short Boy Tall, hidden behind bushes at camp's edge, the others in the wickiups watching the hill where the white men slept.

The two youths at the edge of camp had ridden in three war parties but would not be called warriors until after their fourth fight. If they fought well this day, they would earn the respect of the men and the camp. Crooked Tooth watched the pair from her wickiup. The breeze was cold, but she never saw them shiver, so devoted were they to protecting their people. The other women and two old men were the only other defenders, the two healthy warriors taking positions to guard the horse herd so their animals would not be stolen.

It was an hour after daylight before Crooked Tooth saw movement atop the hill. She glimpsed a head peeking above the snow-covered crest, taking in the village. Then the man came fully into view and found the body before retreating back over the hill. Minutes later a man topped the hill and dragged the body away, leaving a brown slash through the white snow.

Crooked Tooth heard the moaning of the sick and the queries of her women defenders, asking her permission to provide the sick with water and food. "No," she called, refusing all entreaties. "We must protect the camp first and the sick later or all of us will die."

"Listen to Crooked Tooth. She is correct," Gray Eyes said.

Crooked Tooth saw Gray Eyes emerge from her wickiup, unarmed, then pick up firewood, which she cradled in her arm like a baby as she went from wickiup to wickiup. Crooked Tooth heard her offer encouragement and plead for patience among the women defenders.

Gray Eyes at last approached Crooked Tooth's hiding spot and dumped the rest of her wood inside.

"Thank you, Gray Eyes. The other women listen to you."

"Why do they not come, Crooked Tooth? They know we are here."

"Our enemies are weak. They will come because they believe we are weak. One is dead, for I killed him. We shall kill the rest. Be patient."

"Can we kill them all?" Gray Eyes asked.

"We will do our best," Crooked Tooth replied. "Now return to your spot. They will be coming soon."

The sick cried for water and food. Crooked Tooth grimaced at the suffering of her people, but as she had told the other woman, to tend them would lessen the vigilance of their defenders and their chance of survival. Even Mangas Coloradas, great warrior that he was, and his son-in-law Cochise, destined to be a great warrior as well, would depend upon a handful of boys, women, and old men for survival.

Crooked Tooth wished the scalp hunters would advance upon them so they could begin the confrontation. The waiting was harder than the battle itself.

And then they appeared, riding single file over the hill: seven evil men, dark against the snowy landscape. They rode tentatively at first, then gradually with more confidence as they closed the distance to the village. From the darkness of her wickiup, she watched them check their carbines as they advanced. They rode slowly and would make easy targets, even for boys, women, and old men.

Crooked Tooth had instructed the women and the old men to stay deep in the shadows of their wickiups so they could fire without being seen. All the women could shoot carbines and pistols, having learned from necessity. But shooting and shooting while being shot at were two different things. Sometimes an excellent target shooter was a mediocre shot in battle. Crooked Tooth knew she could depend on Gray Eyes, and she felt good about Long Arrow and Short Boy Tall. Once the riders passed those two, the boys were to slip behind them and block a retreat.

As around her the moans of the sick made a mournful chorus, the riders neared. Never had seven men seemed so ominous. They rode like evil. Crooked Tooth held her breath. She wished she had told the women not to fire until the riders were within the perimeter of the camp. She hoped the scalp hunters' slow pace would not unnerve the women.

The lead rider reached the first wickiup, then the second and third.

Crooked Tooth smiled. The women and the boys had done well.

Then the fourth and fifth riders passed. The white men said nothing, their eyes looking for signs of life.

As the sixth rider reached the wickiup Short Boy Tall bounced up from behind the bushes, catching the eye of the last rider.

"Ambush," cried the scalp hunter.

The boy fired his carbine, the bullet striking the sixth rider. He screamed and grabbed his arm.

Long Arrow arose and fired, hitting the sixth rider as well. The rider jerked on his horse's reins and froze as blood dripped from his arm and chest. His terrified horse ran in a circle.

All at once the riders fired, the camp convulsing with the sound of gunfire and filling with the acrid odor of gunpowder.

Crooked Tooth fired at a rider, who flinched, then tried to spin around and find his attacker. His horse spooked and the man could not control him to aim at any of the attackers. Four white men raced deeper into camp, Short Boy Tall and Long Arrow chasing and firing at them.

"Shoot their horses if you can't shoot them," Crooked Tooth cried, leaping outside her wickiup. She fired, winging one of the white men.

Then she heard the volley of the women firing from the wickiups, screaming as they did, cursing the scalp hunters who would attack a sick village.

Gray Eyes emerged from her hut, shouting and shooting. Crying out in anger, she fired her rifle, then took up her pistol and grazed a rider who charged at her.

Two horses were down, thrashing on the ground, terrified and whining. Crooked Tooth counted three men down, leaving four still unscathed. From a wickiup on the opposite side of camp, she saw a man emerge. It was Cochise, still pale and weak. He fired a pistol, then braced himself for a scalp hunter charging at him.

Crooked Tooth jerked her carbine to her shoulder, aimed at the rider's back, and squeezed the trigger. The gun slammed against her and coughed a cloud of smoke that blinded her momentarily.

Uncertain if she had hit Cochise's attacker or not, she bolted forward through the puff of smoke. She saw Cochise on the ground and feared she had failed or, even worse, shot him herself.

She ran across the camp, realizing as she did that she had jumped over the body of the man she had been firing at. Reaching Cochise, she squatted beside him. "Are you hurt?"

"The horse knocked me down," he answered.

"Get to your blanket," Crooked Tooth ordered, standing up, spinning around, and looking for enemies.

Only three were still mounted and they were running in circles around wickiups, shooting and shouting.

Gray Eyes emptied her carbine, tossed it aside, and pulled a pistol from her belt. She quickly fired off all the rounds in her pistol.

"Let's get out of here," cried the leader of the scalp hunters.

The three men on horseback bolted for the hill.

As Crooked Tooth reloaded she watched the trio charge by. She ran after them, hoping for a shot, then saw Short Boy Tall and Long Arrow standing resolutely in front of the oncoming horses.

The boys lifted their carbines and fired, then jumped out of the way as the horses pounded past, catching Long Arrow and spinning him around.

Crooked Tooth fired at the rider in the back, but he ducked and the bullet passed over his head. He and the two others escaped. Crooked Tooth ran to Long Arrow and bent over him.

The collision had knocked the breath from him, but with Crooked Tooth's help he got up, standing wobbly and gasping but otherwise unhurt. Short Boy Tall shouted and raised his rifle over his head. "We shot their horses. They will not go far."

Crooked Tooth smiled. "The scalp hunters will know now that there are two more men among the Apache."

Both boys swelled with pride. "We saved the people."

She nodded, then left the boys to check the bodies of the four attackers scattered around the camp. The one who had attacked Cochise was dead from her bullet or a broken neck. Another man was groaning from a gunshot wound. Crooked Tooth spat in his face, then poked the barrel of her pistol in his ear and fired.

A second shot surprised her and she spun about to see Gray Eyes standing with a smoking pistol over a third white man. Crooked Tooth stepped to the remaining attacker and toed him, but he was dead as well. When she looked for the three who had ridden away, they had disappeared behind the hill. She wished she could trail and kill them, as they deserved to die, but there were sick to care for.

"My warriors," she cried, "was anyone hurt?"

One of the old men stepped from his wickiup, holding his arm. "Their bullet left a scratch, but nothing more."

Crooked Tooth retrieved her carbine and lifted it above her head as she smiled at Gray Eyes. "Tell the women to tend the sick. The scalp hunters don't dare return because they are cowards." She pointed to the two boys. "Drag these dead away and scalp them so you will have trophies from this day."

Crooked Tooth moved to Cochise's wickiup and entered without announcing herself. He looked weak upon his bed and his face was beaded with sweat from the fever. She was amazed that he had found the strength to stand and fire at the enemy. But she knew that strength of body and strength of will are different.

"You are safe, Cochise. The scalp hunters will not return."

He nodded, then spoke weakly. "It was you that shot my attacker from his horse."

She did not acknowledge her shot, for she thought it immodest of herself to say such to a warrior as great as Cochise. "Many were shooting."

"But not all were hitting. You have always been the equal of any warrior."

Again she did not respond by voice or gesture. A brave warrior must never brag of accomplishments. It was unseemly to do such.

"You even take praise like a warrior," Cochise whispered. "Now, please go tell our leader that the danger has passed."

"But I have never entered the lodge of Mangas Coloradas without his invitation."

"You will do him great honor, for you saved our people."

"Thank you, Cochise. I shall do as you say."

She lowered her head in respect to Cochise, then exited his lodge and moved quickly to Mangas Coloradas's wickiup. She entered with head bowed. The old man lay weak upon his blanket, his woman keeping the fire burning by his side.

Crooked Tooth spoke softly. "Cochise has sent me to tell you that the village is safe and we have been victorious over the scalp hunters."

"Who led that victory?"

Crooked Tooth answered, "All that were able fought, but I must praise Gray Eyes, Short Boy Tall, and Long Arrow for their bravery."

"But you led them, Crooked Tooth, that I know. Were you a man, Crooked Tooth, you would vie with Cochise to lead our band when I am gone."

"That will be many years in the future."

"No, my years are already many and the white man's trespass into the land of the Chiricahua will age me more. Before I die, I would like to know that my people will be led by a man of Cochise's bravery and wisdom, not by someone who tells lies like One Who Hears Like a Coyote. Promise me this, Crooked Tooth."

"Anything."

"Support Cochise to be the next leader of the Chiricahua. He is my son-in-law, yes, but he is wise in the ways of men."

"I will, but I am only one woman."

"A woman who will be praised for many moons as a brave warrior."

Crooked Tooth lowered her head again. "I am honored by what you say, but there were seven attackers and three got away."

"Yes," he replied, "but the people live."

One Who Hears Like a Coyote had driven his band hard during the night, much of the time in the snow and sleet, but they had made it out of the mountains and into the foothills before the heavy snows set in.

One Who Hears Like a Coyote suspected it would be at least two days before the soldiers could come down from the mountains, maybe longer, depending on the cold spell. Perhaps that would give his people time to escape to their winter camp in Mexico.

When the darkness gave way to a pale gray sky and the riders could see better, One Who Hears Like a Coyote told his warriors that they must ride harder and faster to get back to camp. They herded the dozen stolen bluecoat horses, which would bring praise from those at the camp, excluding Mangas Coloradas and Cochise, of course.

Though the braves were displeased to have ridden all night and then be ordered to ride hard into the morning, they followed One Who Hears Like a Coyote. When they neared the camp One Who Hears Like a Coyote slowed the pace.

Then he saw in the distance three men, apparently riding hard away from the camp. He pointed to the men. "Trouble," he said. "Half of you ride with me and the rest take the horses to camp."

He angled across the rolling hills to cut off the trio. He wondered what they had done and why they were running so. Though the Indians' horses were tired, He Who Hears Like a Coyote's band gained on the white men, who seemed not to have seen them.

At first he could not understand why his men gained so rapidly, but as he neared he saw that all the horses had been wounded.

As soon as the three white men spotted his band, they panicked and beat their injured horses for more speed, but their efforts were useless.

The men turned in their saddles and aimed guns, but they never fired. One Who Hears Like a Coyote found it strange until he realized they might have spent all their ammunition or never reloaded after an attack on the camp. He frowned. If they had attacked the camp, he did not want to kill them, he wanted to torture them.

"Kill their animals," One Who Hears Like a Coyote cried, "and capture the men."

The five warriors with One Who Hears Like a Coyote whooped and made a sport out of it as they approached the three. Coming within reach of the riders, they poked them with their carbine barrels, then peeled away from their fading horses, laughing and taunting the riders, whose eyes widened with fear.

When they had finished toying with the riders, the Apaches fired their carbines into their horses. The first animal staggered, then tripped and tumbled headfirst, tossing the rider aside. He landed hard, too stunned to move.

The second horse took a bullet, then slowed and finally lay down, rolling over on its side, the rider jumping away, then standing between two Apaches who aimed their carbines at him. The third rider jumped off his horse, hoping the Apaches would chase it long enough for him to hide, but there was no place to hide nor any chance to escape. Realizing the futility of escape, the white man stood, his knees trembling as an Apache rode by and dropped a rope over his neck.

One Who Hears Like a Coyote shot the escaping horse, which finally collapsed dead. He rode to the animal and jumped from his horse, jerking his knife free and slashing the reins, halter, and stirrups so no white man would ever use them again.

Cutting the strap on the saddlebag, he rummaged through the contents, pulling and tossing aside a mirror and a razor, some jerked beef, a pair of socks, a handful of cartridges, and a wad of hair.

Angering, One Who Hears Like a Coyote lifted the

four plugs of hair over his head and screamed like a wild animal. These men were scalp hunters for sure. These men were among those who had tormented the Apache for years. These were men he would kill slowly once he returned to camp. Knife still in hand, he waved the scalps over his head, jumped on his pony, and rode back to the others, showing them what he had found.

"Let's kill them," cried He Is Wide.

"They deserve never to take another breath of air," shouted Flat Nose.

"No," One Who Hears Like a Coyote answered. "They do not deserve to live, but they should not die quickly. They should die slowly where the whole camp can enjoy their death."

The warriors saw the wisdom of One Who Hears Like a Coyote. The Apache with the rope around his captive's neck jerked it taut, then cursed the white man.

One Who Hears Like a Coyote slid from his horse, stepped to the terrified man, and waved the scalps in his face. Lifting his knife, One Who Hears Like a Coyote sliced the man's gunbelt so that it fell from his waist. Then he bent and put the blade against the top of his left boot and sliced the side open, nicking the man's heel and drawing blood. He destroyed the man's other boot similarly, then shoved him on the ground and yanked his boots off, tossing them aside. Then he grabbed the socks and pulled them from his feet.

Every time he lifted his knife, the scalp hunter cowered. One Who Hears Like a Coyote wondered how many Apaches had died before this man. He despised him and proceeded to cut his clothes off until the man was naked and shivering in the cold.

One Who Hears Like a Coyote moved to the next scalp hunter, taunting him with the four scalps, then stripping him naked. Another warrior gave One Who Hears Like a Coyote a rope and he looped it around the captive's neck.

The third scalp hunter was still stunned from the fall when One Who Hears Like a Coyote found him. He seemed not to fully understand what was going on. One Who Hears Like a Coyote stripped him and put another rope around his neck. Then the warriors herded the three naked men together and started them the five miles toward camp.

The captives cried and whimpered as they walked, their feet quickly numbing in the cold weather, then bleeding from the cuts and scratches as they walked between the cactus. For fun, one of the warriors yanked the rope and pulled his captive into a cactus, setting him to howling in pain and the warriors to laughing. Then the warriors began a game of it, dragging their captives into the cactus so much that the scalp hunters' hands and legs bristled with thorns.

They came to a hill that stared down into the draw where the camp was situated, and there they found the body of another white man, his throat cut.

"The day has not been good for the scalp hunters," One Who Hears Like a Coyote said.

His warriors laughed.

"And the day that began poorly will end even worse for them," he announced.

The warriors laughed so loudly that when they rounded the hill and came in sight of the Apache camp, the members of his band who had preceded them to camp with the stolen horses raced out to greet them.

The handful of Apaches who were about the camp cheered at the sight of the three captives. A dozen women and children ran out to meet the returning men and to taunt the captives. They danced around them, spitting, throwing dirt and snow in their faces, taking sticks and whacking their buttocks and privates until the men screamed.

"These men are scalp hunters," One Who Hears Like a Coyote told.

The women and children hissed and beat them with their hands.

"They shall be our entertainment for tonight," One Who Hears Like a Coyote announced, and everyone hooted with approval. He stopped his horse in front of Crooked Tooth, who studied the captives.

"They raided our camp this morning, but we drove them off, killing four. These three got away."

"Who was your leader?" One Who Hears Like a Coyote asked, fearing that it might have been Cochise.

"I was," Crooked Tooth answered.

One Who Hears Like a Coyote nodded. "That is good." He pointed to the mountains. "The soldiers will be trapped by the weather for several days, too much snow and too few horses for them to move with speed." He then studied his captives. "These men shadowed the soldiers and must have been told to attack the camp while the soldiers followed the warriors."

"You should tell this to Mangas Coloradas and Cochise," Crooked Tooth said, "so they will know how treacherous the white man's bluecoats are. They send soldiers for the braves and scalp hunters for the women, the children, and the old."

One Who Hears Like a Coyote instructed his warriors to stake out the three men on the ground in the center of camp, then he turned to Crooked Tooth. "And for that, they shall die a painful death."

Captain Jean Benoit was as restless as a caged animal. He wanted to get out of the mountains, away from the cold, away from the reminders of the surprise attack that had left his command impotent. Then the snow and the sleet had turned the mountainside into a hell without heat. The clouds hung low over the mountain most of the day, spitting snow and sleet, keeping the soldiers and horses miserable. They built fires as best they could from the damp wood, but the fires tended to give off more smoke than heat.

To give the men something to do, Benoit ordered them to take turns digging a grave for Lieutenant Webster. The excavation was tough because the earth was as cold as everything else and where the moisture had soaked into the soil it had frozen. In places it was like digging through granite.

Benoit turned to Tim McManus, who was huddled under a tree, sharpening his knife. "You think the Apache'll be back?"

McManus shook his head. "They're sure to have ridden away and back to the village, if there's one left."

Benoit paced in front of McManus. "What do you mean?"

"Morehouse and his gang didn't follow us into the mountains. They likely attacked the village."

"What'll happen if the Apaches catch them instead?"

"It won't be pretty, Cap'n. They can kill a man a thousand times before he breathes his last breath."

Benoit and McManus passed the time by discussing the Apaches, Benoit soaking up as much as he could about the tribe because it kept his mind off the cold and off the worry of what had happened to Inge and his daughters.

Late in the afternoon one of the soldiers reported that Lieutenant Webster's grave was complete. Benoit gave the command for the soldiers to assemble to pay their last respects. He told McManus to help uncover Webster from the snow and put him in his grave.

McManus arose, shoved his knife in his scabbard, and invited a half dozen soldiers to help. Together they brushed the snow from Webster's body and its army blanket shroud, then they pried the frozen body from the frozen ground and carried it to the grave, which was a tad bit short, so they had to angle him in corner to corner.

When Webster was in the grave, Benoit stepped to the head and felt obligated to make a few remarks. Though he had found Webster obnoxious and a discredit to the army, he could not defame a dead man.

"Lieutenant Webster was a soldier. He tried to do his best, and, like all of us, sometimes he failed and sometimes he succeeded."

"Yes, sir," said a soldier softly.

"Last night when the Apaches attacked, Lieutenant Webster, unlike most of us, stood to defend our animals and ourselves. He died trying to protect us. A soldier can come to no more honorable end."

"Amen," said a couple of soldiers.

"Now we commend his soul to the great beyond and hope that when our moment to die comes to us, we will fight as bravely as did Lieutenant Webster."

As his soldiers began to fill the grave Benoit turned and walked away, McManus by his side.

"I figure I'll carve an inscription on a tree by 'is grave so someone'll know that a soldier is buried here," McManus said.

Benoit realized then why McManus had spent so much time sharpening his knife. Benoit walked around the camp the rest of the afternoon, trying to encourage the men.

McManus finished Webster's inscription, then helped drag in wood. Toward dusk he looked up at the sky and cursed. "Dammit, Cap'n, thin clouds, too thin to hold any heat and too thick for the sun to get through if they hold tomorrow. You know what that means?"

"Cold night?"

"Damn cold night. I just hope none of our boys freezes. It could happen to them and some of the horses, if we're not careful."

Harold McRae had never felt so much pain, and he knew the worst was only beginning. His feet were cut, bruised, and bleeding. His legs, hands, and arms were full of thorns.

At least now he was warm. The Apaches had staked out him, Morehouse, and the scalp hunter called Sam in a triangle and had built a fire in the center. McRae knew that he would die before the fire did, but at least then he would be out of pain.

McRae knew enough Apache to know what was going to happen and to understand part of their conversations. And one of the Apaches had recognized Morehouse. McRae knew that would make his demise even more painful, for there was no scalp hunter hated more than Morehouse.

As the fire burned to a bed of embers some of the Apaches got burning sticks and came around poking his body. McRae screamed at the pain, then felt a knife slice off his good ear. Sam was tormented with burning sticks, too, but the Apaches were even crueler to Morehouse, dropping burning embers on him. He would scream and wriggle so the ember would slide off, but then it would be on the ground by his side, and shortly there wasn't a spot where he could lay that he didn't touch a firebrand. McRae could smell burning flesh, and he hoped it was Morehouse's rather than his own.

McRae, having been thrown from his horse and dazed in the chase, had walked to the camp in a fog, but now he knew what was in store for him, especially when he listened to the Apache who had caught him. He had understood his name to be One Who Hears Like a Coyote.

"Which shall we kill first?" he asked the dozen Apache who hovered around them. "These men are worse than vultures." One Who Hears Like a Coyote picked up a pan and scooped up an ember from the fire. He walked to Morehouse and dumped the ember on his manhood.

"Bastards," Morehouse screamed, then squirmed when the ember slid between his legs.

McRae grimaced.

"We shall kill the evil one last," One Who Hears Like a Coyote said, pointing to Morehouse.

He strode between McRae and Sam, then kicked both in the ribs with his moccasined foot. McRae gasped for breath.

"Let one of them live," came a voice barely audible over the crackling and popping of the fire.

One Who Hears Like a Coyote turned. "Cochise, are you well?"

"I am weak, but we must leave one to carry a message to the bluecoats: The Apache will now kill and scalp bluecoats for allowing the scalp hunters to raid our village."

"The evil one dies," One Who Hears Like a Coyote insisted.

"That is agreed," Cochise replied.

McRae caught his breath. Perhaps he might live after all.

"Which one should live?" One Who Hears Like a Coyote asked.

"The one who is the strongest," Cochise replied.

"And how shall we determine that?"

"The one who doesn't cry out like a woman when he is kicked between his legs. He shall live."

McRae almost passed out at the thought. He hurt so much he didn't think he could hurt any more, until he understood what was said. He hoped that Sam did not understand Apache.

One Who Hears Like a Coyote laughed, then stepped between McRae's legs. McRae saw a dark shadow lift his leg. He closed his eyes and gritted his teeth as the Apache's foot crashed into him. He tried not to scream, but pain pulsed through his body like lightning. He writhed and his eyes watered and his ears popped.

Then he heard a terrible scream, but he was in so much pain that he didn't realize Sam had been the source and that his knowledge of Apache had saved his life. McRae passed out.

When McRae came to, he realized they had stood Sam up. He watched as the Apaches seemed to measure the straps that still tied Sam's feet to the stakes. They tied longer leather strips to his wrists. Then two Apache warriors grabbed a wrist strap and ran around the fire, jerking Sam's body into the bed of glowing embers. He screamed and thrashed as he landed facedown in the fire. Almost instantly the sickening stench of burning flesh enveloped the circle.

McRae felt like retching but, having no food in his stomach, merely dry-heaved. Then he began to cry again, knowing that he would be allowed to live.

Sam's agony lasted but a few seconds as the embers consumed him.

McRae prayed for his soul and further thanked God that Sam had not understood any Apache. With the smell of Sam still enveloping the camp, the Apaches turned to Morehouse. Four warriors surrounded him, one at each of his extremities. Each carried a knife and a flat stone.

The warriors squatted, then placed the stones beneath his hands and feet. Then a warrior lifted a knife and slammed the blade against the stone.

"My finger," screamed Morehouse.

McRae looked that way long enough to see the warrior toss the finger in the fire with Sam's body. One by one the warriors declawed Morehouse, first a finger, then a toe, one after another for twenty times until he had but bloody stumps for hands and feet.

Then One Who Hears Like a Coyote dumped another ember upon his manhood. Morehouse bellowed for God, but McRae knew Morehouse had not lived the kind of life God would save.

Then One Who Hears Like a Coyote pulled his own knife and bent over Morehouse and sliced at his groin. McRae closed his eyes so he would not see what happened next. He heard Morehouse scream, then mutter and gag.

A warrior rode up on a horse, striding over McRae and tossing a rope to One Who Hears Like a Coyote, who quickly cut the straps binding Morehouse's legs to the stakes, then tied the rope around his legs. He whooped and the horse started pulling.

Morehouse screamed again as the rope tightened and pulled against the stakes that secured his hands. The bindings cut into his wrists until they bled.

One Who Hears Like a Coyote jumped to Morehouse's head, slicing the bindings on his left hand. The horse pulled the rope tighter, all its strength being held by Morehouse's right hand. Then One Who Hears Like a Coyote cut the right hand free. The horse bolted forward, dragging Morehouse around the camp.

The scalp hunter screamed as the horse pulled him out of the camp and toward the thorny plants and cacti beyond. At first Morehouse fought death with lusty screams, but his shouts gradually weakened to cries and then moans. Finally Morehouse made no sound. All that McRae heard were the sounds of the chattering Apaches and the hoofbeats of the horse, dragging him to unconsciousness, if not death.

As the horse returned to the fire McRae raised his head and stared, then wished he hadn't. Morehouse's body was raw and red, virtually all the skin scraped off by the desert earth.

McRae averted his eyes and looked skyward, hoping the Apaches did not change their mind that he should live. As he looked at the dark sky he heard Apaches gather around Morehouse. They removed the rope from his legs, picked him up, and tossed him in the embers atop Sam. The embers crackled and popped, propelling a thousand glowing spots of fire skyward in the updraft.

Then the Apaches heaped firewood atop Morehouse's body and retreated to their lodges, leaving McRae alone to his thousand aches and his tortured thoughts. For a couple of hours the fire kept his naked body warm, but the burning flesh nauseated him. Then as the fire died away and the warmth receded with it, McRae shivered in the frigid night air.

There was nothing he could do but wait and hope and pray that he would be permitted to carry his message back to the soldiers. The night seemed interminable, and McRae seemed to fade in and out of sleep or consciousness. It did not matter which, as both brought momentary relief from the agony.

Morning came after a night that stretched for eons through McRae's crazed mind. Then he was slapped across the face and shaken until he cracked his eyes and saw the face of the Apache known as One Who Hears Like a Coyote.

Another Apache stood behind One Who Hears Like a Coyote, peering over his shoulder. One Who Hears Like a Coyote spoke Apache, and McRae understood that he was to carry the message to the soldiers that there would be a bounty on their scalps now that the bluecoats had allowed the scalp hunters to ride with them and attack the people.

Then the Apache behind him began to translate into broken English the words that One Who Hears Like a Coyote had just spoken. "Tell soldiers, Apache take scalps, avenge attack on camp. White man and white soldiers not to be trusted."

McRae nodded, then tried to speak. He was shocked at his words, which sounded so weak, rough, and distant that he did not recognize his own voice. "I understand."

One Who Hears Like a Coyote spat in McRae's face, then spoke in Apache. "You would die, were it not for Cochise." He stood up and ordered the other Apache to untie him. "I will never again let a white man walk away from our camp."

The second Apache cut McRae free, then retreated,

leaving him alone. For a moment he was too numb to
move, the cold and the torture having left his fingers,
muscles, and joints so stiff that even fear for his own life
could not get them moving. Gradually he wiggled his
fingers, then his hands and arms, which ached as he tried
to bend them enough to push himself up. He looked at
his body, examining the blisters where he had been
poked with fire, the bruises where they had beaten him,
the welts where thorns still protruded from his flesh. He
rubbed his face and whimpered at the thorns that were
embedded in his hands. He looked at his swollen, blood-
caked hands and began to pull the thorns out of his
palms with his teeth.

When he saw the Apache who had freed him standing with a horse, McRae feared the man had come to
drag him across the desert, as the warriors had done to
Morehouse the night before. Then McRae understood
the horse was for his escape to civilization to carry his
message to the soldiers. The horse was an army mount
still saddled, a canteen on the side and a set of saddlebags over the animal's rump.

The warrior tossed McRae the reins. "Leave now,"
he commanded. "If Apache ever see you again, Apache
kill you for what you did."

McRae nodded and tried to rise, but his legs were so
stiff he couldn't. As he struggled to get up, the Apache
warrior stepped to him and withdrew a knife from his
scabbard. He grabbed McRae's hair and jerked his head
back, then sliced off the tip of his nose.

Blood gushed out of the wound and trickled into his
mouth. The moisture, though sticky and foul-tasting, felt
good upon his swollen tongue.

"Now you are marked man," the Apache said. "All
Apache will know you by your nose. And all will know

to capture, torture, and kill you if you ever enter the land of the Apache again."

The warrior turned and walked away.

Terrified at what might happen next, McRae forced himself to stand. He teetered for a moment, then lunged toward the saddled horse. He grabbed the saddle and held on for a moment to get his balance.

Then, mustering all the strength he could, he pulled himself into the saddle. Leaning over the horse's neck, he grabbed the reins and slapped the horse's neck so it would get away from camp as soon as possible, but the horse barely reacted. The horse was broken and worthless, ridden so hard that it could barely trot, much less gallop.

McRae moved as quickly as the horse would carry him away from the Apaches. He cursed the Apaches for torturing him, and he cursed the soldiers who had not let the scalp hunters ride with them.

When he was a couple of miles away from camp, he reached for the canteen, hoping for a drink, but the water inside was frozen. He then twisted around in the saddle and opened up the saddlebag, hoping some clothes might be inside. He found a pair of socks and a pair of long johns. He struggled to put them on without stopping his horse. Slow as the animal was, McRae knew it would take days to get back to Mesilla with his message.

But McRae wasn't going to deliver the message. The army be damned. He would not warn them of the Apache message, for they had contributed to his torture. McRae vowed to have his revenge, if not against the Apache, then against the army.

8

As the sky lightened, bringing an end to the miserable night on the mountainside, Captain Jean Benoit and his troops shivered, waiting for the sun's relief. The morning sun, though, was weak and impotent against the frigid air, which seeped through the men's uniforms and into every pore in their bodies.

McManus was up first, building a fire that seemed to cower before the chill. Gradually the cavalrymen gathered round the fire, hopping from foot to foot and holding their hands toward the flames. Their uniforms were caked with frozen mud, snow and ice. As the fire melted the snow on their clothes, water soaked through the uniforms, increasing the men's suffering. They were a beaten bunch of men, misery residing in their empty gazes. Their faces were red and chapped from the cold, their joints as frozen as the water in their canteens, their hope as weak as the fire's heat fighting against the cold of the early winter storm.

Benoit moved around the circle, informing the men they would move as quickly as the weather allowed. He explained they could not leave until the sheet of ice melted or they would injure more of their depleted herd of horses. The men nodded understanding but not acceptance. They were too cold, too miserable, too disgusted with the Apache and their wiles for that.

McManus alone among all the men seemed to carry on as usual, unperturbed by the turn of events. He whistled a jaunty Irish tune as he fed the fire, then moved around the camp, checking men and animals. But when he reported to Benoit, the news wasn't all good.

"Cap'n," McManus said, "can I speak with ya alone?"

Benoit frowned and followed McManus beneath a tall pine that swayed and creaked from the weight of wet snow upon its branches.

"We lost three horses overnight, Cap'n. I 'spect it'll be another day at least before it thaws enough to leave."

"Shouldn't we head out today so we won't lose more time or horses?"

McManus scratched his chin. "It's a gamble. My experience tells me we'll be havin' a warm spell followin' a storm this early. It'll be easier travelin' once there's some meltin', easier walkin' and less injury to horse and man. What time we lose by stayin', I think we'll gain by waitin' on better conditions."

"The men are restless and hungry."

"Then keep 'em busy and feed 'em, Cap'n."

Benoit shrugged. "And how do you propose to do that?"

"The horses."

"What?"

"The horses, Cap'n. Two of the dead ones haven't frozen yet. Have the troopers butcher 'em for food. We'll have plenty of horsemeat to get us by a day or two. Then we have others forage for grass to keep the horses with food in their bellies. Unless we feed the horses, they'll get so hungry that they'll start gnawin' at the bark on trees. If that happens, we'll all be walkin' for Fort Fillmore. Too, it'll keep the men busy. Worst thing that we can do is let them stand around discussin' their misery."

Benoit agreed and rejoined his soldiers. "Men, we'll wait at least another day to start down the mountain, hoping for warmer weather."

The men grumbled.

"McManus tells me two of the horses that died last night haven't frozen. I want volunteers to skin and butcher them for meat until we leave."

Seven soldiers stepped forward.

"Get started before the meat freezes."

The soldiers retreated to the carcasses and attacked them with knives, axes, and a saber.

Benoit turned to the remaining soldiers. "The rest of you need to find grass for the horses. That means we'll have to scrape snow down to the ground, pull up what grass you can, and feed the horses. It's hard work, but it'll help us on the trip back. Gather what firewood you can while you're looking for grass. We'll need plenty to cook our horsemeat and to melt water for the animals and us to drink. We want to keep them healthy and strong."

Soon all the men were busily working. By the end of the day the men were tired, but the plentiful horsemeat cooked over four fires replenished their strength. At first the soldiers bit tentatively into the horse steaks, but soon they were biting off hunks of the sizzling meat and talking among themselves. They washed down the meat with plenty of coffee, then retired to their blankets to endure another cold night.

The hard weather lasted another full day, with four more horses dying. By then some of the men were in bad shape, most experiencing frostbite on their toes, fingers, and faces. Benoit identified those who were worst off and made sure that their duties did not require them to get too far from the fires, which they kept burning all day and throughout the night.

On their fourth day on the mountain the sun rose bright and strong. By noon the trees began to drip melting snow.

Benoit congratulated McManus for reading the weather and ordered everyone to be ready to start the return trip by one o'clock. Benoit moved among his soldiers assessing their problems. Two had taken sick with fever; eleven had frostbite, and of those, four had feet so bad they could not walk. The major problem was that Benoit had only three horses for every five men.

He approached McManus. "We don't have enough horses, and not all the men can walk."

The scout nodded. "I done sent some men out into the woods to cut young trees we can use to make travois, like the Indians do, by hookin' two poles over a horse and tyin' hides 'tween the poles at the other end, makin' a bed for belongings or people."

Benoit was familiar with travois from the northern plains but didn't interrupt McManus's description.

"Goin' will be slow, ya understand, Cap'n, because a few men will still have to walk, but we'll get out of here and back to Fort Fillmore. I 'spect we'll use ten travois; we can load one with horsemeat to feed us. We'll want our strongest horses pulling travois, but we'll want our lightest riders on them so we don't exhaust them."

"Can we be ready in an hour?"

"Sure can, Cap'n. The men're dyin' to get off this damned mountain."

In an hour the procession started down the mountain, eight men on travois, nine walking, and the rest mounted. Those riding and those walking switched off periodically so no man had to walk all the time. Benoit, though, feeling responsible for leading his men into the storm, led the way afoot, declining to switch out with a rider.

Benoit walked through snow up to his knees. The snow crunched, then clung to his uniform, melting and draining into his boots. His feet were numb with cold, but he was determined to lead his men out. By dark the men's spirits, though not their bodies, felt better. They were escaping the mountain of misery. They made camp in a snow-covered clearing and soon McManus had a campfire roaring. As Benoit warmed himself McManus approached.

"Cap'n, take off your pants."

Benoit shook his head. "You sound like the senator's wife."

"Wouldn't know about that, Cap'n, but I know if ya don't get those pants dried out and your feet warm, ya'll be riding a travois tomorrow."

Benoit nodded, undressing quickly, giving his boots, socks, and pants to McManus.

"Need your undergarments. Won't do any good to dry these if we don't dry them."

Benoit shook his head, then obliged, taking off his blouse so he could remove his underwear. He stood naked before his men.

"Don't none of ya fellas peek, the cap'n being a modest man and all," McManus teased.

Shortly a couple of other soldiers stepped to the fire and undressed. Like McManus, they hooked their clothes on broken limbs of firewood and held them over the fire.

"They'll smell like wood smoke, but at least they'll be dry," McManus said. He spotted one of the soldiers holding a boot similarly over the fire. "Now with the boots, ya've got to be careful, as wet as they are. If you dry 'em too fast over the fire, they'll shrink on you and you'll never get 'em back on your feet. Just warm 'em, don't fry 'em."

When the soldiers finished drying their clothes, they cooked more horsemeat and went to bed exhausted. The next day they continued toward home, taking three days to reach the foothills, everything going slower with insufficient horses and ailing men. It took an additional day for them to reach the spot where the Apache trails diverged, one going to the mountains, the other to the village.

Benoit recognized the spot, then turned to McManus. "Here's where our trouble began. The Apaches have outfoxed me every step of the way since we left Fort Fillmore."

"Don't think ya're the first or the last that's ever happened to, Cap'n. Ya were just followin' Colonel Sullivan's orders and my instincts. Both were wrong, and I ain't got excuses, havin' grown up with them."

Benoit studied the trail. "In the morning I want to see if the camp is still there."

Even though many Apache were still sick, himself included, Cochise knew they should not linger in camp. They must move south toward Mexico and their winter camp, where the weather would not be as cold. Cochise had waited two days after the scalp hunter had ridden away with his message, but he was worried about the bluecoats One Who Hears Like a

Coyote had led into the mountains. The snows, though bad, might not keep them long in the mountains. With revenge on their minds, they might find and attack the camp.

Though his strength was returning, Cochise was still weak when he forced himself from his bed and walked out of his wickiup in the morning light. The snow would be melting this day.

He saw Crooked Tooth carrying firewood to the wickiups of the sick at the same time she saw him. "Cochise, are you well?"

"Better but not well. Let everyone know that we must break camp and head south this morning."

Crooked Tooth nodded. "What about the sick?"

"They must ride as best they can, even Mangas Coloradas."

Crooked Tooth dropped her firewood. "I will tell the people," she acknowledged, and began moving from lodge to lodge, telling of Cochise's orders.

When she came to the wickiup of One Who Hears Like a Coyote, she saw him astride his woman, riding her as men do women, lunging wildly like an animal.

"Cochise says to break camp so we can ride for Mexico," she announced.

One Who Hears Like a Coyote rolled off his woman and glared at Crooked Tooth. "Who has made him chief?"

"I did not ask him."

"Mangas Coloradas is still our chief. Only he can tell us when to break camp." One Who Hears Like a Coyote dressed quickly, putting on his breechcloth, leggings, and shirt, then striding from his lodge, leaving his woman naked and gaping until she pulled the blanket up.

Crooked Tooth watched as One Who Hears Like a Coyote headed for Cochise's wickiup. Crooked Tooth despised One Who Hears Like a Coyote because he had the heart of his namesake. He could never be trusted except to lead the Apache astray. Cochise was a cautious man, his only concern being the safety of his people. One Who Hears Like a Coyote was concerned only with himself.

"Cochise, Cochise," cried One Who Hears Like a Coyote, "we have too many sick to break camp."

Cochise emerged from his lodge. "The bluecoats might come."

"No, I left them in the mountains. They are weak and ignorant of the ways of survival in the desert or in the mountains."

"But Mac-man-us is with them. He is wise in the ways of both and in the ways of the Apaches."

"He is not wise or he would never have abandoned the people."

"I have given word to break camp."

"But I demand to see Mangas Coloradas. He is the man I follow, not Cochise."

Without waiting for Cochise, One Who Hears Like a Coyote marched to Mangas Coloradas's lodge. Crooked Tooth watched Cochise follow, slowly but with determination, and she headed for the wise chief's wickiup as well because she wanted to hear for herself what Mangas Coloradas had to say, rather than trust the word of One Who Hears Like a Coyote.

From outside Crooked Tooth peered into the lodge, the fire casting just enough light for her to see Cochise's face.

One Who Hears Like a Coyote began complaining about Cochise even before Mangas Coloradas asked him to speak. "Cochise has taken it upon himself to be chief of the Chiricahua. The people have not given him that right. When Mangas Coloradas speaks, the people will follow. But many sick, like you, Mangas Coloradas, cannot travel."

Then Cochise spoke. "The soldiers in the mountains may return. Had you stayed in the mountains and occupied the bluecoats, then we could stay, but One Who Hears Like a Coyote returned. So can they."

"I captured the three scalp hunters who had attacked the camp."

"After the women and children drove them away. Crooked Tooth, Gray Eyes, Short Boy Tall, and Long Arrow killed more than you captured. The camp was safer then, without you, than now, with you, because we do not know where the soldiers are."

"The soldiers are where I left them."

From his bed, Mangas Coloradas lifted his hand. "Silence." He stared at One Who Hears Like a Coyote. "No man can know where the bluecoats are unless he sees them with his eyes, hears them with his ears, or touches them with his hands."

One Who Hears Like a Coyote crossed his arms in anger.

Mangas Coloradas pointed a finger at him. "You care more for yourself than for the people."

"You care for Cochise more than you care for the people," challenged One Who Hears Like a Coyote.

"Caring for Cochise is the same as caring for the people. Were I a young man, I would challenge you. If you stay with the Chiricahua while I am alive, you will follow Cochise. The people, though sick, will move. It is easier for the sick to travel than for the dead to do so."

One Who Hears Like a Coyote spun around and

marched past Cochise, the anger brimming in his eyes
and in his swagger as he stormed to his lodge. Crooked
Tooth watched him enter, then heard the cry of his
woman as he finished his time with her.

Word spread quickly around the camp of the confrontation and the decision to move toward Mexico. The
camp quickly broke apart, the healthy gathering belongings, loading parfleches with food and dishes and
weapons, packing horses with blankets, bedding, and
clothes. Then they helped the sick from the wickiups
and then onto horses. And when all were loaded,
Cochise gave the word to start toward Mexico. Rather
than give the honor to a male warrior, Cochise instructed Crooked Tooth to burn the wickiups, as was the
custom when Apache abandoned camps, so no enemy
might use them.

As the caravan pulled away the fires took hold and
the lodges turned to flame and smoke. The Chiricahua
stretched out in a long line. Last in that line rode One
Who Hears Like a Coyote. Even the warriors who had
ridden on his last raid refused to ride beside him.

Under a warm sunrise Captain Benoit and Tim
McManus led a dozen soldiers away from the camp
and along the trail toward the Apache village. They
rode a great way before coming to a hill where
McManus pointed to a body near the crest.

The scout rode to inspect the corpse. He did so without dismounting, then rode to the top of the hill.
McManus looked down a wide draw and saw black, circular splotches where lodges had been burned. He
retreated to Benoit. "They're gone. They burned their
camp and headed toward Mexico."

"What about the corpse?"

"Dead several days, likely one of the scalp hunters."

Benoit ordered an advance, and his men moved around the hill toward the abandoned camp. Upon reaching the site, McManus dismounted and checked the ashes. They were cold and dust had settled on them, telling McManus the placed had been abandoned two, maybe three days earlier. He was drawn to a large circular fire bed in the middle of the camp and studied the debris, making out two charred clumps among the ashes. He stepped into the circle and kicked the nearest bulge. It rolled over and he saw a line of blackened teeth.

"Cap'n," he called, "here's two more scalp hunters."

Benoit came over and stared into the empty eyeholes of the blackened skulls.

"The 'paches tortured them. I'd like to think one of them was Morehouse. I can't think of a more deserving fellow."

One of the soldiers rode up to Benoit.

"Captain, there's four more bodies up the draw."

McManus laughed. "That's seven of the eight."

"Then odds are," said Benoit, "one of them's Morehouse."

"I'd want 'im dead whether I was livin' with the 'paches, the white men, or the rattlesnakes." McManus told the soldier to lead him to the other four bodies. The scout examined them, but none was Morehouse.

"Is there anything else we need to do here?" Benoit asked.

The scout shook his head, then grinned. "We can tell Colonel Sullivan that we found the 'pache camp and left seven dead and the lodges in ruins. That ought to satisfy 'im."

Benoit didn't care to jest about this failed expedition. He merely motioned for the soldiers to rejoin their comrades. He found the other soldiers in a defensive perimeter in case the Apaches attacked. When Benoit announced that the Apaches had headed for Mexico, the men cheered and relaxed.

That knowledge made the rest of the journey to Fort Fillmore less worrisome. They made pitiful time because of the weak horses. Two more died, but the men didn't take time to butcher them, wanting instead to reach Fort Fillmore as quickly as possible.

Even so, they could move only a third as fast as they had giving chase to the Apaches, and they did not reach Fort Fillmore until three weeks and a day after they had left.

Harold McRae knew he was about to die. The pain he had adapted to, but that had been nothing compared to his thirst. He had consumed what water had been in the canteen once it had thawed, not conserving a drop for later. Thirst had driven him to the brink of insanity, his tongue swollen, his lips cracked and bleeding. Thirst would finish what the Apaches had started.

After riding deliriously for miles upon miles, McRae was so confused that he was totally lost in the desert. He could no longer make sense of east and west, sunrise and sunset, day and night. He thought only in terms of glare and shade, heat and cold, none of which was comfortable. In his deranged mind, he thought the other scalp hunters were luckier than himself, for at least they were dead and beyond the tortures of heat and cold and thirst and hunger. His skin was so blistered by the sun that he felt the rest of him was about to burst through his skin like a chick out of an eggshell.

Finally understanding that he was so crazed he would never save himself, he dropped the reins of his horse and let the animal walk, following its senses. His horse, already weakened from lack of nourishment, suffered the thirst with him. McRae knew he could not save himself without his horse. He hoped in his rare moments of clear thought that the horse might lead itself to water and save them both. He merely held on to the saddle horn and slept in the saddle. Awake and asleep, he kept recalling the horrors of the Apache camp and the terrible screams of Sam and Morehouse.

Occasionally as he rode he bit his swollen tongue, hoping that the blood would moisten his mouth and bring him relief, but that did not work either. His mouth remained as dry as sand and his hope of survival even drier.

Gradually his vision, like his mind, blurred. He could no longer understand what was happening to him. At times he shivered with cold and at other times burned with the heat, but the two extremes lost all connection with night and day. Gradually his eyelids began to cake shut, so it was painful to blink.

Finally everything went dark. He just remembered tumbling from his horse and landing hard against the earth. Whether his horse went on or died beneath him he could not tell. His mind was blank and his pains were gone.

Then when he began to revive, he knew he must be in heaven. He felt moisture on his lips and a cool cloth against his forehead. He tried to open his eyelids, but they pained him still. He did manage to blink a couple of times, enough to see in the glare a tiny white-shrouded figure standing like an angel over him.

Heaven was so tranquil and peaceful and wet, he thought as water trickled down the side of his cheek. He tried to open his eyes again, seeing the golden wall of his heavenly mansion. He had heard a preacher once talking about the mansions in heaven and he realized he had earned one. Then he heard the angel speak.

"*Venga pronto, Mama.*"

McRae was dumbfounded. The angel was Mexican.

He blinked his eyes again, then squinted against the brightness coming through the square of a window. A golden shaft of daylight slanted across the room, but the light was all that was gold. The walls around the window were not golden after all, merely the shade of dirt. This was not a mansion but an adobe hovel, and the angels were Mexican peasants. McRae would have spit had his throat not been dry.

What he had thought was an angel was actually a young girl no more than twelve years old. Her hair was black, her eyes were dark, and her skin was bronze. McRae turned away from her. She reminded him of an Apache.

He heard the shuffle of moccasins across the hard-packed floor and a voice. "*¿Cómo se siente? ¿Está bien ahora?*" asked the Mexican woman.

McRae turned to face her, opening his eyes to see the woman smiling over him. He shook his head in ignorance. He did not know enough Spanish to answer; Morehouse had always handled the Spanish when he was alive. Now McRae was alone without anyone to translate. He did not respect them enough to learn their language; he didn't have to know the language to scalp them. He looked at the woman and the young girl, figuring how much their scalps might bring. Then he shook his head. To get the bounties he would have to go to

Mexico, and he did not care to go anywhere ever again where he might encounter Chiricahua.

"*¿Cómo se siente? ¿Está bien ahora?*" the woman repeated. McRae shrugged.

"*¿Durmió bien?*" the woman asked, then took the moist cloth from her daughter. She knelt on the floor and dipped the cloth in the clay pot by the corn-husk mattress where McRae rested. She squeezed excess water from the cloth and brushed it across his face.

McRae lifted his left hand and saw that all the thorns had been removed. Then he lifted his right and saw it too had been treated.

The woman spoke to him but he did not understand. He touched his face and ran his fingers across his lips. They had been swollen, cracked. Now they just felt rough. His fingers touched the woman's as she brushed the cloth softly across his face.

He gazed up at her, ignoring the tenderness in her smile and focusing instead on the silver crucifix around her neck. He knew it must be silver. He smiled at the thought of the silver necklace.

"*Muy bien,*" she said, "*muy bien.*"

McRae lifted his fingers to his mouth to indicate that he was hungry, and the woman nodded, then issued instructions to her daughter. The girl ran into the adjacent room. In a few moments she returned with a rolled tortilla and offered it to McRae. He snatched it from her fingers so quickly that she jumped back, her lip trembling. The mother removed the wet cloth from McRae's forehead and comforted her daughter.

McRae gobbled the tortilla filled with boiled meat and beans. It was not the best food he had ever eaten, but it was the first in several days and he would've eaten it no matter the taste. The tortilla did little to fill the pit that was his stomach. He pointed to his mouth again, signaling his unsatisfied hunger.

"No mas," the woman answered, *"no mas."*

McRae grabbed the woman's arm and pulled her toward him. "Food, more food."

The little girl backed away and cried.

"More food or I'll eat the girl," he growled, flinging the woman's arm away and pointing at the little girl.

Though she could not understand English, the girl ran screaming into the other room. Her mother backed away and out the door.

McRae flung back the blanket to go after her. He tried to get up, but he was still weak. He managed to rise, but he needed to lean his hand against the wall to steady himself a moment, as his dizziness seemed to make the room whirl around him. As his eyes gradually focused he looked at himself and realized he was naked. He saw he had been bathed and his wounds tended.

The long johns and socks that had been his only clothes were washed and neatly folded on a bench against the wall. He walked gingerly on bandaged feet to the bench and yanked on the long johns, then stepped toward the door into the next room just as the woman burst through, carrying a handful of tortillas.

She offered him the food as a supplicant would try to appease an angry god.

McRae grabbed the tortillas and stuffed them in his mouth, gobbling them down. "Water," he mumbled through the tortillas.

"No sabe," the woman said.

He pushed her aside and strode into the next room, where the young girl cowered in the corner. He scowled and saw an olla on the table in the center of the room. He grabbed the clay pot, lifted it, found that it was empty.

He dropped it on the table and it shattered. He saw a goatskin hanging from a peg in a *viga* overhead and he yanked it down, jerked out the stopper, and held it to his mouth, sucking the moisture like a breastfeeding child. He tossed the goatskin on the table, knocking some of the pottery shards onto the hard-packed floor.

He studied the room, looking for weapons but seeing none besides the butcher knife and the cleaver used for preparing food. He stepped to the opening at the opposite side of the room and pushed aside the blanket that served as a door. Crammed into a small room were two small pallets, another corn-husk mattress, and a cradle, where an infant slept. He figured the family had slept in that room while he recovered alone in the room at the opposite end of the adobe house. He wondered how long he had been unconscious. He thought it could have been four or five days. He limped to the wooden outside door and lifted the latch. As he swung the door open the bright sunlight blinded him momentarily. He shielded his eyes with his hand and stepped outside, examining the place of his benefactors.

The adobe house was built on a small rise that overlooked a river that could only be the Rio Grande. He heard a rustling in the cornfield just down from the house and shortly saw a man he took for the woman's husband emerge from the yellowed stalks, carrying an armload of corn. He was slight and slender and his face broke into a smile as he saw McRae.

"Buenas días," he said.

"Shut up," McRae said, gauging the size of the Mexican and considering whether his clothes might fit. The man was too small.

The man's smile faded just as a boy emerged from behind his father, carrying an ear of corn under each arm. The boy froze when he saw McRae and stood with wide eyes.

McRae turned away and walked to the opposite end of the house, where he saw a corral that held the broken-down army horse he had ridden from the Apache camp, plus a mule and a milk cow. McRae returned to the house, the little girl scurrying from the kitchen into the side room, waking up her sibling.

"Whiskey? You got whiskey?" He wagged his finger menacingly at the woman.

"No sabe."

"Tequila? You got tequila?"

The woman's brow furrowed.

McRae lifted his thumb and hand to his mouth and tilted his head back as though he were drinking from a whiskey bottle. Lowering his head, he grinned. "Tequila."

He saw the butcher knife on the bench by the fireplace and slid toward it. His movement startled the woman and she squealed just as McRae grabbed the knife.

He lunged for her, grabbing her arm and pulling her to him. She screamed in terror.

Her husband bolted inside, jumped into the bedroom, and emerged with an old flintlock pistol in his hand.

McRae laughed at the weapon and lifted the butcher knife to the woman's chin.

She whimpered as her husband stared in horror.

"Put it down. The gun," McRae said, "or she dies."

Though the man could not understand English, he understood the threat to his wife. He bent and placed the weapon on the floor.

McRae laughed, then lowered his knife hand and

spun the woman around. With one swift motion he swiped the silver crucifix and chain from her neck.

She cried and protested, but her husband calmed her with his words.

"Shut up," McRae said. "Now give me money." He shoved the woman away.

She ran to her husband and clung to him.

"Money, give me money. *Dinero*," he said.

"*No dinero,*" the husband answered.

McRae shoved the woman aside, then charged into the adjacent room, grabbing the baby from its crib. The baby started crying, as did its mother when McRae emerged in the kitchen, the knife at the baby's throat.

"*Dinero.*"

The husband nodded. "*Sí, sí, dinero.*"

He stepped to the fireplace, bending to grab the poker used to tend the fire. McRae stiffened for fear the man would turn the weapon on him, but instead the Mexican strode to the wall and began to strike the adobe. Quickly chips of adobe began to fall away, exposing a little niche with a tiny leather bag inside. The man dropped the poker and yanked the bag out. He started toward McRae, his hand extended.

McRae reached for the bag, but the Mexican shook his head, gesturing that McRae first give up the baby. The mother rushed to take her infant, and McRae released the tot.

The father tossed the bag to McRae.

McRae snagged the bag out of the air and laughed.

"Now I want your moccasins and some clothes."

The man shrugged that he didn't understand. He motioned for his wife to leave the house, but she hesitated. He commanded her to leave, and she burst outside. The man stepped cautiously past McRae and into the bedroom, quickly herding his daughter outside to join her brother.

McRae laughed as he saw a few coins and what looked like a couple of nuggets of silver in the bag. He added the crucifix to his haul, then went into the bedroom. He took a pair of moccasins from beside the bed and a pair of baggy work pants that might fit. He then grabbed a blanket from the floor and with the knife cut a slit in the middle and slipped it over his head for a poncho. After putting the pants and moccasins on, he returned to the kitchen, taking the goatskin with him and walking outside.

The family was huddled by the corral. When McRae started in that direction, they moved hurriedly away, like a covey of quail before a hunter.

McRae opened the gate, grabbed the army saddle and bridle, then quickly saddled the Mexican man's mule.

The Mexican said nothing.

McRae shoved the bag of coins in his saddlebag, then mounted and rode out the gate.

"*Gracias*," he mocked as he rode past them and turned the mule south toward Mesilla.

The land did not change. The cactus was the same, the vermin identical. There was no mountain range, no trees, nothing but an imaginary line running between periodic stone markers placed there by army surveyors who knew more about a map of the land than the land itself. Yet on one side of this imaginary line was Mexico and on the other was the United States.

Cochise let the procession ride past him as he studied the imaginary line, which the soldiers of both countries respected as if it were a wall a hundred feet high.

The white man wanted to own the country, not to know it. He wanted to plunder it rather than live from it. Already men who called themselves miners had entered the land of the Apache in search of metals that the Apache had long ignored. There were the metals the white man called copper and silver, and most of all there was gold, which the white man sought with the ferocity of a rabid animal. Cochise did not understand the white man's greed in pulling these metals from the earth. He did not understand the white man's need to put an imaginary boundary around the land and claim it for his own, because no man lived as long as mother earth. The Apache knew that. The white man did not.

Maybe all white men were like One Who Hears Like a Coyote, who did not see the foolishness of his ways. Until the previous week the bluecoats had never sent scalp hunters against the Apache, the way the Mexicans had. Cochise hated the Mexicans, for they had harmed many of his people, and he knew he could grow to hate the white men as well. Their ways were strange, their beliefs inexplicable, and their greed unlike that of any other people he had seen. Even the Mexicans, as much as he hated them, were not nearly as greedy as the white man.

As the last of his band crossed the imaginary line into Mexico, Cochise sat atop his horse, which stood astride both countries. He had not wanted to fight the white man too, for there were many more of him than there were Apaches.

Cochise did not want to find his people caught between two stronger peoples—or countries, as they called themselves. He did not know that his people could survive, but they would never give up, that he was certain of.

From his band of Chiricahua, one rider turned away and retreated to join him. It was Crooked Tooth. He respected her foremost among all women, because she was as brave and wise as a man.

"Are you well, Cochise?" she asked, reining her horse up beside his.

"My body is better, but my heart is sick."

"How can that be?"

"We must fight two peoples, and I do not know that we can survive. It is a fight against the white man that I had hoped to avoid."

"Do you blame One Who Hears Like a Coyote?"

Cochise nodded. "He attacked the bluecoats first. Everything that followed was started by him."

"Then you should blame me too, for I rode with him and killed more bluecoats than did One Who Hears Like a Coyote."

"You only followed your leader."

"But I did not mean to bring harm to my people."

"We shape what we do, but what we do shapes us."

"I do not understand."

"Some things are not meant to be understood."

"And some people, such as One Who Hears Like a Coyote," she replied, studying Cochise intently.

"I know but one thing now about the white man," Cochise said as he rode into Mexico.

Crooked Tooth turned her horse and joined him. "And what is that, Cochise?"

"Now that the white man has attacked us, he will never forget the fierceness with which we will fight back."

9

Captain Jean Benoit led his demoralized command onto the parade ground at Fort Fillmore just after the noon mess. Some men walked, others rode double on cavalry mounts, and a few, their feet too swollen to walk or ride, reclined on the travois. Benoit knew the expedition had been a failure and that a reprimand might be entered upon his record, but he worried most about his wife and daughters. Had any news from Fort Laramie arrived during his chase of the Apaches? He hoped desperately that General Barksdale, drunk though he often was, had allowed Lieutenant Frank Coker to forward any mail from Fort Marcy to Fort Fillmore. Benoit ordered his troops to take the wounded to the hospital and the others to take horses to the stables and tend them before reporting for mess. He dismounted and ordered a soldier to take his own mount to the stables while he reported to Lieutenant Colonel Jeremy Sullivan.

As he walked across the parade ground Tim McManus fell into step with him. "It's like walking to your own execution, reporting to the colonel after this expedition," Benoit said.

When they walked into the headquarters building, Benoit nodded at the desk lieutenant, then saluted Sullivan, who was standing in the door of his office. "From what I saw out the window, Captain, you're missing horses and men," Sullivan said, turning to retreat into his den. "I want the full report, and I don't need you, McManus."

"Sure ya do, Colonel. The cap'n bein' a modest man, he might forget to tell you somethin'."

"One man killed by Apaches, Colonel—Lieutenant Webster, one who came from Fort Marcy with me. Several men are sick or suffering frostbite."

"Frostbite? How the hell did that happen?"

McManus stepped forward. "Let me answer that, Cap'n. We was chasin' 'paches, the very ones that attacked the senator's wife, hope she be doin' well, yes I do, and we followed 'em into the mountains, where the storm trapped us. We couldn't get out for a few days, and it was my fault for gettin' us snowed in."

"Did you catch the Apaches?" Sullivan asked.

"No, sir," Benoit replied.

"Not in the mountains," McManus interjected. "A lesser officer would've given up, but not the cap'n. When the snow melted enough for us to travel, we backtracked to the desert with sick and hurting men, frostbite mostly."

Benoit stared at McManus and just shook his head.

Sullivan eyed them both. "Go on, McManus."

"Well, sir, even though our strength was halved, the cap'n there led a dozen soldiers to find the 'pache camp and extract our revenge. He found it."

"And what happened?" Sullivan asked.

"Well, sir, by the time we left, I counted seven dead—all men—and no injuries to us. We left the camp burned and destroyed."

Benoit grinned. He'd heard men shading the truth before, but never with more ease.

"Is that true, Captain?" Sullivan asked.

"Every word of it."

Sullivan smiled. "Good. I'll want a full report by the end of the day tomorrow." The colonel then picked up an envelope from his desk. He shook the missive in his hand as he pursed his lips.

Benoit's heart sank like a stone in water. He feared he had lost part or all of his family. Numbly he waited for the colonel to speak.

"Captain, I'm afraid I've got some terrible news for you."

Benoit clenched his jaw. Was it his children or his wife? Or worse, both?

"I've received word from up north . . ."

Benoit closed his eyes.

". . . that General Barksdale died four days ago."

The news caught him so off guard, considering what he had expected, that Benoit had to cover his mouth with his hand to hide the smile that slid across his lips. "I'm most sorry to hear that, Colonel, as any soldier would be to lose his commanding officer."

"Is it true he drank as much as they said?" Sullivan inquired.

"Well, sir, I never saw him . . ." Benoit paused.

"Drink?" Sullivan supplied.

"No, sir. I never saw him sober."

"He wasn't an Irishman, was he?" McManus laughed.

Benoit shrugged. "A South Carolinian."

"Is it true he was planning to take over New Mexico Territory if war broke out?" asked Sullivan.

"Can't say, sir."

Sullivan eyed Benoit. "I forgot, you're from Louisiana. No wonder you can't say."

"I took an oath, Colonel, like you. I intend to abide by it."

Sullivan smiled "You are good with words, Captain. I admire that in a man. It's a sign of quick thinking."

"And how is the senator's wife?"

"Alive and better, though weak."

"I'm glad to hear that, sir."

"Well, she's been asking about you, wanting to see you."

"I don't care to see her, sir."

"She's not the only one who's been wanting to see you."

"And who would that be?"

"Senator Couvillion himself."

"Cle Couvillion," Benoit said, the name dripping like poison off his tongue.

"He's sure interested in seeing you."

Benoit shrugged. "Can it wait until tomorrow? I'm exhausted."

"You'll have a lot to do tomorrow. I'd prefer you do it right now. He's with his wife in the quarters where she stayed before her departure."

Sighing, Benoit saluted, figuring it was best to get the encounter over with. As he turned to march out the door Sullivan gave him further instructions.

"Check at the desk. The lieutenant's holding a couple of letters for you."

Benoit bounded out the door and snatched the letters from the lieutenant, then caught his breath. One was from Dobbs and the other from Inge.

Benoit burst out of the building so quickly that he left McManus behind. He ripped open Inge's letter and

began to read it hurriedly, wanting to know the fate of
his daughters.

> *My dear Jean,*
>
> *I am sorry that I have not written sooner to cele-
brate the joyous occasion of the birth of our girls, but
I was weak from the ordeal. The girls arrived early
and small. The labor was long and hard for reasons
Jace does not understand, but there is much about
the miracle of life we will never comprehend.*
>
> *They were tiny, barely fifteen inches long, and
each scarcely weighing four and a half pounds. Jace
said he wished they had been heavier but that the two
of them probably took up all the space there was in
my big belly and they had to get out. At first I did
not produce milk, and for a couple of days Jace fed
them with what he called sugar tits. He would put a
couple of tablespoons of sugar in a thin cloth and tie
twine behind the sugar, which he dipped in milk.
Then he would hold the ball of sugar at their lips and
they would suck away at the sweetness. They lasted
on sugar tits for two days until I recovered enough
from the ordeal to be able to feed them.*
>
> *Jace thinks the worst is behind them and they
will survive, but I know he still worries, because he
is always here checking on me and them. Mother has
been a big help, changing the babies, bathing them,
and rocking them when I need the rest.*
>
> *The girls are so beautiful, Jean. They are fair
like us and have eyes that are the bluest I've ever
seen. When they cry at night, I know they are crying not just for their food but for their father as
well. I cry for you, too, and wish that you were here
to hold your daughters and to hug me. I have missed*

*you so much and have not named the girls so that I
could talk with you about it. There are many people
whose names they would carry well, but I doubt
they would be here without Jace Dobbs. I know he
has felt an extra responsibility to care for them —
and me — because of his enduring friendship with
you. I would like to name the girls for his late wife,
Colleen, and his intended, Ellen, who was killed.
You and I never knew his wife and I know Ellen
was a woman of bad repute, but taking their names
is the only way I can come up with that might in
any way repay Jace for bringing our girls success-
fully into the world.*

*Jace has been good to Erich as well. My poor
brother still cannot walk; his legs are as lifeless as
his spirit. He says little and eats less, and his powerful arms and shoulders have withered away to nothing, like his legs. He sits in his chair and stares
toward Laramie Peak, saying nothing. Jace has
offered him some of the periodicals and newspapers
he receives, but Erich reads poorly and ignores him.
Sometimes, I am ashamed to say, I am scared of my
own brother, he broods so. I keep guns from his
reach, as I fear he might shoot himself. Mother, bless
her heart, cares for him as best she can, but it is one
thing to clean the diapers of our infant daughters
and quite another to clean those of her adult son. He
is embarrassed by it and I think that is one reason he
eats so little, even when we offer him much. There
are times I can hardly bear to look at him. Isn't that
a terrible thing to say?*

*I have so much more to tell you, but one of the
babies is crying and I am weak yet. Remember that I
love you, and though I cannot hold and hug you, I*

*can at least love your daughters until we are
together again. I shall sleep tonight dreaming of you.*

Your loving wife,

Inge

Benoit felt like shouting and crying at the same time,
relieved that his daughters had survived and his wife
was going to live as well. He folded the letter and put it
back in its envelope. He quickly opened Dobbs's letter.

Dear Jean:

*The worst appears over and I think your daugh-
ters will survive to see their father. I was worried at
first, them coming early and being likely the tiniest
babies I've ever delivered. Small though they were, I
think that had I not operated we would have lost
both Inge and the babies.*

*I was surprised that the first one to emerge
brought a sister with her. This is the first time I ever
delivered twins. Inge was too weak to feed them, so I
improvised until she came around and started lactat-
ing. It is a miracle, Jean, that a woman's body can
change so quickly to nourish a child or even two.*

*I will attend Inge and the girls faithfully because
I want to get them healthy enough to withstand the
winter. We have already had one early storm that left
a couple of inches of snow on the ground, but it
melted away quickly. Inge's mother has been making
quilts to wrap the babies in during the cold, so they
should be fine.*

*Jean, the fort is not nearly as interesting with-
out you. At least you would listen to my ramblings
on every topic under the sun. Though we disagree on
states' rights and slavery, I'd almost change my*

*positions on those issues just to have your company
back here. I have put in for a transfer to see if I can
join you in New Mexico. The weather's surely
warmer and the Indians certainly more civilized
than those we must contend with here.*

*With darkness setting in, I must finish this mis-
sive and find something to eat. I hope this reaches
you well and brings some relief to your mind.
I know my last letter was perhaps unduly worrisome, but I did not know what I was dealing with
for certain at the time. I do now and they are two of
the cutest little girls I've ever seen. I can't wait for
you to see them.*

Jace

Benoit let out a deep breath. His girls were better, and
knowing that made him feel better. He folded Jace's letter
and put it back in the envelope. He shoved the two letters
in his pocket with the first he still carried. At least now he
could face Cle Couvillion without a troubled mind.

Before moving to the senator's quarters, he checked
his wounded at the hospital. After making sure his men
were recovering, he headed across the parade ground to
meet Cle Couvillion again. Nearing the quarters, he saw
the *New Orleans Picayune* reporter leaving. He despised
the man.

J. Ernest Hardley, his nose in the air, strode past
Benoit. "The senator knows how you failed to protect his
wife on the trip to Santa Fe and has learned how you
bungled the search for her attackers."

"Make sure you're never in Apache country when
you need the cavalry, Hardley, because I won't be coming to your rescue."

Hardley halted to articulate a response, but Benoit

kept walking, teeth clenched, fists balled. "I don't understand what the senator sees in you, Benoit, that could
benefit Louisiana when it becomes a free state."

Benoit could not respect a man so obviously
Couvillion's lackey. Reaching the door, Benoit hesitated
before knocking, dreading the encounter, certain his
own values would be tarnished by mere proximity to the
senator. Reluctantly he pounded on the door until an
orderly opened the door and saluted.

Benoit replied with a lazy salute, then removed his
hat.

"This way, Captain," said the soldier.

Benoit followed the man down the hallway, past the
parlor on the left and a bedroom on the right. The soldier
halted at the dining room on the left, and Benoit entered,
finding the senator at the table reviewing a stack of
papers through the half lenses of reading glasses.
Couvillion glanced up, smiled slightly, nodded at the
soldier, then removed his glasses.

"Thank you, soldier," he said. "Now that Captain
Benoit is here, why don't you take a break for thirty minutes or so?"

The soldier disappeared out the back door.

Couvillion said nothing else until he heard the door
shut behind the departing trooper. Then he cocked his
head. "Well, well, Captain, it's always good to see you."
He leaned back in his chair.

"I'm surprised to see you here."

"I bet you are. Seeing as how you've been diddling
my wife."

"Not since you married her, Cle."

"Rumors are that some officer's had her here."

"Don't know about that, Cle, but it wasn't me."

"Most men call me 'Senator' now."

"Whatever you say, Cle."

The senator smiled. "Jean, I can make your life miserable."

"You already have, Cle, with your treasonous leanings."

"It's what's best for Louisiana, Jean. And you will do what's best for Louisiana or I'll ruin your career. With General Barksdale's death, you could be the most important man in New Mexico Territory. If war breaks out, we want to take this region for the South, find its gold and silver to finance the war. Mining can help us pay for a war. By gathering information for us, you'll be helping Louisiana and the South."

"I'll be committing treason against the Constitution, which I swore to uphold and defend."

"Well, well," Couvillion said, crossing his arms. "Let me explain a few things to you. There are many reasons you will do what I say. First of all, there's your brother, Theophile. He will be graduating from the Naval Academy soon. He is not nearly as worried about treason nor as judicious as you, Jean. He has already sent me a letter proclaiming his willingness to join the southern cause when the time is right. I have that letter safely hidden in Washington. Should you not go along with my wishes, I can simply reveal it to the War Department. Treason is punishable by hanging, as I recall. I would hate to do that, Jean, because your brother is a fine young man who understands his allegiance to his state first. Right now you are of more value to us than your brother."

Benoit shifted uncomfortably.

The senator leaned forward and slapped the table with his palm. "Don't think I wouldn't turn on him if I had to for Louisiana."

"I have no doubt about it."

Couvillion grinned. "Then you understand the predicament you put your brother in."

Benoit shook his head. "Theo created his own problems. It will be up to Theo to work them out."

"Tsk, tsk," Couvillion mocked. "Won't Theo be disappointed to know that his own brother was responsible for his hanging."

"I am not my brother's keeper."

"Quoting scripture now, are you, Captain? Well, how about the Ten Commandments? Thou shalt not commit adultery—just what were you doing with Marie when the Apache attacked?" Couvillion bolted up from his chair and stood glaring at Benoit. "I've heard the stories. Now I want to hear your version," he screamed.

"I did nothing."

"Is it true she was half naked when she was shot?"

"She wanted to bathe. She wanted me to stand guard."

"Damn poor guard you were."

"She threw herself at me."

"I killed one man for adultery with my wife and I can kill you. And another thing, Captain—I'm powerful enough now that I can even have you killed, so that I don't get my hands dirty."

"It's all lies and you know it, Cle."

"No, there was a witness, Captain, a Lieutenant Webster, who said you attacked her."

"He lied, but he's dead now and won't do you any good."

"Is that so? Well, let me tell you, Captain, in politics a dead man is of more value than a live one. My good friend J. Ernest Hardley of the *Picayune* can make a great story out of that. The one man who witnesses your assault on my wife winds up dead in an expedition you led."

"Every soldier there knows Apaches killed Webster."

Couvillion laughed. "And how many men was that? Fifty, sixty, a hundred? Once Hardley decides to print a story, thousands will believe otherwise."

Benoit had known for years that Couvillion was evil, but he had never realized the depth of the senator's wickedness until now. There was no bottom to the senator's malice.

"So," Couvillion reminded him, "you'll spy for me. I can have your brother hanged for treason. I can have you killed for assaulting my wife. Or I can have Hardley print stories about your incompetence chasing Apaches, your questionable relationship with my wife, and your killing the subordinate officer who dared to report your evil deeds with my sweet Marie. Once the *Picayune* starts attacking you, you'll wish you were dead."

Benoit let the threat hang in the air, eyeing Couvillion, wondering if he, Louisiana, and the nation might not be better off with the senator dead.

"I take it by your silence that you have seen the wisdom in cooperating with me, Captain. And I understand you now have children. It would be such a shame for their father to die or live with a reputation that would cloud their own names for decades."

Couvillion would stoop to any low in the name of politics. Marie had always said politics was his real mistress, but Benoit realized that in truth, politics was his whore.

"You're a snake," he said, his voice quiet but with an edge.

"And you are little more than a chess piece in a

grand game I am playing, Captain. One day Clement Couvillion will be a name known throughout this continent. You'd do well to remember it, because I will be able to do you more good over the long run than you will be able to do me."

"You have had your say, Senator. Now, are you done with me?"

Couvillion answered by reaching for his reading glasses again.

"Maybe he's through with you, but I'm not," came a voice that surprised Benoit. It was Marie.

Benoit turned to see her standing in the doorway, her face colorless, her smile as limp as the hand holding her robe together.

"How are you, Marie?"

"They say you saved me by riding all night to get me to the doctor. I doubt my husband," she said sarcastically, "has even thanked you for that."

"I am glad you are better."

"You know my husband sent me to spy on you and that damn reporter to spy on me while I'm spying on you."

"Go to bed, Marie, you're delirious," instructed the senator.

She laughed. "He wants his own wife to call him 'Senator.' You tell me who's delirious, Jean."

"I am glad you are mending, Marie, truly I am," Benoit offered, backing away as she walked inside.

"My husband, the senator, came from New Orleans when he learned I was shot. Had Congress been in session, he'd have stayed there to attend to his politics. You know his politics—southern this, southern that, Louisiana this, Louisiana that."

"Marie, hush your mouth and go to bed."

His wife walked to the table, leaned across it, and brushed his papers onto the floor. "Everybody else may lick your boots, Senator, but not me. I am the daughter of a senator, so I know about power. My father was a statesman. He tried to hold things together, rather than tear them apart."

Benoit watched Couvillion redden.

"You harlot," Couvillion cried.

"Damn you to hell, Senator."

Couvillion leaned across the table.

Thinking Cle was about to slap her, Benoit took her arm and gently pulled her away.

"Marie," he said, "please get your rest."

She smiled gently at Benoit, then glared at her husband. "I hate you, Senator."

"The people of Louisiana love me."

"Not all of them," she cried back.

"But a majority," he smirked. "The majority that keeps you a senator's wife."

Benoit tugged Marie's arm. She grimaced and turned from her husband. Benoit helped her down the hall and into the back bedroom. He helped sit her on the bed. Her hand dropped from her robe and it fell open, allowing Benoit a glimpse of the fresh scar where the arrow had exited.

Benoit then averted his eyes, as she made no effort to close the robe.

"Stay with me, Jean, and visit."

"I must go."

"Cle doesn't talk to me. I never loved him. I loved you."

"You loved his position, Marie, his prestige. He was a congressman. I was just an army officer. Now he's a senator and I'm still an army officer, one who made captain only because of strings he pulled. And it's true whether I like it or not." Benoit turned to walk away. "Good luck, Marie." He stepped out the door.

Marie sobbed in his wake.

Benoit marched down the hall, stopping in front of Couvillion's makeshift office. "Your wife needs you, Senator."

"So does my country," he answered pompously.

"Not as much as your wife." He turned and marched out the door, glad to escape the senator and Marie.

Though he was tired, there was plenty of time left before the evening mess, so he returned to headquarters to write Inge a letter and, if he felt like it, complete his report on the failed expedition. Sullivan was out when he arrived, so he took up paper and a desk in an empty office and began to write his wife.

Fort Fillmore

My darling Inge, mother of my daughters,

Your letter brought me such wonderful news, but tell me more about my daughters. I do not know the day they were born and how you can tell them apart. I want so much to know everything about them, and as I can't see them for a while, please send me a lock of hair from each.

I agree they should be named Colleen and Ellen for Jace's sake. He is the best friend a man could ever have, even if he has abolitionist leanings. He has patched me up many times and now has saved my wife and my twin girls.

I am sorry that I have not written you sooner, but I was posted to Fort Fillmore from Fort Marcy with orders to escort Marie Couvillion to Santa Fe. It was not an assignment of my choosing, but apparently the senator had so requested. On the trip she was wounded by Apaches in a raid that killed two of my men. We chased the Apaches into the mountains, then were trapped several days in an early snowstorm. We lost one man, but several suffered frostbite, and we came back without having drawn the blood of a single Apache.

We arrived back today and I received your letters. My joy in the good news of your and the girls' health was complete. I learned, too, that Senator Cle Couvillion had arrived. I think he was more interested in spying on New Mexico Territory than he was in seeing about Marie. Their marriage is loveless and at times I think they deserve each other.

The senator is still trying to force me to gather information for him. If I don't, he will use any possible means to do his bidding. But I cannot disavow my oath as an officer of the United States Army, so you must be prepared not to believe anything that you may hear about me, because he will start cruel rumors to destroy me.

But do not worry—I have more to live for than ever before with you and the girls. I will do nothing to dishonor your names and mine.

I must close to write my report, but do write when you get the chance and do give thanks to Jace for saving my family. And please let Erich know that I am thinking about him daily.

Never forget, Inge, that I love you.

Your husband, Jean

Until mess call, Benoit wrote out his report on the futile three-week chase of the Apaches. He provided a chronology of events, then detailed the death of Webster, the loss of horses, the sudden early snowstorm, the frostbite of the men, and the return to Fort Fillmore. About the trip to the abandoned Apache village, he wrote exactly what McManus had said: that they had found the village and left behind seven bodies and a burned-out camp. He was tired and didn't care to go into more detail. He left the report on Sullivan's desk, then stepped outside, deciding to walk about the fort until it was time for supper.

As he strode by the flagpole he spotted McManus scurrying toward him. "Cap'n, Cap'n," the scout called, "could I have a word with ya, if ya don' mind?"

"What is it?"

McManus seemed nervous, shifting on his feet, looking all around. "It's the horses, Cap'n. I need your opinion."

Benoit studied McManus. "This on the level?"

"I wouldn't waste your time 'less it was."

McManus turned in beside Benoit and they started for the stables. When Benoit was certain they were beyond any who might overhear their conversation, he addressed McManus. "What's this all about, McManus?"

"Geldin', sir. I need some advice about geldin' an animal."

Benoit knew there was only so much you could pull from an Irishman and that he had gotten all he would for the time being.

McManus pointed to one of the stables and Benoit headed that way, opening the door and stepping inside, where the aroma of hay, fodder, and horse manure min-

gled comfortably. From the back end of the stable, Benoit
heard what sounded like mumbling.

"Anybody here?" cried McManus. When no one
answered, McManus said, "Good."

He pointed to a back stall, and Benoit followed.
When they reached the stall, Benoit saw a bound and
gagged man on a bed of hay.

"Cap'n, I know this be a mite unusual," McManus
began, "but I overheard this smarty-pants newspaperman asking cavalrymen on our expedition just what
happened at the 'pache camp."

Benoit grinned when he realized the gagged figure
was J. Ernest Hardley, bound helpless on the hay.

"I know he's been a pest since he arrived, whinin'
and all, figurin' he deserved special treatment, bein' a
newspaperman. Well, sir, I figured I'd make a geldin'
out of him." McManus pulled his knife.

Benoit shook his head, barely keeping from laughing.

"Ya know, Cap'n, when a stallion is rowdy and
making too much trouble, all it takes is a slice of the knife
to fix his problems. Think it'd work on a man?"

"Can't say for certain."

"I figure it's worth a try."

Hardley shook his head and pleaded incoherently
through the gag.

"Ya can't even understand' 'im now. I figure he'll
talk plainer once he's gelded."

"He talked pretty plain this afternoon, threatening
to ruin my career," Benoit said.

"That a fact? I'm sayin' you lied to Colonel Sullivan
about what happened at the 'pache camp, that sure is
botherin' me. I'm the one that said what happened. And
there's more truth in what I said than in a thousand of

his newspapers. So I'll tell him the truth right now: If he don't mind his own business, I'll see to it that he talks like a girl."

McManus laid the side of the blade on the newspaperman's cheek. Hardley flinched at the touch of cold steel. Then McManus slid the blade under the gag and sliced the cloth.

Hardley spat out the cloth and started jabbering like the nervous man that he was. "I'll get you two for this."

"Not without riskin' your privates, ya won't." McManus waved the knife in front of his nose. "Ya just remember that what the army knows is what goes in the report. Ya say anythin' different and you'll be walkin' around a tad lighter in the pants."

"Wait until I tell the senator."

"Ya jus' do that and ya and the senator will be able to play marbles with your privates. Ya understand?"

Hardley nodded vigorously.

Then McManus cut the bindings from his feet and from his wrists. The newspaperman jumped to his feet, pushed his way past McManus, and darted for the door.

"The senator'll hear about this."

"Go to hell," McManus yelled.

Benoit laughed. "You'll get me in big trouble before all this is over."

"Hell, Cap'n, from what I've seen, the senator'll get us all in big trouble before this is over."

After a meager supper Benoit retired to his room. He took off his boots, then fell into bed still wearing the rest of his uniform. He dozed right off but slept maybe three hours, no more than four, before he awoke and could not go to sleep again. There was so much to worry about.

His wife.

His twin daughters.

The paralyzed Erich, who might never walk again.

His brother, Theophile, and what might happen to him if the damnable Couvillion decided to make his letter public.

Senator Cle Couvillion himself. No telling what he might do.

Marie Couvillion, who was unpredictable in mood and action.

The *Picayune* reporter.

His own army career, which could be destroyed by the senator's long tentacles.

After tossing in bed, unable to return to sleep, Benoit realized hunger was still gnawing at his stomach. He sat up, pulled on his boots, and walked outside onto the parade ground. On impulse he decided to go to Mesilla to find food and drink to fight his hunger. He remembered the cantinas and figured one could provide him a decent meal and a little whiskey to wash it down with.

Briskly he walked to the stable, identified himself to the guard, and told him he needed a horse. The guard was sullen, not wanting to get up and ready the animal, until Benoit said he would saddle his own mount; then the guard smiled.

Benoit found a horse and saddled it quickly. He knew he shouldn't ride to Mesilla without reporting to Lieutenant Colonel Sullivan first, but this would be a harmless little trip for food and a little whiskey, not enough to get drunk. He carried his pistol on his hip, but no other weapon, and doubted he'd need the pistol.

He saluted the guard as he rode out of the stable and

turned north toward Mesilla. The riding was easy in the bright moonlight which made the Rio Grande shimmer like a giant silver serpent. As he rode he began to ponder his career. He had been made a captain at an early age, but only because of the pull of a man he despised. He had led a failed expedition against the Apache after allowing a senator's wife to be shot on his watch. He wondered if the army was really the place for him to stay, but what else would he do?

Up ahead he saw Mesilla, its adobe buildings glowing gold in the soft moonlight. As he neared he heard the strum of a guitar and the moan of a fiddle coming from a cantina on the square. Cantinas and stores were intermingled on three sides of the square, but on the north stood a cathedral. A pair of lovers walked hand in hand along the plaza, staring at the moon. Benoit wished that Inge was with him to share this moment.

He found himself aiming his horse toward the cantina from which the music was drifting. He dismounted and tied his horse beside three others at a hitching rail. He lifted his hat and ran his fingers through his hair, then stepped inside.

There were a handful of customers—four Mexican men, a dance girl, and three Anglos. The bartender serving drinks waved Benoit inside, and even the two musicians nodded a welcome to him.

Benoit stepped up to the bar. "Food?" he asked.

"*Sí,*" replied the bartender. "*Chile con carne, frijoles, tortillas.*"

"Whiskey?"

"*Sí,*" replied the bartender.

Benoit pulled a pouch from his pocket and dumped a couple of coins on the counter. The bartender smiled. "*¡Dinero! Americano muy rico.*"

"Food and whiskey," Benoit repeated, taking a table by himself.

As he did, he felt the hard gaze of a white man at a corner table. He was wearing a blanket as a poncho and his eyes seemed to be glazed over. His beard was unkempt, and there was something about him that was vaguely familiar. Too, both his ears were missing.

The bartender arrived with a bottle of whiskey and a shot glass, placing them both in front of Benoit. As he retreated to the bar Benoit uncorked the whiskey and filled the glass. He lifted the jigger to his lips and poured the amber liquid down his gullet. It slid down like molten lava, and nothing could have felt better.

When he glanced at the corner, he saw the bearded man eyeing him suspiciously.

Benoit knew he had seen the man before but couldn't quite place him.

The bartender returned with a tray and unloaded a bowl of chili, a bowl of refried beans, and a platter of tortillas.

As he started eating he glanced occasionally at the bearded man, trying desperately to remember where he had seen him.

The food was spicy and tasted good, not nearly as bland as army fare.

Then the bearded man stood and walked deliberately to his table. The fellow stared oddly at him.

At that moment Benoit recalled the face. This was one of the scalp hunters, the one called McRae.

~*10*~

Harold McRae looked up from his whiskey bottle as a
cavalry captain sat down at a table across the cantina.
McRae recognized him immediately: Captain Jean
Benoit. McRae strangled his bottle as he lifted it to his
lips and gulped down the whiskey. He hated the captain, blaming Benoit for what the Apaches had done to
him, but at least he had lived. Jim Morehouse and the
others had died. If the captain had allowed Morehouse's gang to ride with the soldiers, then the others
would have survived, McRae's whiskey-muddled
mind told him. He'd be damned if he would carry the
message from Cochise to the soldiers. After all, the soldiers were responsible for the loss of his companions,
and this captain was the cause of Morehouse's death,
as well as of his own terrible ordeal.

His anger simmering, McRae slammed the bottle
against the table. He knew he must kill the captain. He
pushed himself up from the table, mad at the captain,
annoyed by the musicians, who wouldn't be quiet long
enough for a man to think. McRae steadied himself
against the table with his left hand while he slipped his
right under his poncho and fingered the handle of his

stolen butcher knife. Then he moved slowly, deliberately, across the room, making certain he concealed the knife.

The captain, eating hungrily, watched him approach but did not stop filling his mouth with food until McRae was opposite him across the table. McRae bent over and rested his left hand on the tabletop. "I know you," he sneered.

Benoit put down his spoon and nodded. "And I remember you. You're the scalp hunter, the one that survived the Apaches."

"It's your fault, you bastard."

Benoit pushed himself away from the table and stood. "How's that?"

"You wouldn't let us ride with you. They tortured me, almost killed me, because of you."

"If you live like vermin, you die like vermin."

McRae drooled with anger, and when he spoke he sprayed spit out with the words. "You bastard. You're all bastards, you and your soldiers. You know what they did to us? They stripped us naked and forced us to march barefoot in the cold. They staked us around a huge fire, dumped coals on us, branded us with burning sticks, cut us with their knives, kicked us between the legs.

"They threw Sam on the fire, roasting him like a side of beef. Morehouse, they chopped off his fingers and toes, then tied him behind a horse and dragged him across the desert until his skin was peeled away and he was raw and bleeding. They tossed him in the fire and he died. And all because of you and your cowardly soldiers."

"They got what they deserved. A shame you got away."

McRae studied Benoit, then looked around the room at the customers, the bartender, and the musicians, who had stopped playing. Much as he wanted to kill the captain right there and then, he knew he must wait until there were no witnesses. Too, with only a knife he knew he would stand little chance against the captain's pistol. He would wait until the captain left the cantina to kill him.

"I got away because they let me leave with a secret," McRae admitted. "And I'll tell you something else—I'll get you for what you did and what you let happen. You'll know what it felt like to be tortured when I'm done." McRae pushed himself from the table, stared at the captain a final time, then staggered to the door before shuffling outside and into the moonlight.

He studied the four horses tied to the hitching rail and picked out the captain's by the army saddle. He pulled his knife and sliced the reins, then waved his hand and spooked the horse, which trotted off toward the church. He followed the animal, planning to jump the captain when he came looking for his mount.

With the captain dead, Morehouse and the other scalp hunters would be avenged.

Benoit watched the scalp hunter slip outside into the night. He was drunk and would likely sleep it off somewhere.

The bartender approached. "*Señor McRae muy mal.*"

Benoit sat back down and grabbed his spoon, pointing at the bowl of chili. "*Bueno,*" he said.

The bartender smiled and motioned for the musicians to resume.

Though the food was spicy, it settled nicely on

Benoit's stomach, so much better than had all the horsemeat in the mountains. After he finished the first bowl,
the bartender brought him a second, which he ate
between bites of beans wrapped in tortillas. When he finished his second bowl of chili the bartender offered him
a third, but Benoit waved it away. The bartender
returned instead with a tin of goat's milk and a platter.
As Benoit drank the milk the bartender placed the platter
in front of him. It was covered with fried tortillas sprin-
kled with sugar and cinnamon and drenched in honey.

He thought he would take merely a bite or two, but
the sweetness was a fine complement to the spicy foods
he had just eaten, so he cleaned the platter. *"Muy bueno,"*
he said to the bartender, drawing a smile.

Standing, Benoit stretched. He was sluggish from
the food and knew that by the time he reached the fort he
would fall asleep easily and sleep soundly. He thanked
the bartender again for the food and drink, then
marched outside. He looked both ways down the plank
walk, checking for McRae, then stepped to the hitching
rail.

"Damnation," he cried when he saw that his horse
was gone. Just his luck for his horse to be stolen and for
him to have to walk back to the fort. He admitted to himself, though, that his luck had been running poorly for
the last few weeks, so why should he have expected any
change?

As he stepped toward the plaza he saw a horse
standing by the low stone fence surrounding the church
and realized it was his. He didn't think he tied the reins
so carelessly that his mount could have wandered off,
but at least now he wouldn't have to walk back to the
fort.

He stepped across the dusty street and moved

toward the church. His horse stood calmly watching him, never flinching until he was within reach. The animal shook its head and blew as Benoit grabbed the reins hanging beneath the horse's jaw. *"Merdé,"* he said to himself when he realized the reins were shorter than normal. They had been cut.

He turned the horse about and was about to mount it when he heard the swish of moccasined feet on hard-packed ground.

His horse reared, but he held the reins momentarily. Benoit slipped when the horse landed, butting its head against his chest. He fell to the ground and the horse trotted off. Stunned for a moment, Benoit lay motionless, not realizing that a man towered above him. The man raised his arm in the air. Benoit saw the motion, then realized the danger from the avenging scalp hunter. He saw the knife blade glimmer in the moonlight. The knife came down, but Benoit rolled away as the blade sliced the air where he had been.

The attacker cursed. "Be still, you bastard."

Sluggish from the food in his belly, Benoit scrambled up, then jumped aside as the attacker lunged at him with his knife.

"You're dead, you bastard," cried McRae. He lunged at Benoit with the knife but stumbled over his own feet and landed full against the stone wall.

McRae spun around, lowered his shoulder, and plowed into Benoit's stomach, knocking the officer backward.

Benoit tripped and fell on his back.

McRae pounced upon him, grabbing a fistful of Benoit's army blouse with his left hand and waving the knife with his right.

Benoit grabbed the knife hand with both of his

hands, then struggled to wrench the weapon from McRae's grasp.

The knife started down in spite of Benoit's efforts to stop it.

"Bastard," cried McRae, "I got you now."

Benoit bucked against the weight of the scalp hunter. McRae was momentarily off balance, his grip on Benoit's blouse ripping a button free as the knife continued toward Benoit's neck. But in that moment Benoit twisted McRae's wrist enough that the knife changed its course toward the scalp hunter's stomach.

With all his might, Benoit shoved the blade at McRae, then felt the knife enter flesh. McRae screamed, gasped, and released the knife. Then Benoit rammed the blade all the way into McRae's stomach. Like a ripped bellows, McRae deflated quickly, crumpling over on the ground beside Benoit.

Benoit pushed the dying man away, then got to his feet. He backed away, looked around the plaza for witnesses, then went for his horse to get away quickly before anyone realized what had happened.

Hurriedly he walked to his horse, grabbed the shortened reins, mounted, and started back for Fort Fillmore. By the time he got back to the stables, the guard had changed, but the new man had apparently been informed by the previous guard of Benoit's departure. Benoit quickly unsaddled his horse, rubbed him down, then retired to his room. Exhausted and confused from the fight in Mesilla, he removed his gunbelt and his boots, then fell into bed and a deep slumber that carried him through reveille at sunrise and drill mount at ten-thirty.

Benoit was roused from his sleep not by a bugle call but by a sergeant and four soldiers with carbines pointed at him.

"Captain," the sergeant said, "the colonel demands to see you immediately."

Benoit knew what the colonel wanted to talk to him about: the visit to Mesilla and the fight. He nodded, reaching for his boots and pulling them on quickly. Standing, he moved past the sergeant, then stopped until the soldiers with the carbine parted so he could exit his room.

"Why the guards, Sergeant?" Benoit asked. "I've never required an armed guard before when I was summoned by a superior officer."

"I can't rightly say, sir. I'm just following orders."

Benoit stepped out into the hallway, waiting for two of the guards to take positions on either side of him. Then he marched out the door and into the morning light. It was a brisk morning and the chill felt good.

Once again Benoit paused so the guards could take positions on either side of him and so the sergeant could step to the front of the procession. Then they started toward the headquarters building, crossing the parade ground, moving past the flagpoles and by the many soldiers who were riding horses on drill. He could see them whisper among themselves, likely wondering about the cause of Benoit's trouble.

An orderly held the headquarters door open as he approached. Benoit marched straight into Lieutenant Colonel Sullivan's office. With the guards still on either side, Benoit saluted the colonel. "Sir," he said.

Sullivan did not return the salute. Standing up from his chair, he walked around his desk and stood eyeball to eyeball with Benoit.

"Captain, did you leave this fort last night without permission?"

"Yes, sir."

"And what was your reason for this breach of rules?"

"Sir, I awoke early and was hungry. I decided on my own to ride into Mesilla for food."

"Army food not good enough for you?"

"At the time it didn't seem to be."

"I'm glad you didn't deny leaving the fort without permission, because I've two stable guards who reported your borrowing a horse, then returning it to the stables with cut reins. While you were in Mesilla, Captain, did you kill a man, a civilian named Harold McRae?"

"I can't say, sir."

"What do you mean, you can't say?" Sullivan raged.

"I mean, sir—"

Sullivan lifted his arm and pointed at Benoit. "Silence."

Benoit let the sentence hang incomplete in the air.

"Look at your blouse, Captain."

Benoit glanced down and saw blood smears and a tear where a button had been ripped away.

Sullivan turned to his desk and retrieved something, then spun back around to face Benoit. In his open palm he held a button from an army uniform. "This was found in the hand of the dead man this morning in front of the church in Mesilla. You seem to be missing a button from your uniform. How do you explain that, Captain?"

"I defended myself against an attacker who had threatened me in the cantina where I ate. There were witnesses. He was a scalp hunter, the only survivor of the Jim Morehouse gang, the rest of whom were tortured and killed by the Apaches. Plenty of people saw it. When I went to leave, he attacked with a knife. I defended myself and didn't stay around to see what condition he was in. I knew I shouldn't've been away from the fort, so I rode back."

"A civilian's dead, Captain, and it appears you killed him. That's not the kind of situation an officer of honor runs away from."

"He was a scalp hunter, for God's sake."

"He was a civilian, Captain, and as a consequence of that, I am ordering that you be confined to the stockade until this matter can be examined and resolved."

Benoit saluted. "Yes, sir. Will I be allowed mail or any correspondence?"

Sullivan shook his head. "No, Captain."

Benoit felt his shoulders sag.

"There's several issues here that need to be resolved, Captain, and your cooperation will be helpful and will certainly enhance your chances of minimal punishment."

"And how long will I be in the stockade, sir?"

"Until justice runs its course, sir. I must take up these matters with headquarters at Fort Marcy and with the civilian authorities in Mesilla."

"Yes, sir."

"Captain, your time at Fort Fillmore has been unfortunate. If the outcome of our investigation points favorably to you, I would hope that you will learn from this and become a better officer than you have thus far been."

The words were like salt on a wound.

"One other thing, Captain. Is your report on the expedition after the Apaches finished?"

"Yes, sir. It's there on your desk."

"Good." He turned to the sergeant. "Please escort Captain Benoit to the stockade."

Benoit was taken to the stockade and locked in a small dark cell, the only light coming from a tiny opening barely six inches by six inches at the top of the adobe wall. The door was solid wood. He had a blanket on the floor for a bed, a pail with water for his thirst in one corner, and a bucket in the opposite corner for use when nature called.

He sat down on the hard floor and waited, having no idea how long the wait would be or what the army's decision might be. Noon came and went without rations; then for supper he was delivered a half loaf of bread and a tin of coffee. He ate the bread ravenously, then drank the coffee.

After the guards came to pick up the coffee tin, Benoit tried to stretch out on the blanket on the floor. The cell was too small for him to lie straight, and he positioned himself diagonally across the cell so that he could lie down without bending his knees.

Sleep came as slowly as the passing of the minutes.

J. Ernest Hardley of the *Picayune* accompanied Senator Cle Couvillion to a meeting with Lieutenant Colonel Jeremy Sullivan. The senator relished the news of Jean Benoit's misfortune in Mesilla two days earlier. Benoit's troubles had played right into the senator's hands. He could force Benoit to spy for him, or he could ruin his career, or at least he could see that the captain was jailed for years. No longer would Benoit have an option other than to do what Couvillion desired.

As he approached Sullivan's office he was pleased to be able to add one more little problem to Benoit's plate. It was the matter of the report on Benoit's visit to the

Apache camp and the subsequent threat by McManus and Benoit to emasculate the newspaperman.

The colonel stood at the door waiting. Couvillion eyed him, wondering if his wife had seduced him, the way she had done with so many other men. Even though it was distasteful having a wife with such proclivities, it was not without its advantages, because it gave him power over those other men. He could certainly ruin the career of any man who had slept with his wife.

Couvillion greeted Sullivan warmly. "Afternoon, Colonel."

Sullivan nodded to both the senator and the reporter. "And how is your wife?"

Couvillion measured his response carefully, wanting to gauge the colonel and his relationship with her. "She is better, much better."

"I am glad to hear that."

"She speaks very kindly of you."

Sullivan shifted on his feet, and his cheeks reddened.

"She said she felt like she got real close to you in such a short time."

Sullivan avoided the senator's eyes for an instant.

Couvillion smiled. Now he knew that the colonel was the Fort Fillmore officer who had bedded his wife. That would be valuable knowledge in the days ahead.

"Please come into my office," the colonel managed with a nervous sweep of his arm.

"Thank you," responded the senator. "We have much to talk about."

Sullivan swallowed hard.

Couvillion grinned. Couvillion and Hardley took their seats while the colonel paced back and forth behind his desk.

"Please, Colonel, be seated," Couvillion said. "You have nothing to be worried about."

Sullivan nodded. "It's just that so many things have gone wrong since your wife came—I mean arrived. I must assure you this is not typical of my command. Seems much of this responsibility rests on the shoulders of Captain Jean Benoit."

Couvillion nodded. "Colonel, I must share some responsibility for that. He was a childhood friend of my wife, blessed angel that she is. I thought it might do her spirit good to see him on this trip out west. She has been quite fragile these days, the strain of life in Washington weighing heavily upon her. My intentions, though noble, had but the opposite effect, alas, and now she seems even more fragile. Colonel, she even said some things about you that I could not find it in my soul to believe."

Sullivan whitened.

"So don't you worry a bit, Colonel. All will be worked out eventually, and if I had known that Captain Benoit's presence would lead to so many difficulties, I never would have requested he accompany Marie to Santa Fe. As it is, I fear she shall never see Santa Fe, for I must take her to New Orleans, where she can fully recover. Later, when she is up to it, I will get her back to Washington and to the life that she loves."

Sullivan nodded. "I will do whatever I can to assist you on that."

Couvillion smiled. "I'm sure you will. Now, about Captain Benoit. I have some serious reservations about his leadership capabilities. And I understand you are working with the civil authorities to see whether or not he should be prosecuted on charges of murder in Mesilla."

"That's true, Senator."

"Then let me explain why I brought Mr. Hardley of the *Picayune* along with me. I understand that Captain Benoit has finished his report on the punitive expedition to avenge my wife."

"That's correct."

"Hardley has a special interest in that report, being that he's talked to the men who accompanied Captain Benoit, and their accounts lead us to believe Captain Benoit might not have been fully forthright."

"And how is that?"

"Colonel, I think it best to let Hardley tell you." Couvillion turned to his companion.

Hardley grinned. "Colonel, in spite of what you may have been told about casualties at the Apache camp, there was no attack and no Indian casualties. The camp had already been burned to the ground, and the seven dead they left behind were a band of scalp hunters killed by the Apaches. You can check with the troops who were there. They will confirm that, all save Captain Benoit and the scout, Tim McManus. They have fabricated a story to satisfy you, to make you believe that they carried out your orders. Perhaps they were scared of the Apaches."

Sullivan shook his head. "I cannot believe that about McManus being scared. I've used him many times as a scout and he has never turned from danger."

"Perhaps," Hardley said, "Benoit ruins everything he touches."

"That may be so," said the colonel, marching to the door. He told the orderly to bring him Benoit's report of the expedition.

"While you're waiting, Colonel," Couvillion started, "let me also inform you that McManus and Benoit threatened Hardley with a horrible punishment if he should advise you of their lies."

"They threatened him?"

Couvillion laughed, drawing Hardley's icy glare. "Colonel, the most delicate way to say it is that they promised to make a steer out of him if he spoke with you. And me too, if he informed me of the threat."

Sullivan shook his head as the orderly handed him Benoit's report. Sullivan returned to his desk and scanned the short report until he reached the section on the Apache camp. He began to read aloud the pertinent paragraphs.

"'The next day we came to the spot where the trail of the raiding party veered toward the mountains and away from the trail to the Apache camp. Posting half of my healthy men to set up a perimeter and to guard the sick and wounded, I took the other half to find the Apache camp. We found the camp at the end of a wide draw, the site of more than forty or so lodges. We rode into camp looking for the enemy. When we were done, we left seven bodies behind as well as the camp burned to the ground. Returning to the men we had left behind, we then continued on for Fort Fillmore and were bothered no more by Apaches."

Hardley crossed his arms and nodded. "It's all false and misleading, Colonel. I am a reporter and accustomed to finding the truth from the lies. There was no attack, no fight. The men that were dead were white scalp hunters. If you don't believe me, you can ask some of the men. They will back my account. Now that Benoit is in the stockade and can do them no harm, they will be honest."

Sullivan nodded.

"And," Couvillion added, "I should like to ask that

you consider charges against Benoit in connection with
the threat to Mr. Hardley. A free country will be free only
as long as a free press is not threatened by governmental
authorities such as the irresponsible Benoit."

"I shall do that, Senator."

"Excellent. Just one more request, Colonel."

"Anything."

"Tomorrow I would like the opportunity to visit
with Captain Benoit, to see if I can show him the error of
his ways."

"That can be arranged."

"And Colonel, please have him brought to my quarters."

"Yes, Senator."

"In chains."

The guards rattled the key in the lock, then swung the
door open. Jean Benoit sat propped against the back
wall, staring at the door as the guards marched in.
They were carrying chains, which clanked as they
moved.

Benoit had lost track of time and days. He did not
know if it was morning or afternoon. Time had seemed
to stand still to the point that Benoit was too confused to
tell the difference between the days.

The sergeant who had initially come to arrest him
entered. "You're looking a mite pale, Captain," said the
sergeant, "but it's time to take you for a little walk."

"Where?"

"I was told not to tell you, just to put some jewelry
on you and escort you to your destination."

Four more soldiers approached Benoit, one carrying
leg irons and another wrist shackles.

Two squatted to grab his ankles, one yanking off his left boot, then the other yanking off his right. They quickly locked the irons on his feet and stood up. The metal rested heavily on his heels, scraping his ankles as he tried to move.

The two other men grabbed his hands and locked the wrist shackles in place. As he stood there Benoit wondered whether this had been Couvillion's idea or Sullivan's.

Next the soldiers led him out of his cell and into the bright morning sunshine. The glare of the light blinded him. He lifted his hands to shade his eyes but could barely hold them up for the weight of the chains. He realized how weak he was.

Feeling dizzy, he paused for a moment, but the soldiers nudged him ahead and he half walked, half stumbled across the parade ground, the leg irons biting into his flesh, making each step painful. He wanted to hold his head up so that the soldiers who stood watching him would realize he was not a defeated man, but he did not have the energy. By the direction in which the guards ushered him, he knew they were taking him to see Senator Couvillion.

As he walked he gritted his teeth against the pain, vowing to keep enough energy so that he could stand proudly before Couvillion instead of groveling. Though he no longer cared for her and hadn't for years, he hoped Marie would not see him like this, at least not in front of her husband.

Benoit lifted his head and saw Couvillion standing in front of his quarters, his arms folded across his chest, an evil smile upon his lips. When Benoit came within speaking distance, the senator stepped back inside.

Benoit wondered if he would have the chance to kill

Couvillion. The idea raced through his mind, then he discarded it for the foolishness that it was. He was already in trouble for killing one man in self-defense. He would have no defense for dispatching the senator, short of the fact that he actually needed killing, like some poisonous snake.

The sergeant led Benoit inside to the dining room Couvillion was using for an office. The senator was seated behind the table, reviewing a stack of papers, as though he didn't know what was going on. He looked up and nodded at Benoit. "Morning, Captain."

The sergeant stood beside Benoit with arms crossed.

"That'll be all for now, Sergeant," the senator said. "Keep your men outside until I call for you."

"You sure you'll be okay, Senator?"

"Certainly," Couvillion replied. "Captain Benoit and I go back a long way together."

"Whatever you say, Senator." The sergeant herded the other men out into the hall and then outside.

Only when the door shut did Couvillion speak again. "You're looking a bit pale, Jean. The stockade's not been good for you."

Angered, Benoit lifted his arms. He considered striking Couvillion or wrapping the chain around his neck regardless of the consequences.

Couvillion shook his head. "Don't make it any worse on yourself, Jean. You've already got a murder charge hanging over you, and since we talked last time, you've gotten a few more problems facing you."

Benoit shook his head. "It can't get any worse."

"Sure it can, Captain. Let me explain."

Benoit said nothing.

"Now, you're the only one who knows what happened in Mesilla, but you murdered a civilian. From what I understand, he was one of the scalp hunters who followed your expedition."

"He should've died with the others."

"Maybe he should have, but you'd have done better to leave it to someone else to kill him."

"I didn't have much choice when he came after me with that knife."

Couvillion waved off Benoit's words. "And if that isn't enough to make you do what I want, there are a couple of other developments you should know about."

Benoit thought of Hardley and knew the *Picayune* reporter would figure in it.

"You've been accused of making false statements and filing an erroneous report with your commanding officer. That's a serious charge in and of itself, one that can ruin your army career forever, Captain.

"On top of that, you and Tim McManus have been accused of threatening to maim or kill both Hardley and myself. That's a serious charge as well.

"In addition, I don't know that I need you any more, Jean. As I grow more powerful I won't need the people I needed before. Maybe you'd better understand that."

Benoit laughed. "You'll always need others to do your dirty work."

"You shouldn't insult a man who's trying to do you a favor. As it is, I feared I would need you, but the War Department's appointed Brigadier General Arnold Smedley to command the Ninth Military District. If you ever get back to Santa Fe, he will be your new commander. General Smedley just happens to be a third cousin of Jefferson Davis. I'll be able to find out everything I want to know about the military in New Mexico Territory through him. You'd best grab on to me while I'll still let you, or you'll be on your own, and we've already seen you're not real good on your own. Fact is, you wouldn't be a captain without me, and the way things are going you'll be nothing if you don't do what I say."

"There are too many people doing what you say as it is."

Couvillion nodded. "And they'll do what I say on this, including Colonel Sullivan."

"You got it all figured out, don't you, Cle?"

Grinning, Couvillion agreed. "I do, and *you'd* better figure it out soon, before I lose my patience."

"I'll think on it."

"Sure, put up a strong front, try to save face, Jean, but you don't have a face to save anymore. I can squash you like a bug and leave the grease stain on the ground. I'll be returning to New Orleans and then Washington in a week. I want an answer in five days. Either you play with me and do what I say for the glory of Louisiana and the South, or you'll regret it the rest of your life, however long or short."

"I hate you, Cle, for what you're doing to Louisiana."

"Hate whom you like, Jean, but just remember that right now I control events and your future. If you wait much longer and I lose control, then nobody, not even God himself, can help you."

Benoit nodded, knowing Couvillion had a stranglehold on him but not wanting to admit it. Benoit turned from the senator. "Don't bother," Benoit said. "I'll see myself out."

Couvillion laughed. "That'll be the last decision you make on your own unless you do what I say. Good day, Jean."

The sound of the senator's laughter stung his ears as he stepped outside.

Benoit knew he had no choice but to do what Couvillion wanted if he was ever to get out of his predicament, but he didn't want to admit it to himself. He ate supper that night in the dark. The weather was turning cold, and the single blanket was not enough to keep him warm.

Well after midnight, he heard a familiar voice calling him through the high window.

"Cap'n, Cap'n," came the hushed voice, "it's me, McManus. I brought ya some things."

Benoit stood up but was disoriented for a minute. Then he heard the sound of something falling from the tiny window.

"I brought ya a present, some food. It's not much, but ya looked a little pale today when I saw ya in irons."

"Thanks," Benoit said, his voice sounding dry and distant.

"I'm also bringing ya another blanket. It's gonna get cold tonight."

"Okay."

"Cap'n, I heard what the senator and Hardley done to ya. Do ya want me to kill 'em?"

"It won't do any good, McManus. That'll only make matters worse for both of us. My only option is to do what Couvillion wants."

"Okay, but don't say I didn't offer. I'd better go before I get caught. I'll bring ya more whenever I get the chance. Ya just hold on."

"Thanks, McManus."

After that, McManus came every other night, leaving food for Benoit. Gradually Benoit regained some of his strength. He would feel better, he thought, if he could just bathe and shave.

He passed the time thinking of Inge, rereading her letter and dreaming of having her in his arms. He thought of his two girls and tried to imagine what they looked like, how they cried, and how their tiny hands would feel in his. He carried on imaginary conversations with Jace Dobbs, talking about everything he could think of.

And on the fifth day after his visit with Senator Couvillion, the guards came to get him again. They locked the chains on his feet and wrists, then marched him across the parade ground again.

Couvillion didn't watch from the door this time, just waited inside.

The sergeant stopped at the door. "You know your way," he said, "and the senator didn't want me coming in this time."

When he entered, Benoit found Marie seated in the parlor, wearing her robe. Her face was clouded with defeat and then concern when she saw Benoit's ragged figure.

She did not get up from her chair, just smiled weakly and spoke softly. "Please, Jean, do what he says. Not only for yourself and your family, but for Louisiana and the South."

Benoit dragged his chains down the hall and turned into Couvillion's office.

"Well, well, Captain. Good to see you again. I believe you remember our last conversation."

Benoit nodded.

"Then it's time you make your decision. Either you gather the information that I want and see that I get it or you stand trial for murder."

Benoit sighed. He didn't want to do this, but he

wanted to see his girls, he wanted to see Inge again, and, as much as anything, he wanted his decent name and his army career back for the sake of his family.

"What's your decision?"

"You win, Cle. I'll provide the information you want."

Senator Clement "Cle" Couvillion sat at the table that served as his desk and awaited the arrival of Lieutenant Colonel Jeremy Sullivan. The stony silence between the senator and his wife, sitting in a rocking chair behind him, left J. Ernest Hardley uncomfortably tapping his fingers on the wood of the table.

Periodically Hardley glanced at Marie. There was a hardness about her gaze that he had never noticed before. Previously he would have thought it the strain of the arrow wound and her recovery, but now he was certain the pain was deeper than that. It was the pain that only a husband could inflict upon a wife or a wife upon a husband. And Hardley knew that more pain was about to be inflicted upon this marriage, because the senator had confided in him how he planned to resolve the delicate matter of extracting Jean Benoit from his predicament.

Hardley found the relationship with Couvillion mutually beneficial. As the senator's confidant, he shared information that the senator did not even share with his wife. In fact, the senator was about to humiliate his own wife for his political purposes. The information the relationship produced gave Hardley scoops that translated into readership for the *Picayune* and made him one of the most widely read reporters in the South. The senator, in return, could use the *Picayune* for political purposes, which would ultimately benefit the South and Louisiana. Too, Jefferson Davis and many of the other southern leaders were aging, whereas Cle Couvillion was a young, ambitious politician with a future, characteristics that might one day make him president, either of the United States or, even better, the new nation that the South might form if the Union were dissolved. Couvillion was going places, and J. Ernest Hardly intended to go with him. Marie would probably go with the senator as well, being enamored of the trappings that went with being a senator's wife, but she would not go as happily.

At the knock on the door, Hardley arose and stepped out to admit Lieutenant Colonel Jeremy Sullivan. The colonel seemed nervous being summoned to the senator's quarters. Hardly played on the officer's discomfort by merely nodding in answer to his salutation. Hardley motioned to the senator's makeshift office, then followed Sullivan down the hall.

"Good afternoon, Senator," Sullivan said as he entered the room. "And Mrs. Couvillion, glad to see you are better."

As he took his seat Hardley saw Marie nod slightly, without any emotion. The senator, however, didn't look up from his papers, making the colonel even more nervous.

When finally he did lift his head from his papers, he gave the colonel a narrow smile, which did little to ease the officer's fears.

"Colonel," Couvillion said, "I've not been apprised

of the status on the problems of Captain Benoit. And it has been a few days since we talked."

For a moment the colonel seemed relieved. "I have worked it out for him to be tried in a civilian court for the murder. And I initiated the paperwork for a court-martial."

Couvillion shook his head and frowned. "The situation has changed, Colonel."

Sullivan shifted nervously on his feet. "And how is that?"

The senator stood up, planted his hands on the table, and leaned toward the colonel. "I want you to get the charges dropped against him. I want you to cancel the court-martial proceedings. And I want you to give Captain Benoit a suitable commendation for bravery and leadership in service to his country."

"But sir, I don't understand. I will look bad if I go back now to both the civil authorities and my superiors to reverse this."

"Colonel," Couvillion said, "you'll look worse if you don't."

"Sir?"

"You'll look worse. Mr. Hardley will see to that."

Hardley smiled and gave a slight nod.

"To speak plainly, Colonel, unless you do what I suggest, I'll ruin your career."

"But Senator, I have had an exemplary career, following the spirit and the intent of my superiors and the army code of conduct."

"Perhaps so, Colonel, but I don't think it is conduct becoming an officer and a gentleman when he commits adultery with a senator's wife."

Hardley saw the colonel deflate, his shoulders slumping.

Sullivan sighed.

"You can deny it, Colonel, but my wife told me all about it when I questioned her."

Sullivan hung his head.

"I killed a man once for diddling my wife, but he was only an Indian agent, not an officer in the army. As I told you before, my wife has been fragile. I had hoped the trip out west would help her recover emotionally. Now, she admits to initiating this adulterous encounter, but if you don't attend to Captain Benoit's trouble as I request, I can easily change that charge to one of rape. How do you think that would look on your record? Your career would be ruined, a promising career at that."

"I did not make undue advances toward your wife, Senator."

Couvillion smiled. "I would never suggest that, Colonel, as long as you do what I say."

Sullivan still seemed reluctant to go along with Couvillion's wishes.

Couvillion motioned to Hardley. "Colonel, you probably wondered why I asked Mr. Hardley to join us."

Sullivan shrugged, as if to say he hadn't thought about it.

"Well, there are two avenues I can take if you cannot arrange what I wish. One is to go through army channels, and the other is to go through Mr. Hardley's newspaper, the *Picayune*. If the army doesn't ruin you, the newspaper stories will. Mr. Hardley can do things to your reputation that the army can't come close to doing."

Hardley smiled at the colonel.

"But didn't he want something done about the threat to you and him by McManus and Captain Benoit?"

"Yes, he did, but he has since come to realize that frontiersmen have a rugged sense of humor. It was little more than a joke. And he is willing to forget, Colonel, unless . . ."

"Unless I don't drop the investigations into Captain Benoit."

"Exactly," replied the senator.

"The way I see it," the reporter interjected, "if you don't save Benoit, the threats against the senator and myself become just one of many examples I'll use to expose how poorly you've run Fort Fillmore, such as posting an insufficient guard for the senator's wife on her journey to Santa Fe, sending out an ill-fated expedition to chase her attackers, even putting on a bullfight that was solely for her amusement and cost a young native his life. At the *Picayune,* we buy ink by the barrel and paper by the ton, so there's plenty available to ruin your career if you don't salvage Captain Benoit's."

"But only a few days ago you wanted to ruin Captain Benoit's career yourselves."

"Just consider it politics, Colonel. Now, are we clear on your options?"

Sullivan hesitated before answering, looking first at Hardley, then at the senator, and finally at Marie Couvillion. She seemed as helpless against the senator and the newspaperman as did he.

"You leave me no choice."

"Not if you value your career." Couvillion smiled.

Sullivan clenched his teeth. He had done everything he could to impress the senator's wife, but because of her loose morals and his weakness in a single moment, he found himself a pawn in the senator's game. He had no choice except between right and his career. He chose his career.

"I'll cover for Captain Benoit and for you," he told the senator.

"You'll be doing it for yourself, Colonel, don't forget that."

Sullivan nodded. "For myself."

"Now, Colonel, Marie should be well enough to travel in a couple of days. I want a wagon for her and a wagon for her baggage in two days. I will expect an army escort at least until El Paso for my wife and myself. I would not want a reoccurrence of the attack on my wife."

"Yes, sir. And what about Captain Benoit? I suppose you want him released from the stockade."

Couvillion laughed. "Just because I'm interested in his career doesn't mean I'm interested in him. Let him stay there until the morning Marie and I leave. I want him out to see us off and then I want him ordered back to Santa Fe immediately."

"Yes, sir. Is he to have an escort? I still have the men who came down with him from Santa Fe."

"No, send them back to Fort Marcy and let him fend for himself."

"Yes, sir. Anything else?"

"Just one thing, Colonel: Don't ever discuss this conversation with anyone or we'll ruin your career just the same. Understood?"

"Very plainly," Sullivan said, then saluted with contempt.

After his deal with Senator Couvillion, Captain Jean Benoit lingered in the stockade for several more days. Then, as suddenly as he had been roused from his bed and detained originally, he was given his freedom without explanation.

When he walked outside into the soft early morning light, he saw a line of sixty cavalrymen behind two wagons on the parade ground. He noted Cle Couvillion astride a horse and Marie Couvillion propped up in a bed in the lead wagon.

The sergeant who had arrested him stood outside the stockade, holding the reins to a cavalry horse. "Here's your mount, Captain. Your pistol and belongings are in the saddlebag. I am also instructed to give you orders to return to Fort Marcy immediately."

His knees still rubbery, Benoit marched around, trying to gauge if he even had the strength to get on the horse. He pointed to the wagons and line of cavalrymen. "Where is the senator headed?"

"El Paso, to begin the trip home to New Orleans for his wife."

"I'm glad," Benoit answered, "that we're going in opposite directions."

"Maybe so, sir, but the senator wanted to see you before you left. Word is he pulled strings to have your record cleared and all charges ignored. Colonel Sullivan's none too happy about that. That's why I understand he's not providing you any escort back to Fort Marcy."

Benoit took the reins, then hauled himself into the saddle. "Maybe I'd better get going before the colonel changes his mind."

"Don't forget to see the senator."

Benoit shook the reins, aiming his mount for the senator.

Couvillion sat regally in the saddle, smiling at Benoit as he rode up. "Well, Captain, I see they finally let you out of the stockade. Don't forget the deal that got you out. I'll expect regular updates from Santa Fe."

"I won't forget, Cle. There's a lot of things I won't forget."

"Remember, Jean, you're doing it for Louisiana and the South."

"No, Cle, I'm not doing it for Louisiana or the South. I'm not even doing it for you. I'm doing it for my wife and twin daughters, that's all."

"That's your business, Jean. Just don't forget that you wouldn't have had the chance to do it without my pull."

"Believe me, Cle, I won't forget what you've done." Benoit jerked the reins and turned his horse about, then rode toward the line of cavalry. He stopped at the wagon to speak to Marie Couvillion.

She smiled softly at him. "I hope your wife and daughters do well. I'll always wonder what might have happened between us if Father hadn't seen to it that you were transferred from the War Department to Fort Laramie."

"Why do you stay with Cle? You don't love him."

"There aren't many senators available for husbands, Jean."

Benoit nodded. "At least you've got a senator, even if you don't have love."

He saw her eyes moisten. He turned his horse about and rode away, not wanting to see the tears. She had been a fine young woman at one time, but Clement Couvillion had changed her.

Benoit hoped Couvillion hadn't changed *him*.

"Good-bye, Marie, and good luck," he called over his shoulder.

Benoit aimed north and rode away from Fort Fillmore, hoping he never saw the post again. He planned to ride to Mesilla, find a room, take a bath, fill his belly, then ride on to Santa Fe.

Halfway between the fort and Mesilla, though, he spotted a rider coming toward him. He wasn't in the mood for company until he realized the rider was Tim McManus, the scout.

McManus rode up and fell in beside Benoit. "Mornin', Cap'n. I heard ya might be ridin' this way and I thought I'd join ya."

Benoit smiled. "For how far?"

"Clear to Santa Fe. I figured ya could use company."

"I didn't make many friends at Fort Fillmore."

McManus shook his head. "I can't figure it all out, Cap'n, me not being an educated man. One day you're about to be charged with every crime and sin known to God, and the next day you're free."

"You ever heard of Faust?"

"Who?"

"Faust. He made a pact with the devil."

McManus shrugged. "Ain't heard of him."

"I made a pact with the devil."

"The senator or his wife?"

"The senator."

"What're ya gonna do?"

"Figure my way out of it, but not until after I've spent a night in Mesilla and bought me a bath and some food."

McManus shook his head. "I'd advise against doin' that, Cap'n."

"Why?"

"I don't know how things were resolved for the murder. Could be the colonel didn't settle things with the civil authorities. You'd best ride on as far as ya can tonight and get away from Mesilla. Bathe in the Rio Grande and then go on to Santa Fe."

"Why you riding with me?"

"Seems Colonel Sullivan can't be trusted anymore."

"That all?"

"Well, I figured I got ya in the mess you were in by leading ya up into the mountains and gettin' trapped by the snowstorm. I owe ya one better."

"I'm glad to have your company."

"I wouldn't say that, Cap'n, until I get ya to Santa Fe without frostbite."

"I've got faith in you."

Over the ensuing days they rode deeper into the chill of autumn, arriving in Santa Fe to the smell of burning pinyon wood.

McManus looked around. "It hasn't changed much since I was here before. I know where there's a saloon. I'll buy ya a drink."

Benoit declined the invitation. He was anxious to meet his new commander, though he dreaded the result. "I'd best report to General Smedley. You staying long in town?"

McManus grinned. "I might winter here, see if I can get some work with the army in the spring."

"I'll put in a good word for you. In fact, come around tomorrow and I'll introduce you to the other officers."

McManus nodded. "Make it the day after tomorrow. I plan on bein' drunker than a skunk tomorrow." McManus rode away from the plaza down a side street, looking for a saloon.

Benoit turned his horse toward army headquarters and went past the governor's palace. Dreading his meeting with General Smedley, he sat in the saddle a minute, then dismounted, tied his horse, dusted his uniform as best he could, and stepped into the squat adobe building.

He was pleased to see Frank Coker with Sergeant Phipps at the front desk. Coker's face split into a grin, and he grabbed Benoit's hand and shook it warmly. "Glad to have you back, Jean."

"It's good to be back."

"Hear you had a rough go of it."

Benoit nodded. "Apaches are a tough breed."

"I never cared much for Tom Webster," Coker said, "but it was a shame to lose him anyway."

"Getting snowed in the way we did, we were fortunate he was the only one."

"We'll have time to visit over supper. I've got a couple of matters to attend to for General Smedley," Coker said. "I think you'll like him. He's got an honorable head about him, even if he is a southerner."

"What was that, Lieutenant Coker?" came a booming voice behind Benoit.

Benoit turned to see a strapping man in the uniform of a brigadier general. Benoit saluted Smedley.

Coker saluted. "Just saying you got a good head about you, General."

"My ears aren't that bad, Lieutenant, and I'm not drunk, like General Barksdale always was," Smedley said, studying Benoit. "Captain Benoit, I gather you heard your former commanding officer died. He battled hundreds of bottles of Taos Lightning, I'm told, before losing the war. A man of such proclivities should never be given command of a mule, much less a soldier."

Benoit took in the general's thin frame and the wide handlebar mustache that made him seem even thinner. His uniform was clean and pressed and his manner was military. Though his face was stern, there seemed to be a twinkle in his brown eyes. Or perhaps it was doubt.

"It's not for me," Benoit said, "to criticize my former commander, sir."

"Not to his replacement, anyway." Smedley grinned. "Now, if Lieutenant Coker would get on with his assignments, I should like to visit with you, hear a report of your troubles in Fort Fillmore and with the Apaches." The general stared at Coker.

Coker saluted and started out the door.

"He's got a good head for a Pennsylvanian," Smedley said with a laugh.

Benoit felt at ease with the general but didn't know if he could be at ease with his politics.

Smedley motioned for Benoit to step inside his office. When he did, the general closed the door and asked Benoit to take a seat. Smedley sat down in the chair facing Benoit rather than in the seat behind his desk.

"Tell me about the Apaches and the trouble."

Benoit explained his assignment and how things had gone wrong from the beginning, including the attack on Marie Couvillion, the foray into the mountains, the snowstorm, the return, the scalp hunters, and the abandoned Indian camp.

"What about the killing?" Smedley wanted to know.

Again Benoit went into detail, giving his side of events.

"I must be candid with you, Captain—there's been some odd goings-on related to you. First you get a promotion before your time. A senator demands that you escort his wife to Santa Fe. Your punitive expedition fails against the Apache, about which you turn in a false report and are being considered for a court-martial, and after that you kill a man and are subject to a trial; then the murder goes away as though it never happened and the court-martial is dropped as nothing more than a simple misunderstanding."

"There's a simple explanation, sir."

"Well, son, I'd like to hear it."

"Senator Cle Couvillion."

Smedley shook his head, arose, and pinched the bridge of his nose with his fingers. He walked back and forth behind the desk, almost in disgust, though Benoit could not ascertain if it was disgust for him or for the senator.

Finally Smedley spoke. "Enough said."

"Sir?"

"I'm a southerner and damn proud of it, but politicians like him make me ashamed to admit it. I got this appointment because of him. He's been bullying the War Department trying to get southerners appointed to key positions so that if we have a war between the states, the South will have officers in places to help the treason. He thinks that just because I'm a third cousin to Jefferson Davis, I agree with everything the honorable senator from Mississippi says. I don't."

"Yes, sir."

"Let me tell you something, Captain. There's a lot of talk about war between the South and the North. Like you, I'm a soldier, a West Point graduate. I learned enough there to know that the South will never win a war against the North. The South can't manufacture the guns or powder it'd take to win a war. We produce the bulk of the world's cotton, but we don't have a decent mill in the South to weave fabric. That means we can't even produce our own uniforms, much less weapons and powder.

"Cle Couvillion and all the other firebrands think we can win a war based on the righteousness of our cause. Maybe they'd be right if we were throwing rocks and hitting each other with sticks, but not with the weapons of today."

Benoit nodded. "General, Couvillion got me my appointment as captain, raising me over several other deserving men. I know that, but I didn't ask for it. He's been trying to force me to spy for him, send him information on what's going on in New Mexico Territory."

"I feared as much. And how are you going to respond?"

"I took an oath when I joined the army, sir, and it means something to me. A man's name is no better than his word. Couvillion is proof of that. I had resisted his demands. The murder charge and the threat of a court-martial were his leverage to get me to do what he wanted."

"Which is to spy on the army—am I correct, Captain?"

"Yes, sir. To feed him regular reports."

Smedley laughed. "He wouldn't know valuable information from worthless drivel. What do you propose to do, Captain?"

"Sir, I swore to uphold and defend the Constitution of the United States, and I shall live up to that oath."

Smedley smiled. "Then there are at least two sensible southerners in the U.S. Army. I will help you, Captain."

"How's that?"

"I'll help you provide information that is worthless. He'll never know the difference."

Benoit grinned. "I'll be glad to shake myself free of Senator Cle Couvillion and his underhanded ways."

Smedley nodded. "I don't care what a man's politics are as long as he is honest with me. Senator Couvillion hasn't been honest since the day he was born. I expect you to be honest. As long as you are that, you will have me as your champion."

"Thank you, sir."

Smedley motioned for him to rise. "I know you've had a long ride over the last few days, so get some rest. We can talk about this more tomorrow. And by the way, check with Phipps on the way out. You've several letters from Fort Laramie."

Benoit retired to his quarters and hurriedly read the letters. Colleen and Ellen were fine and Inge was doing okay as well, thanks to help from her mother and Jason Dobbs, who regularly visited their quarters to check on them all. Winter had arrived at Fort Laramie, Inge reported, but the quarters were warm and her mother's cooking was good. The only bad news was Erich, his legs no better, his mood worse. For now Benoit would think only of his wife and daughters. There would be other days to think about Erich.

Though it was still midafternoon, he was tired as he took the pen in his hand and begin to write his wife.

My darling Inge,

Four letters were awaiting me when I returned to Santa Fe. They brought such good news about you and my daughters. And I have good news as well. My new commander is a southerner and he feels as I do about Cle Couvillion. For once I finally feel out of reach of Cle's claws. So much has happened over the

last two months that it does not bear going into now,
but when we are together again I shall tell you all.
Just believe me when I tell you that this new com-
mander makes me feel so much better about my
career in the army, and you make me feel so much
better with the delivery of my two girls that I think
we can look forward to a wonderful future together.

Benoit wanted to write more, but the aches in his
arm and fingers told him how tired he was. It would be
good to sleep in a decent bed again. He put down his
pen, knowing he would finish the letter the next day,
then undressed and went to bed. He slept as he hadn't
slept in weeks; when he finally awoke, it was almost
noon the next day.

For the first time in months he felt rested. And for
the first time in years he felt optimistic. Whether or not
the Union was dissolved and war came, he would have
his family. And, in spite of Cle Couvillion, he would
have his honor.

AUTHOR'S NOTE

This is a work of fiction set in a historical context. Some characters, such as Cochise and Mangas Coloradas, will be recognized as historical figures, but most are fictional, though often loosely based upon actual people who lived and died in New Mexico Territory prior to the Civil War.

A historical novel such as this would not be possible without the groundwork provided by historians and scholars of the Old West. Consequently a great debt is owed to those whose works provided background and ideas for this book. Among those writers whose works were most useful were A. C. Greene for *900 Miles on the Butterfield Trail*, from which an 1850s San Diego newspaper account listing equipment passengers should take on a trip west was most helpful; Kimberly Moore Buchanan for *Apache Women Warriors*; and Edwin R. Sweeney for *Cochise: Chiricahua Apache Chief* and *Merejildo Grijalva: Apache Captive, Army Scout*.

Others include John G. Bourke for *On the Border with Crook*; Ruth McDonald Boyer and Narcissus Duffy Gayton for *Apache Mothers and Daughters*; Ross Calvin for *Sky Determines: An Interpretation of the Southwest*;

John C. Cremony for *Life Among the Apaches;* W. W. H. Davis for *El Gringo: New Mexico and Her People;* Roland F. Dickey for *New Mexico Village Arts;* Francis L. and Roberta B. Fugate for *Roadside History of New Mexico;* Josiah Gregg for *Commerce of the Prairies;* William E. Hill for *The Santa Fe Trail: Yesterday and Today;* Frank C. Lockwood for *The Apache Indians;* Max L. Moorhead for *New Mexico's Royal Road: Trade and Travel on the Chihuahua Trail;* John A. Murray for *The Gila Wilderness: A Hiking Guide;* David Grant Noble for *Pueblos, Villages, Forts and Trails: A Guide to New Mexico's Past;* John Sherman for *Santa Fe: A Pictoral History;* C. L. Sonnichsen for *The Mescalero Apaches;* Dan L. Thrapp for *The Conquest of Apacheria* and *Victoria and the Mimbres Apaches;* Robert M. Utley for *A Clash of Cultures: Fort Bowie and the Chiricahua Apaches;* Paul I. Wellman for *Death in the Desert;* and Donald E. Worcester for *The Apaches: Eagles of the Southwest.*

Without their works this volume in the Tony Hillerman's Frontier series would not have been possible. As readers of this series know, the story of Jean Benoit and the other colorful characters chronicled in this and the preceding volumes would not have been possible without the imagination of Ken Englade. My thanks to him for the opportunity to carry on this saga with a few touches of my own and to be associated with the name of one of the best of all southwestern writers, Tony Hillerman.

I must also acknowledge with gratitude the opportunity this book has allowed me to continue working with HarperPaperbacks senior editor Jessica Lichtenstein, whose deft touch on six previous novels has certainly enhanced the finished product each time. I must also acknowledge Ethan Ellenberg, my agent, for solid advice and his many contributions to my writing career.

Finally I must thank my wife, Harriet, whose support, encouragement, and understanding over the years have allowed me to invest the time and energy it requires to become a novelist. Whatever successes I have had would not have been possible without her love and patience.

Will Camp
Lubbock, Texas
January 1998

Here is an excerpt from

COMANCHE
~TRAIL~

by Will Camp
coming soon from HarperPaperbacks

Coahuila, Mexico
April 1859

On the north bank of the Rio Sabinas just before it received the waters of the Rio Nadadores stood six-year-old Armando Sardinas, chunking rocks into the river while his father and two brothers paused for a smoke. They rolled the tobacco in fine corn husks, then touched twigs to the dying embers of the fire that had warmed their lunch. When the fire took hold, the men touched the flame to the tips of their cigarettes and inhaled. The dry cornhusks flared up and the three sucked in the bitter smoke, then exhaled quickly. The cornhusks burned quicker than the papers the mayor-domo could afford for his cigarettes, but he was muy rico and could even afford such luxuries as well as fine cigars which burned sweeter than nectar.

When Armando saw his brothers, Miguel and Jesus, squatting around the fire with their cigarettes. He squatted too and picked up a twig which he broke into the length of a cigarette and poked in the corner of his mouth like his father, Manuel Sardinas. Armando

could not have been prouder to be with his father and
brothers. He ignored their snickers when they saw his
dry smoke.

"Don't choke on your fine cigar," cried Miguel.

Armando could tolerate his brother's insults
because now he was one of them for he was of an age
where he could help with the shearing of the sheep.
He was an age where he could consider himself a man.
Miguel, barely fourteen, was shearing sheep for his
first season and Armando had assumed his chores in
the process. Jesus at sixteen had manned shears for
two years and was getting as adroit at his father at
snipping away the wool without cutting the pink flesh
beneath it.

Beyond the men with their cigarettes, his father's
sheep circled nervously under the watchful eye of
their dog, Blanco, who skittered back and forth keeping the flock from escaping the makeshift pen. The
men had driven stakes into the ground with their axes,
then circled the stakes with their lariats tied together.
The sheep could easily have jumped over the ropes or
ducked beneath them, were it not for Blanco, ever vigilant that no animal might escape. More than two hundred and thirty sheep, half already sheared and the
other half nervously waiting for their punishment for
surviving the winter, milled about. The sheep bleated
their protests and stamped their tiny hooves in anxiety
but made no effort to escape for they could not outrun
Blanco.

Once the sheep were sheared and the wool bagged
and delivered to the mayordomo's hacienda, Manuel
Sardinas would receive his pay for a winter's work.
The mayordomo would grow richer and have money
for cigars while Manuel Sardinas would barely have

enough to make it until the fall, but at least they had mutton to eat and an occasional beef the mayordomo would slaughter for his shepherds and vaqueros to share with their families.

As the men smoked their cigarettes to nubs, Armando tossed the twig from his mouth into the river. He jumped from the bank to a large flat rock in the edge of the stream. He teetered for a moment before he found his balance, then quickly squatted and dipped his cupped hand into the water. The water was cool and he splashed another handful on his cheeks for the work was hot and dusty, leaving a film of grit across his face. He looked at his reflection in the water. The river was a distorted mirror, his eyes seeming to sparkle and dance like a candleflame. His black hair was matted to his forehead. He had never felt more tired nor more proud than this moment for now he was surely a man. Even if he didn't shear the sheep like them, he treated the nicks where the sharp shears had cut flesh instead of wool. He gathered the wool and put it in great sacks, stuffing as much inside as his aching muscles would allow before his father or one of the other men would use their strength to compress the wool even more.

"Armando," called his father, "it is time to go to work."

He scooped up another handful of water and tossed it down his throat, splattering most of it on his face and shirt. He pounced off the rock, then bounded up the shallow bank and toward the shearing stations the men had set up in the soft shade of the trees standing in clumps along the river. The nubile spring grass where the men sheared the sheep had given way to he flaying hooves of the terrified sheep.

Herding sheep was a poor man's occupation, requiring little equipment: shears and a whetstone for sharpening the blades regularly; axes for cutting wood for kindling or stakes for temporary fencing; a copper cauldron for rendering tallow; knives for slaughtering sheep; poison for combating wolves, coyotes and other predators; and a dog well trained. With a dog a man didn't require a horse for he could easily work the animals by foot.

Since Manuel Sardinas could not afford a flock of his own, he rented one from the mayordomo and shared the profits. He was proud that he had brought the flock through the winter without a loss to weather or predators. This would be his best year ever. With the years of apprenticeship under his eye, Manuel could at least be proud that his sons would know an occupation that could provide for their families.

Manuel took up his shears and began to sharpen the blades until the metal was shiny. The shears were two blades joined by a "u" shaped handle of the same metal. The handle was stiff and squeezing it required a man's strength, or at least the strength of an older brother.

Armando had grabbed Miguel's shears when his brother had gone to fetch his next sheep and had squeezed at the handle, but the spring action was stiff and soon his hand ached. Proud though he was to be helping, Armando knew his small hand would be of little use in actually shearing the sheep. One day, though, he would be strong enough and he would shear more than his brothers ever did.

His father handed the whetstone to Jesus, then started to the pen to grab a sheep. Jesus worked quickly to sharpen his shears then get his next animal.

Their father demanded that his sons produce by age, Jesus being older was expected to have sheared more sheep than Miguel. When each boy finished, he notched a broken limb he kept at his feet. At the end of the tally, his father would add up the totals and make sure they tallied with the sheep in the pen.

Armando watched his father walk in the narrow opening they had left between the two stakes that closed the circle. He lunged for the nearest unsheared animal, grabbed its hind leg and dragged it out of the pen. The animal kicked, stamped and tried to escape, all the while bleating to no avail. Reaching the shade of the tree with his struggling ewe, he threw it on its side, jammed his knee against the animal's hindquarters and wrapped his arm around the animals neck and began to clip the greasy coat. The wool fell away in sheets.

Armando ran to the tree where he had left his bucket beside the musket the mayordomo had loaned them to protect against predators and, if the need be, against Comanches. He stood beside the gun which was taller than him by a head, proud that he could actually reach out and touch the weapon.

"Armando," called his father, "bring the bucket. I have nicked this ewe."

Heeding his father, he grabbed the rope handle of the bucket and raced to his father. Armando's job was to daub the cuts with a tarry concoction that looked black as night and smelled worse than anything short of death.

At his father's side, he grabbed the stick with its end wrapped in a cloth that was now saturated with the black goo. The stick made a popping sound as Armando pulled it from the despicable salve. He swabbed the bleeding cut on the animal's shoulder, making sure that he completely covered the wound and its perimeter.

Proud though he was to be with his father and brothers, the job was boring and he was tired. He knew it would be at least four hours before his father quit for the day and that would only happen when it got too dark to see or they finished the flock.

"Pay attention, Armando. Yours is the most important job of all."

"How can it be, papa?"

"You know that I made it through the winter without losing a single animal, not even a lamb."

"I know that, si. You are a good herdsman."

"But each cut can destroy an animal?"

"How?" Armando asked, but before his father could answer, Jesus called out.

"Nick!"

Armando rushed from his father to his oldest brother and dabbed the tar upon the cut. Darting back to his father, he almost bumped into Miguel, who was struggling to pull his next sheep to his station in the shade.

"If we do not dope the wounds, the blowflies will be drawn to the blood and will lay their eggs in the open wound. The eggs will become maggots which will eat away at the animal's flesh and kill it."

"Nick!" called Miguel and Armando jumped to treat his animal before returning to his father.

"Maggots, papa, what are they?"

"They are like the grubs you dig from the earth, like short fat worms. Have you ever seen a dead animal after a few days, it's swarming with flies and maggots."

Armando nodded.

"You, Armando, are like a doctor. You put the medicine upon the sheep and it keeps them well. There is nothing more important in shearing for it does not matter that the animals make it through the winter if they all die in the spring after the shearing. And if that happened, a poor family like ours would be even poorer. So your job is important, the most important of all."

Miguel cried out for assistance and Armando ran quickly to him, then returned to his father."

"Sheep are God's best animal gift to man, my son."

"Why, papa?"

"Because they give you wool and lambs. You must kill the cow to get his hide, but you can shear the sheep twice a year, just as we do in late March or early April and again in August. And, the lambs come twice a year in January and July. Even Jesus Christ was a shepherd, so the padre says."

As soon as his brothers released their animals, Armando gathered the wool and stuffed it in the bags. He was tired, but he enjoyed being a little man and learning from his father. And though his father never missed a beat of work while talking, he seemed to enjoy teaching his son the knowledge that he knew.

His father, just finishing his animal, motioned for Armando to come to him and inspect the animal, daubing anything that looked like a scratch before turning the animal loose. Armando slapped the rag stick in the tar and pulled it out, then touched the animal in several spots.

Behind him at the sheep, he heard Blanco growl, then start barking wildly. Blanco's excitement flustered the animal, which fought harder.

Armando stabbed at him with the tar, but the animal broke free from his father. That had not happened before. "Papa," he said as he looked up at his father.

Manuel Sardinas had collapsed upon both knees, snapping the shears in his right hand. Armando did no understand. Then he saw the arrow.

Miguel screamed.

Armando looked at the arrow, staring at the feathers beneath the notch, then following with his gaze the slender wooden shaft that ended in his father's chest.

"Comanche" cried Jesus.

Armando saw but did not understand.

Blanco was going crazy barking and the sheep were bleating wildly. Suddenly, everything was noise and confusion. A half dozen gunshots were followed by screams that seemed to be inspired by the devil himself.

Manuel Sardinas looked from Armando to the arrow in his chest, then back to Armando. Then his eyes rolled up.

"No, papa, no." he cried as his father began to pitch forward.

Armando dropped the bucket and threw his hands toward his father's shoulders, but the butt of the arrow jabbed him in the chest and when jumped aside, his father collapsed on his chest, driving the arrow throw his back.

"Papa," he cried, "papa."

But his father was dead, the only thing coming from his mouth was a trickle of blood.